ALL THE
DEAD
GIRLS

ALSO BY A.M. STRONG AND SONYA SARGENT

THE PATTERSON BLAKE THRILLER SERIES

Sister Where Are You

Is She Really Gone

All The Dead Girls

Never Let Her Go

PATTERSON BLAKE PREQUEL

Never Lie to Me

ALL THE DEAD GIRLS

A PATTERSON BLAKE THRILLER

A.M. STRONG
SONYA SARGENT

**WEST
STREET**

West Street Publishing

Cover art and interior design by Bad Dog Media, LLC.

ISBN: 978-1-942207-35-1

To my grandmother, Grace, who gave me the idea for this story!

PROLOGUE

ESTHER CUTLER LAY in the darkness and listened, hearing only the muted knock of a hot water pipe from the townhouse next door. Having lived in the same building for more than seventy-five years, ninety-eight-year-old Esther could identify every creak of a floorboard or whistle of wind through a badly sealed window. The knocking pipe was familiar, like an old friend. The sound she was listening for now was not, having manifested itself only in the last twelve months. And it was not a product of the aging building she resided in.

Esther had moved into the home fronting Santa Fe Avenue the week after she got married, when it was still newly converted to townhomes from an abandoned warehouse constructed in the 1880s and originally owned by the Santa Fe Railroad. She had been there ever since, through the death of her husband twelve years before, and the onset of crippling arthritis, which had confined her to the downstairs living room turned into a makeshift bedroom. Practically bedridden since that time, she now had caregivers who came in four times a day to ensure the old lady was taken care of, thanks to the rapidly

1

shrinking remnants of an inheritance left to her by an uncle in the 1970s.

Esther shifted in her bed. Years of spending half her day sitting in a chair near the front window and the other half lying in bed meant she suffered from almost constant lower back pain. She reached for the switch that would raise the bed to a half-sitting position and waited for the motors underneath the bed frame to do their work. For a moment, the whirr of gears broke the silence, masking any other noise that might come.

Esther's eyes flitted to the old wall clock in an alcove next to the fireplace. It read a quarter to one in the morning.

The clock had belonged to her grandfather and was probably worth money, especially since it still kept perfect time, but the sentimental value was far more. Still, if she lived much longer, the inheritance would run dry, and she might have to part with the much-loved heirloom. To tell the truth, she hadn't expected to live anywhere near this long. And apart from the arthritis, she was in otherwise good health, which meant Esther could very well outlast the dregs of her inheritance. That would leave only the paltry amount of Social Security she got from the state. Not enough to live on and also pay her caregivers. And Esther had no intention of ending up in assisted living. That was one thing of which she was sure.

Esther closed her eyes, pleased for the momentary respite from her back pain. At some point, she would be forced to lower the bed again, but for now, she was comfortable.

At least until her peace was interrupted by the unfamiliar sounds that had plagued her during the night for the past twelve months. The creak of old hinges followed by a light shuffle that sounded like furtive movement.

Her eyes snapped open. She craned her neck to look toward the doorway and the dark passageway beyond. Out of sight to the right of the door was the kitchen and a small walk-in pantry that also served as a pass-through to the basement below. To the left were stairs leading to the now unused upper floors and, finally, the front door.

"Who's there?" Esther asked in a timid voice. Her primary caregiver, Jesse, had come in at ten to help her go to the lavatory and make sure she was settled for the night. The young man who worked for the senior care service called Home Helpers would not be back until eight the next morning when Esther would eat a light breakfast, drink one cup of coffee, and then settle into the chair near the living room window for most of the day.

The first time Esther had heard the late-night noises, she had assumed that Jesse had returned for some reason. Maybe he had forgotten his cell phone or was stopping by to double-check on her after his last call of the night. But it hadn't been Jesse then, and Esther was sure it wasn't him now, either.

"Is someone there?" Esther asked again as another light footfall breached the silence.

She received no answer. She never did, no matter how many times she called out. In the morning, she would tell Jesse about this latest incident, although it was unlikely she would be believed. There was never any sign of an intruder in the house, nothing was ever disturbed, and the front door was always locked. Even her granddaughter had told Esther she must be mistaken. Maybe she was dreaming the sounds or hearing someone moving around in the townhouse next door.

Except it wasn't just footsteps. More than once, she had caught a glimpse of movement through the doorway. A dark figure that passed by quickly. The figure had even hesitated once, lingering to look at her. Even then, she could make out no features—just a silhouette standing in the doorway. But the intruder was male. Esther was sure of that. She could tell by his build and how he walked.

This was no trick of an aging and addled mind. She was not paranoid. Someone was creeping around her house at night.

Once, she had heard him sneak upstairs. One of the treads halfway up gave a distinctive squeak when stood on. She had recognized the sound because she had heard it for decades when she went up to bed. Of course, that was when she could still get upstairs.

But as always, no one had believed her. Her granddaughter had gone up and looked around, then came back down and said everything was fine. She had even checked the third floor, which hadn't been used since Esther's daughter moved out more years ago than Esther cared to remember, and even poked her head into the basement.

Esther reached for the pad that controlled the bed and pressed the button to raise it higher behind her back. This afforded her a better view of the doorway.

Craning her neck, she squinted into the darkness, a prickle of fear climbing her spine. She hated to look but couldn't stand the thought of not doing so. And as her eyes adjusted to the deeper gloom of the hallway, the breath caught in her throat.

The figure was back, standing at the threshold and watching her. He never spoke. Never made a sound. Except for a slight exhalation of breath that sent the hairs on the back of Esther's neck standing on end.

She whimpered and reached for the lamp sitting on the nightstand beside her bed. She fumbled for the cord, glancing down momentarily to find the attached switch, then clicked it on.

A pale-yellow glow dispelled the gloom in a diminishing pool around the old woman. It barely reached the door but provided enough illumination for Esther to view the intruder better. Perhaps if she could describe the man, see his features, her granddaughter would believe her at last. But when she looked back at the doorway, it was empty. No one was there. The only clue that she had not been alone in the house was the faint musky aroma of cologne that hung in the air, barely perceptible.

Esther reached for the telephone sitting on the nightstand next to the lamp. She picked up the receiver, almost dialed her granddaughter's number, then thought better of it. By the time anyone got here, the scent would be gone, and Esther would be one step closer to being labeled senile. So instead, she dropped the receiver back on its cradle, pulled the blankets tight around her wire-thin frame, and waited for dawn to come and bring with it the safety of a new day.

ONE

FBI SPECIAL AGENT Patterson Blake climbed from the car, stretched, and cast her gaze across a flat grassy landscape overgrown with small trees, brush, and low-growing shrubs. A wire fence ran next to the remote and narrow county road, mostly to stop any stray cattle that found their way here from entering the highway. The midday sun beat down from a cloudless blue sky. The temperature was already creeping toward ninety degrees and would likely go higher through the early afternoon before there was any relief.

They were an hour and a half outside of Dallas and twenty miles north of Decatur in a remote spot of national grasslands that Patterson would never have guessed existed if she hadn't received a call earlier that morning from the Dallas field office, to which she was temporarily assigned. She had intended to head into the office and catch up on police files relating to the assignment SAC Walter Harris had dumped on her a few days before, depriving her of the opportunity to move on with the search for her sister, Julie.

It was a murder investigation that had taken a turn into serial killer territory with two dead girls and a third pre-teen missing. Dallas PD had requested the FBI's help, and Walter Harris decided to cash in the goodwill earned by his assistance with her own investigation into Julie's disappearance. Patterson was in no position to say no, but hoped it would be resolved quickly, allowing her to follow the new leads she had uncovered at the conclusion of her previous case hunting for a missing witness to her sister's time in the city. With this morning's phone call, that possibility appeared to shrink.

No sooner had she hung up than another call came in. This time it was from her recently acquired temporary partner, Special Agent Marcus Bauer. He had received a similar notification from the field office and was already on his way to pick Patterson up, mostly because he disliked her car, a battered Corolla with faded lime green paint and oversized rims that her boyfriend and line boss Jonathan Grant had arranged for her by calling in a favor with an old colleague. It was a seized asset previously used by the Chicago field office for undercover work and would have ended up at a government auction if she hadn't taken it. She understood why Bauer did all he could to avoid riding in the Green Dragon, as he sarcastically labeled it. His official ride, a shiny new Dodge Charger, was more comfortable and less noticeable so she had given up protesting his insistence on driving. Besides, she kind of liked being chauffeured around.

Bauer came around the front of the car and joined her. In front of them, parked along a narrow verge, were more vehicles, including three cruisers from the City of Decatur Police Department, a pair of unmarked units that Patterson surmised would be the detectives from Dallas PD who were running the serial killer investigation, a forensic crime scene unit, and a van from the medical examiner's office.

Leaning against one of the unmarked units was a plainclothes Dallas PD officer Patterson recognized from their prior investigation. Detective Bob Costa had allowed them to interview a man named Ryan Gilder, who was not only the boyfriend of the woman they had been searching for but also turned out to be a dangerous killer driven by jealousy.

Patterson still bore the battle scars of her final encounter with Gilder and his hunting knife more than a week before. There were eight stitches in her right forearm under a fresh bandage applied the previous day. The wound was healing nicely, and the other aches and pains received during that investigation had mostly vanished. She wasn't one hundred percent but no longer needed the pain meds prescribed by the doctor who patched her up.

"Special Agents Blake and Bauer," Costa said as they approached. "So pleased you could join the party."

"Want to fill us in?" Patterson asked, gazing out over the scrubland beyond a wire fence, which had been cut open to allow access. While there was no real path through the foliage, Patterson could see trampled grass and scrub where police and forensic technicians had entered the grasslands on their way to and from the crime scene.

"Sure." Costa pushed himself away from the car. "How about we walk and talk? It's a bit of a hike."

"Works for me," Patterson said. Knowing they would be heading out into the wilderness, she had possessed the forethought to wear a pair of sturdy hiking boots and applied a liberal coating of sunscreen to her face, neck, and arms. In her pocket was a small can of bug repellent, which she hoped would not be necessary. "How far away is the scene?"

"Almost a mile." Costa stepped through the break in the fence.

Patterson and Bauer followed, and the three set off across the rugged grasslands.

Costa cleared his throat and spoke again. "This entire area is designated a national grassland. It's administered by the Forest Service, and it's free to enter. Huge, too. Over twenty thousand acres, used mostly for recreational activities like hiking, camping, horseback riding, and fishing. Farmers use it for cattle grazing in some places. They get hunters up here once in a while during the season, but vast swaths rarely receive visitors, which is probably why our perp dumped the body here."

"The longer a victim remains undiscovered, the harder it is to ID them," Bauer said.

"Exactly. Especially in a location like this. Given the average daily temperatures at this time of year, we can expect the victim to be skeletonized within a couple of weeks. Three at most. Factor in scavenging by wild animals and bone disbursement, and you have a scenario where the body might never be found, let alone identified."

"Speaking of which, how *was* the victim found?" Patterson asked as they ducked under a low tree branch and took a turn to the right.

"Dumb luck. A couple of hikers on their way back from a five-day trek had packed up their camp and started the long walk back to their car parked at the trailhead. They decided to leave the beaten path and take what they thought would be a shortcut. Came across the remains in a shallow depression not long after. Took them another hour to find cell service and call it in. If it wasn't for those hikers veering off their planned route, I doubt we would have ever found the victim."

"This dumpsite is different from the others," Patterson said. The case Walter Harris had assigned to her was troubling. Three teenage girls snatched from their bicycles while cycling home from school. When the first girl, Shawna Banks, went missing in September of the previous year, attention focused on those closest to her. In such scenarios, a family member or friend was almost always involved. The body was found four months later on a piece of waste ground near downtown, hidden under an old tarp, which only heaped more scrutiny upon the family. At least until thirteen-year-old Lauren Rigby was snatched in mid-March. When her body was found two months later on another piece of waste ground, Dallas PD realized they might be dealing with a fledgling serial killer. This was confirmed when Susie Tomlinson went missing under the same circumstances. After more than five weeks of fruitless investigation and no tangible leads, they had asked the FBI for help. That was forty-eight hours ago. Now there was a third body lying ahead of them on the trail.

"Are you sure this is related to the previous murders?" Patterson asked when Costa didn't comment on her observation.

"About as sure as we can be without a positive ID on the victim." Costa batted a flying bug away from his face with one hand. "Apart from the dumpsite, everything else fits. She matches the description of thirteen-year-old Susie Tomlinson, who was abducted while riding home from school just like the previous vics. Same hair color and height as Susie. Same build. And she's been dressed in a similar fashion to the other victims."

"Neither of whom were wearing clothes their parents recognized when they were found," said Bauer.

"Correct." Costa nodded. "They were both wearing knee-length dresses. One green, the other red. Both dresses had butterfly patterns on them. Neither one has been manufactured in a while. In fact, the company that made them, Style Bug, has been out of business for several years. They were mostly in malls and couldn't hang on during the retail apocalypse."

"Meaning the killer could have bought the dresses at a thrift or consignment store," Patterson surmised.

"Or already had them on hand more likely, given the similarities between the garments."

"Except Susie has only been missing for six weeks," said Bauer. "A shorter period than the others."

"Granted, that is less time than the previous two abductions, but our killer shortened the captivity period between victims one and two, so that could just be an emerging pattern."

"And what about the dumpsite? It doesn't fit the previous locations." Patterson knew it was a myth that serial killers never altered their modus operandi, but most preferred a tried-and-true routine. There was safety in familiarity.

"Maybe the perp didn't like how fast the bodies were discovered," Bauer said. "The killer is changing MO to better hide their crimes."

"That's some change," Patterson replied. "The last two bodies were disposed of in Dallas. This one is almost ninety minutes north. And our perp would have needed to hike a mile off the road in difficult territory with the body."

"Unless he hadn't killed her yet," Costa surmised. "He could have walked her in here and then done the deed."

Bauer nodded. "Makes sense. Easier than carrying a dead weight, pardon the unintentional pun."

"Not that it did him any good," Patterson said. "The body was still found."

"But it wouldn't have been if those hikers hadn't come along. One in a million chance," the detective replied. "We won't be as fortunate next time, I'll wager."

"Agreed. What else can you tell us?" Patterson asked as they hiked a narrow path up a small rise covered with rough-leaf dogwood and black walnut. "Do we know how long the victim has been here or how she died?"

"I'll let the medical examiner answer those questions," Costa said as they crested the rise.

Below them was a shallow depression thick with foliage and underbrush. The whole area was a hive of tightly coordinated activity. A couple of uniformed officers maintained a perimeter just in case any other hikers wandered by, while officers in plain clothes and masked technicians in white coveralls buzzed around under a small black willow tree competing for sunlight with a couple of nearby Hackberry.

It was only when Patterson descended the inner slope and pushed her way through the bushes to the crime scene that she saw what they were fussing over. The body of a petite girl in a light blue butterfly print dress. She was lying in the shade. Her dead eyes, at least what was left of them, stared sightlessly up into the blue sky above. Eyes that would never see anything, ever again.

TWO

SHE HAD BEEN PRETTY ONCE. An innocent child with brunette hair and porcelain features. Now she was anything but. The body lay face up under a willow tree in a meager patch of shade as if she had settled down there to avoid the midday heat and never stood back up. Her knee-length dress must have been stylish once, with a cute butterfly pattern that Patterson thought she herself would have liked at that age. Now the garment was stained with dirt and torn, which was not unusual given the exposed location. Her arms were arranged so that her hands met across her stomach, her right palm resting on the back of her left hand. Her eyes, at least what was left of them, were open.

A drift of fallen leaves and other detritus had blown against one side of the corpse, within which Patterson could see insects crawling, mostly red ants that also scurried up over the body in search of an easy meal. Flies buzzed around. A black-winged damselfly with an iridescent thin blue body flitted across Patterson's field of vision, took a sharp turn around the tree, and disappeared from view.

The stench of putrefaction was overpowering whenever the

breeze whipped up, causing Patterson to turn her head and suck a gulp of fresh air before facing forward once more with her mouth pressed shut and a hand over her nose. It was all she could do not to gag.

"You okay there?" Bauer asked.

Patterson nodded but didn't dare speak. She observed the body with a mixture of sadness and horror. She knew from her own excursions as a trainee to the FBI Body Farm in Knoxville, Tennessee, just how quickly a body could decompose. Costa was right. Out here under this sun and exposed to the elements, a corpse would be reduced to a skeleton within weeks. This one was halfway there, which meant it must have been placed here at least seven to ten days ago, by her estimation.

The medical examiner soon confirmed Patterson's suspicion. She was a stocky woman in her mid-forties with a mass of short curly black hair that sprang up as soon as she drew back the hood of her coverall after stepping away from the immediate vicinity of the body to greet them. Her name was Gina.

"What can you tell us based on your first impressions?" Bauer asked after the introductions were done.

Gina glanced back toward the body. "I'd put the time of death at around a week and a half ago, given the state of decomposition and insect colonization, but that's just a preliminary finding, so don't quote me."

"Can you confirm whether or not she was killed here or brought to this site after death?" Patterson asked, bringing her gag reflex under control.

"Not in her current state," the medical examiner replied. "If the body was fresh, lividity might tell us. We could look at how the blood settled in the body and see if there was any contact blanching, which I would expect if she was moved and laying on a hard surface like the trunk of a car or a truck bed for any period of time shortly after death."

"Can you tell us how she died then?" Patterson stepped

aside for a forensic photographer, who mumbled a quick thank you behind his mask as he headed away from the crime scene to make the mile-long trek back to the road with his gear slung over his shoulders.

"That one's a little easier, but only in as much as it lets me rule out certain things. The body is badly decomposed. We can thank the humid environment and exposure to the elements for that. But there's enough left for me to tell you she wasn't stabbed or shot. I don't see any outward signs of strangulation either."

"That takes care of the most obvious ways she could have been killed," Bauer said. "Do you have any theories?"

"Not until I get her on the autopsy table. There aren't any external indicators of how this poor girl was killed, but she'll tell me her secrets. They always do."

"What about prior to death?" Bauer asked, looking slightly uncomfortable. "Are there any signs of assault?"

"If you're asking was she raped, I can't answer that one yet, either. I need to get her on my table. Even then, I may not be able to provide an answer depending on the level of interior decomposition when I perform my examination."

"Until we know otherwise, we should assume that she was," Bauer said, looking at the corpse, then away again. "The primary motive in most cases like this is sexual."

"I'm aware of that," the ME said. "And I'll get you an answer just as soon as I can."

"Do you have a timeframe on that?" Patterson asked. The ME hadn't been able to say if the previous two victims had been assaulted due to the condition of the bodies, and they desperately needed to pin down a motive.

"How long's a piece of string," the ME responded, sounding slightly irritated. "I'll make her my number one priority back in the lab, so you should hear something in the morning, or maybe tomorrow afternoon at the latest, depending on when the detectives and forensics team release the body. Regardless, I'm sure to be waiting on toxicology and other test results, so I can't guarantee you a full-blown report, but the nitty-gritty of what this girl went through and how she died will be clearer."

"Have Susie's parents been informed that we may have found their daughter?" Bauer asked Costa.

"We've told them we have a body," Costa replied. "We took DNA swabs from both parents, so it shouldn't take long to confirm if this is Susie."

"Poor people. Can you imagine what this must be like for them?" Bauer said, then cast a furtive glance toward Patterson. "Sorry, I didn't mean to—"

"It's fine," Patterson said with a wave of her hand. She knew exactly what it was like. The long hours of waiting and praying there would be news. Waiting that stretched into days, weeks, months, and finally years. The faint hope that your missing loved one would walk through the door or call and say it had all been a horrible mistake. The dread that sat in your gut like a lead weight and never truly went away. The fear of hearing the worst underpinned by the anguish of not knowing. Susie Tomlinson's parents had surely gone through the whole gamut of emotions, just like Patterson and her own parents had done so many years before. The difference was that Susie's parents would soon have an answer, however horrific. Her own family never did.

"Hey, you okay?" Bauer asked, nudging her with his elbow.

"I'm fine." Patterson swallowed the lump in her throat and turned her attention back to the girl lying under the tree. She couldn't help but wonder if Julie had met a similar fate and if she was out there somewhere, her bones still waiting to be found.

THREE

"I DIDN'T MEAN to upset you back there," Bauer said as they drove back toward Dallas. It was four in the afternoon, and the heat was abating, although Patterson was happy to crank the car's air conditioning down and enjoy it in silence.

She watched the grasslands pass in a blur outside the car, her thoughts consumed by the dead teenager in the pale blue butterfly dress.

They had left the scene an hour after the coroner took Susie Tomlinson away. Detective Costa had hoped there might be more clues underneath the body, but forensics came up empty. All they found was a layer of flattened brown grass. They still had no cause of death, but the medical examiner promised to expedite the examination, and Patterson was confident they would know more by the next day at the latest.

"Earth to Patterson," Bauer said when it became obvious his previous statement had fallen on deaf ears.

"Sorry. Miles away." Patterson turned away from the car window. "What were you saying?"

"I was apologizing for what I said back at the crime scene."

"I can handle an off-the-cuff comment," Patterson said with

more annoyance than she meant. "You don't have to treat me with kid gloves."

"Duly noted." Bauer slowed at an intersection and turned left without using his blinker.

Somewhere ahead of them on the road was Detective Costa in his unmarked Crown Victoria. Unlike the pair of FBI agents, who were done for the evening unless there was a sudden break in the case, Costa was on his way back to police head-quarters, where he would spend the next several hours sifting through paperwork, including witness statements from the hikers who found the body and the crime scene log of everyone present, when they arrived and left, and the duties they performed while present at the scene.

As lead investigator, he would also produce what was known as the twenty-four-hour homicide report, which would detail everything related to the most recent murder, including a synopsis of the crime, a summary of witness statements, background information on the witnesses—in this case, the two hikers—and the killer's modus operandi. All this, plus reports from the crime lab, chain of custody for evidence collected at the scene, and more, would be added to the Murder Book. This case file, usually a three-ring binder containing hard copies of every report, was also available electronically.

Patterson had already studied the digital Murder Book entries for the previous victims. She and Bauer would get the updated files as they were produced, including the medical examiner's report and crime lab reports confirming the victim's identity, manner of death, and other details.

In the meantime, she looked forward to a quiet evening back at the hotel. But first, she wanted to eat.

"You want to stop and get some dinner on the way back?" she asked Bauer as they drew close to the city of Decatur.

"Any other night, I'd love to, but I already have plans,"

Bauer replied without elaborating. "But I can stop somewhere if you want to pick up takeout."

"You have plans? Like meeting the guys for a beer sort of plans or a hot date?"

"Never you mind." Bauer didn't take his eyes off the road, but Patterson saw his cheeks flush.

"You have a date tonight, don't you?"

"I'm pleading the fifth."

"Which is as good as a yes." Patterson nudged him playfully, her previous irritation gone. "Come on, tell me. Who is it?"

Bauer didn't reply.

"Let me guess. Is it Jessica in admin? She's been running around after you like a doe-eyed puppy for the last week." Patterson grinned. "Or what about Jocelyn?"

"From the coffee shop near the field office?"

"U-huh. She gave you an extra shot of espresso for free yesterday morning. And she commented on your haircut. Said she liked it."

"Give me a break. The woman must be at least ten years older than me."

"So what?"

"Yeah. It's not Jocelyn from the coffee shop." Bauer stifled a snort. "Besides, she hasn't even shown an interest in me. Not like that."

"Are you sure?" Patterson asked. "I didn't get a free shot of espresso."

"I've been stopping in on the way to work every morning since I arrived in Dallas. She's friendly. I also tip well. That's all there is to it."

"Who is it then?"

"Are you really going to hound me until I tell you?"

"What do you think?"

"Alright, already. It's Phoebe Cutler. Happy now?"

"Who?"

"She's the ASAC's admin."

"Wow. You sure that's a good idea?" Patterson asked.

"There's no rule against dating a coworker," Bauer replied. "Which you should already know, given that your boyfriend is ASAC of the New York Field Office."

"Completely different."

"And exactly how do you come to that conclusion?"

Patterson remained silent.

"Yeah. That's what I thought." Bauer laughed. "And anyway, it's only a second date. It's not like we're a couple or anything."

"Does she know that?"

"I'm not having this conversation anymore." Bauer slowed as they drove through Decatur on Route 287. They passed gas stations and fast-food franchises interspersed with roadside motels. As they cruised by a Chinese restaurant with a red neon OPEN sign blinking in the window, he pointed. "You didn't say if you want to stop for takeout."

"I'll pick something up later." Patterson smirked. "Don't want to hold up your hot night with Phoebe."

"Cut it out," Bauer replied with good humor. "What are *you* going to do this evening?"

"Put on my comfy pants, open a bottle of wine, and read over the Murder Book again. See if anything jumps out of me."

"Or you could take the night off and skip the Murder Book."

"And do what?" Patterson's boyfriend was fifteen hundred miles away on the East Coast, and she knew no one else in Dallas besides Bauer. At least not well enough to hang out with them. "It's not like I have a humming social life here, unlike you."

"Only because you keep everyone at arm's length." Bauer sped up again as they left the commercial corridor behind and found themselves surrounded by flat, scrubby fields dotted with bushes and small trees. "Look, I just think you need to step away from the office once in a while. All work and no play, yada yada . . ."

"I could tag along on your date," Patterson said playfully.

"That wasn't what I had in mind."

"Afraid I'll cramp your style?"

"Oh, I'm sure you will." Bauer chuckled. "Just like I'm sure the evening won't end how I want it to with my partner sitting between us like a third wheel all night."

"Well, the offer is there if you want a chaperone to keep you on the straight and narrow."

"You know what," Bauer said. "On reflection, your idea of sitting in the hotel room with a glass of wine and the Murder Book sounds just fine and dandy to me. Have at it."

"You, too," Patterson shot back.

"That's the plan."

FOUR

BY TEN O'CLOCK THAT NIGHT, Patterson could take no more of looking through police reports. She was in her room on the third floor of a Holiday Inn Express close to the office, which was a far cry from the dingy motel in which she had spent her first several nights in the city.

That had been her only request when Walter Harris, Special Agent in Charge of the Dallas Field Office, had asked her to stay and help with the investigation. Her Bureau per diem barely covered the run-down flea pit on the city's outskirts, and she couldn't face another week or longer staying there, so she took a deep breath and asked for more money. Harris had agreed. So here she was, in a comfortable and clean room with modern furnishings, a big flat-screen TV, and air-conditioning that didn't sound like a runaway freight train.

Patterson yawned and closed her laptop. Outside, she heard the faint rumble of jet engines as an aircraft passed over on its approach to nearby Love Field. She scooped up the remains of her dinner—a burger and fries from the In-N-Out a short five-minute drive away—and deposited the wrapper and empty cardboard fry tray into a trashcan under the desk.

She wondered if Bauer was still on his date and almost sent him a text message to find out, but if things had taken a romantic turn, she didn't want to disturb him, so she resisted the urge.

She got her answer, anyway.

A few moments later, her phone buzzed, and a message from Bauer appeared. 'Hope you enjoyed that wine while your nose was buried in police reports.'

Patterson picked up the phone and fired off a quick reply. 'Skipped the wine. Had a burger instead. What happened to your date?'

'Dropped her off at home ten minutes ago,' came his answer. 'Want to grab a drink at Pioneer Jacks?'

Patterson contemplated this for a moment. It felt too early for bed, and the bar was within walking distance of the hotel. Pioneer Jacks was a favorite hangout of FBI agents because it was also close to the field office. There was even a wall of honor featuring portraits of retired agents, along with an unofficial memorial to those killed in the line of duty since the first special agent was sent to the city in 1914 to investigate price gouging related to the First World War.

Another text came in from Bauer. 'Still there, pardner?'

'Still here.' Patterson had nothing better to do, so she agreed to meet Bauer. 'How far away are you?'

'Fifteen minutes.'

'Perfect. Meet you there.' Patterson put the phone down and went to the bathroom, where she ran a brush through her hair. She changed out of the FBI sweatshirt she often wore when she was alone, and her comfy pants, trading them for jeans and a tee. She deposited her gun in the hotel safe, dropped her phone and room key into a small clutch bag, and headed out.

Patterson rode the elevator down to the lobby and stepped outside into the cool night air. Her car was parked a couple of rows from the hotel entrance, but she went in the other direction, following the sidewalk to the main road.

The temperature had dropped since earlier that day when they were out in the grasslands. It was now a comfortable seventy-five degrees, and she relished the warm air carried on a slight breeze as she made her way across the road to the bar.

Bauer was not there when she entered. He arrived moments after she settled at a high top with a glass of wine. After ordering a beer, he joined her and climbed onto a stool.

"Date end earlier than expected?" Patterson asked.

"Not at all." Bauer shook his head. "It was a very pleasant evening. I was a perfect gentleman."

"So why the sudden late-night call to grab a drink?"

"I was passing by on my way home and figured you might like some company. You looked disappointed earlier."

"Not disappointed," Patterson replied, even though the truth was that she would rather have enjoyed Bauer's company than eat a fast-food hamburger and fries alone in the hotel room. "Are you going to see this woman again?"

"Probably." Bauer looked down at his drink. He picked it up and took a sip. "I like her, and I think she likes me."

"That's always better than the alternative."

"It is." Bauer gave her a quick rundown of his evening while he drank his beer. After ordering a second drink, he turned his attention to business. "Did you find anything new in the police files?"

"No." Patterson shook her head. "But it got me thinking. The first victim. Shawna Banks. We should go and see her family tomorrow. Speak to them again. Dallas PD initially thought the stepfather might be involved in her disappearance because he's got a criminal record, and they approached the disappearance from that angle. It was only later when a second girl went missing under similar circumstances that they realized it might be something different."

"You can't blame them for looking at the stepfather. Family members have the most opportunity, and two-thirds of killers in child abduction cases have prior convictions. But they ruled the family out. Shawna was held captive for several months before she was killed. In ninety percent of child homicide cases, the victim is killed within twenty-four hours. If the family was involved you would expect that pattern to hold. They would have no reason to keep their own daughter captive. Besides, the stepfather had an alibi for the time of the disappearance."

"I know," Patterson admitted. "But maybe they didn't ask enough questions. Maybe we can find a thread to pull on that the police missed. Something the family heard or saw. A detail they didn't think was relevant."

"It's a long shot."

"I know."

"And you risk upsetting the family all over again."

"Their daughter's killer has never been caught. I'm sure they want that person brought to justice."

"Fair enough. We'll go and have a chat." Bauer paused. "After that, you can help me out with something. A personal matter. It won't take long."

"Ooh. Sounds mysterious.

"Nothing of the sort. A friend asked me to do them a favor. It's a quick stop. We can do it on the way back from interviewing the Banks family."

"What favor?" Patterson leaned forward and studied Bauer. "Who for?"

"Phoebe. Her grandmother swears someone has been sneaking around her house in the middle of the night. It's nothing. She's ninety-eight years old and bedridden. Sleeping in the living room because she can't get upstairs anymore. The caregiver comes in four times a day, and he's never seen anything amiss. Phoebe said she's imagining things, but the old woman won't stop complaining about it. She asked if I would drop by and talk to the old lady. Put her mind at rest. You know, reassure her . . . as an FBI agent. I figure you have a good way with people. She might listen if both of us talk to her."

"You're kidding, right?" Patterson looked at Bauer over her wine. "That isn't our job. We're not social workers."

"It's a flying visit to set an old woman's mind at rest. What harm could it do? We can do it during our lunch hour if it makes you feel better."

"It doesn't." Patterson grimaced. "Are you doing this because you really want to help or because you think it will get you further with Phoebe?"

"Ouch." Bauer pulled a face. "Does that mean you don't want to help?"

Patterson sighed. "All right. I'll come with you and talk to your girlfriend's grandmother. But it's a one-off deal. I'm not launching a fake investigation into some old woman's senile paranoia."

"Thank you." Bauer smiled over his beer.

"Is that why you wanted to meet for a drink?" Patterson suspected she had been played. "To ask for help with your burgeoning relationship?"

"It's not about that." Bauer looked genuinely wounded.

"But it can't hurt if you gain a few brownie points with Phoebe, right?"

Bauer shrugged and grinned at Patterson. "Best partner ever."

"Yeah." She hopped down from her stool. "I need another drink."

FIVE

THEY LEFT the bar after midnight. Despite the late hour, the air still retained the day's warmth, but clouds had pushed in, and a light drizzle was falling. Patterson hunched against the rain and was about to walk across the parking lot back to the hotel when Bauer stopped her.

"I'll give you a ride back."

"I'm good," Patterson said. "It's really not far."

But Bauer insisted, leading her to his car. "Come on. Climb in. I have something to give you."

"You do?" Patterson was surprised. "What?"

"Not here. Let's go back to your room first."

"Now I'm intrigued," Patterson said, climbing into the passenger seat. "What are you up to, Special Agent Bauer?"

"I'm not up to anything." Bauer started the car and pulled through the parking lot out onto the road. A moment later, they arrived at the hotel, where he chose the closest available parking spot to the lobby. He went to the trunk and retrieved a hard-sided black carry case, then turned to Patterson. "Let's go."

"This is all very cloak and dagger," Patterson said. "You didn't get recruited by the CIA since this afternoon, did you?"

"Very funny." Bauer led them through the lobby to the elevators. He pressed the button and waited for the car, then stepped inside. "What floor?"

"Three."

Bauer punched it in. A moment later, they were rising. When they reached Patterson's room, he stood aside for her to open the door, then followed her in. He went to the bed and laid the black case on it.

"I arranged this for you last week, but the armorer didn't get it in from Quantico until this afternoon," he said, unlatching the case. Inside was a small pistol cocooned in a protective foam layer. Next to it, in a separate cutout within the foam, was an ankle holster. "It's all above board and approved by the SAC."

"A Glock 27 Sub-Compact." Patterson took the weapon from the case and examined it. It was the same model as the backup piece she carried in New York. A gun that was currently locked away in her wall safe back in Queens.

"After what happened to you in Oklahoma City and then the run-in with Ryan Gilder, I figured you could use this. If you were carrying a backup weapon when Gilder attacked you in the hair salon, you might have taken him out easier."

"You won't get any arguments from me on that one," Patterson said. "I probably should have asked Grant to go around to the apartment and get my backup weapon as soon as I arrived in Dallas, but I wasn't expecting to end up encountering a murderer like that."

"I don't know why not." Bauer laughed. "Trouble has a way of following you."

"That appears to be a recent development." Patterson placed the gun back in the case. "Thank you for this. I really appreciate it."

"No worries." Bauer grinned. "Just do me a favor and wear it when we're on the job from now on. I can't imagine for the life of me why you didn't already have your backup weapon handy."

Because I was suspended and hunting for Julie on my own dime, Patterson thought, but she didn't say that. She wasn't ready to tell Bauer the truth about what had happened back in New York. How she ended up pulled from the field. Or how her SAC, Marilyn Kahn, had hijacked Patterson's unofficial investigation for her own ends and reinstated her to pretend it was all a cleverly planned undercover operation. Instead, she shrugged. "Doesn't matter. I have one now, thanks to you."

"You're welcome." Bauer took a step toward the door. "It's late. I'm going home. I'll leave you and your new friend to get acquainted."

Patterson walked him to the door and bid Bauer farewell. After he left, she returned to the gun case and lifted the Glock back out. It was smaller than her regular weapon but would still pack a punch. Even better, she could conceal it in the accompanying ankle holster, and no one would ever know she was carrying two guns. She felt better for having it. Bauer wasn't wrong. Her lack of a backup weapon could have cost her dearly during her confrontation with Ryan Gilder if the encounter had unfolded differently. She had gotten lucky, and she knew it, despite the knife injury and bruising she had sustained.

Patterson returned the gun to its case, closed the lid, latched it, and slid the case under her bed. Then she undressed and took a quick shower. Fifteen minutes later, she was in bed asleep.

SIX

THE BANKS RESIDENCE was a one-story ranch house on the outskirts of town in a neighborhood that probably hadn't changed much since the fifties. It was nine in the morning, and this was their first stop of the day, other than a quick detour to the coffee shop near the field office. Patterson finished her coffee as Bauer pulled up to the curb.

A color printout of the original missing persons report for Shawna Banks lay on Patterson's lap. She picked it up. Shawna smiled at them from a class photo provided to the police at the beginning of the investigation. She had cascading long brunette hair and sparkling blue eyes. She had neither of those things when they found her four months later under an oil-stained tarp. Patterson had looked through the crime scene photos. Shawna's hair had been cut so that it fell above her shoulders. It was caked with dirt and leaves. Her eyes were empty sockets.

"Let's get this over with," Patterson said, stepping out of the car.

"You're the one who wanted to come here," Bauer reminded her as they approached a white picket fence surrounding the front yard and walked up the path to the front porch.

"Doesn't mean I enjoy talking to bereaved families." Patterson pressed the doorbell. From somewhere inside, she heard an electronic jingle. This was followed by the sound of a latch being drawn back.

The door opened a crack on a brass door chain. A woman peered at them through the gap. "Yes? What do you want?"

Patterson lifted her credentials wallet and showed it to the woman on the other side of the door. "We're looking for Jodi Banks and Duane Snyder?"

"Duane's not here. I'm Jodi. Is this about Shawna?" The woman's eyes clouded with sadness.

"Can we talk inside please, Mrs. Banks?" Patterson asked.

"Of course." Jodi drew the lock back and opened the door wider to allow them to enter. "Have you caught the bastard who killed my little girl?"

"Not yet." Patterson shook her head. "We just want to see if you've remembered anything new about the day your daughter went missing. Any small detail you might have overlooked when you spoke with the police?"

"If I'd remembered anything, I would have contacted the detective in charge of my daughter's case already." Jodi led them down a short corridor into a comfortable but cluttered living room. Photos of Shawna, in different sized frames, adorned the fireplace mantle. In some, there was a second girl who looked younger.

Patterson nodded toward one of the frames. "Shawna has a sister?"

"Yes. Britney. She's taken her sister's death hard. We all have."

"How old is Britney?" Patterson asked.

"Eleven. She was practically a baby when I met Duane. He's the only father she's ever known."

"I see." Patterson had wondered if the younger child was Duane's, but apparently not.

"Where is she now," Bauer asked.

"Staying with her grandparents for the summer. We thought it would do her good to be in a different environment."

"And her stepfather?"

"Duane's at work."

Bauer nodded. "If you don't mind me asking, how come you didn't take his surname? You are married, right?"

"Yes. Going on three years. I figured it was better to keep my old name this time around. Less forms to fill out. Besides, it made things easier with the girls."

"Your daughters were never formally adopted by Duane?" Patterson asked.

"No. Their father, Caleb, lives in Louisiana. Baton Rouge. He went there after the divorce."

"Does he see his daughters often?"

"No. Has no interest. To tell the truth, he wasn't really the parenting type. I think he was relieved when I wanted full custody. Weird, huh?"

"Each to their own," Patterson said. "When was the last time he saw the kids?"

"He doesn't see them. Sends them a birthday card if he remembers, but that's about it. Caleb had nothing to do with her disappearance. He wasn't a great husband or father, but he wouldn't do that."

"I know," Patterson replied. "Dallas PD already checked his alibi. He was over four hundred miles away at the time of the abduction in a meeting with at least five other people."

"That's right. Look, is there something specific you wanted to ask me?" Jodi folded her arms.

"No. Dallas PD requested our help, so we're familiarizing ourselves with the investigation, that's all. As I said, we thought you might have remembered something that didn't seem important back then. Some detail that could help us now."

It hadn't escaped Patterson's attention that Jodi had not offered them a seat. She clearly didn't want this interview to go on any longer than necessary.

As if to confirm Patterson's hunch, Jodi said, "I have nothing more to say than I already told the police. I'm sure you have copies of those interviews. They grilled my husband and me for days. Even took Duane in for a formal interview. They thought he had something to do with Shawna's disappearance."

"We're aware of that," Patterson said.

"He had an alibi for the afternoon she was taken. We both did."

"That's right. He owns an HVAC company. Is that correct?"

"Yes. Installs air conditioning. He was on a job in Kaufman, forty minutes outside the city. He worked all that afternoon and late into the evening. At least until it became apparent that Shawna wasn't coming home. When the second girl went missing the cops showed up on our door again. They wanted to conduct another interview. Dragged him back downtown. Kept him there for hours."

"To rule him out as a suspect," Patterson said.

"Or to pin it on him. Just because he made a mistake years ago, everyone assumes the worst."

"His criminal record."

"Yes. Some girl said he tried to rape her after a party when he was in college. He got a little too forceful, but it wasn't anywhere near like she had made it out to be. He had a few too many beers, that's all."

"He was convicted of assault," Patterson said. "He's lucky the DA back then threw out the rape charge."

"Nothing lucky about it. He didn't rape her." Jodi pulled a face. "Look, this is all in the past. It has nothing to do with Shawna or the other missing girls."

"I'm sorry," Patterson said. "But we have to ask the hard questions. It's the only way to get to the truth."

"You're asking the wrong people. We didn't kill our daughter, or the other girls. Go find the person who did."

"I assure you—"

"No." Jodi shook her head. "I don't see how dragging my husband through the dirt is even remotely helpful. It doesn't bring my Shawna back or help those other grieving families."

"We're not dragging your husband through the dirt, Mrs. Banks. But like I said—"

"I think you should leave now."

Bauer stepped between the two women. "Mrs. Banks, we're on your side."

"I mean it. Go." Jodi pointed at the door. "Get out of my house."

SEVEN

"YOU WERE a bit hard on her in there, don't you think?" Bauer asked as they climbed back into the Charger.

"I was just doing my job." Patterson pulled her seatbelt on and glanced back toward the house in time to see a curtain move in the window to the left of the front door. Jodi was watching them, no doubt making sure they actually drove off.

"You made it sound like her husband was still a suspect."

"I was just following the one line of inquiry we have. I looked up the original complaint against Duane Snyder. Regardless of what his wife says, I have no doubt he would have raped that girl back in college if she hadn't gotten away from him."

"It could be like she says. Too much to drink and bad judgment. He was just a kid. Not that I'm making excuses, because I'm not."

"And if the DA had pressed charges, then Duane Snyder would be a registered sex offender right now. How would that change things?"

"It wouldn't. Dallas PD took a long hard look at him and decided their efforts were better spent elsewhere. He had an alibi." Bauer started the car. He glanced over his shoulder, then pulled away from the curb.

"True. An AC installation in Kaufman. The homeowner met him at the property to let him in. But here's the thing. She wasn't there the whole time. She went home during her lunch hour to give him access to the house and then returned to work. The homeowner didn't see him again until six-thirty that night when she returned."

"You think he ducked out unseen in the middle of the afternoon?"

"I have no idea. But he could have. And remember, the installation took longer than expected. He was still working at eight-thirty when Shawna was reported missing by her mother."

"Detective Costa and his colleagues thought it unlikely he was their man. Especially after the second victim. A complete stranger to him. And he had an alibi then, too."

"Just because he didn't know the second abductee doesn't mean the man is automatically innocent. He might have taken and killed Shawna because she was easy pickings, then decided he liked it and went looking for prey further afield."

"And where would he have kept the girls for so long?"

"I don't have an answer for that. Doesn't mean it didn't happen."

"Doesn't mean it did, either." There was a disbelieving note in Bauer's voice. "Come on, Patterson. He had alibis for all the abductions. The police have moved on from him. We should be looking for the real killer."

"That's what I'm doing."

"You're clutching at straws."

"No. I'm following up on every lead to the best of my ability. Which is more than the LAPD did with Julie."

"Then this is about your sister?"

"Only inasmuch as I don't want to let a killer walk simply

because we didn't look hard enough. When Julie went missing, the LAPD decided she must be a runaway. They told my parents that with no evidence of a crime, it was more likely she simply didn't want to be found. They jumped to conclusions and probably missed an opportunity to find her."

"Look, I know you have a low opinion of the investigators in your sister's case, but not everyone in the LAPD is like that. And look at it from their point of view. There wasn't even any evidence that your sister arrived in Los Angeles."

"They didn't bother to interview her roommate, Stacy. She told me they were going to send a Chicago PD detective to speak with her, but no one ever showed up. If they had followed up with her, they might have discovered the hotel registration cards that led me to Dallas and would have been on my sister's trail within weeks of her disappearance. They might even have found her alive."

"I'm sure Eddie Caruso did his best."

"Really? Is that what you think?" Patterson tried not to let the anger show in her voice. Eddie Caruso, now retired, had been the lead detective on her sister's case out in California. It was his decision to stop actively looking for Julie when it became apparent no one had seen her in Los Angeles. Even though Patterson no longer believed her sister had made it that far before something bad happened, she couldn't help thinking that a competent investigation back then might have saved her sister's life or at least given the family closure.

"Eddie was always a straight up guy when I knew him. He cared."

"Not enough to find my sister."

"He probably had a large caseload and needed to prioritize. I know it's not what you want to hear, but it's the truth. It's also in the past and cannot be changed."

"I suppose." Patterson took a deep breath. She knew this conversation was going nowhere and decided to change the subject before they ended up in a real argument. "Do you still want to stop by and speak to your girlfriend's grandmother?"

"If you're up for it," Bauer replied. "And she's not my girl-friend. Not yet."

"You sure about that?" Patterson asked as they slipped into stop-and-go traffic on I30, heading back into the city.

"Not really." Bauer put his blinker on and slipped into the high occupancy vehicle lane.

They started moving faster.

"What's her name?"

"What, the grandmother?"

"Yes.

"Esther. And apparently, she's pretty sprightly for the ripe old age of ninety-eight."

"Except for seeing phantom figures sneaking around her house."

"Apart from that." Bauer was using the car's infotainment system to scroll through the address book on his phone. He came to a number and stopped. "I'm going to call Phoebe. It's her day off. She can meet us there."

"Sure." Patterson settled back in her seat and closed her eyes as Bauer made his call. She wondered if she had been too hard on Jodi Banks. Certainly, she hadn't handled the interview with her usual aplomb. She had put Jodi on the defensive right from the start. Perhaps that had been a mistake. Yet the police file on Jodi's second husband and his brush with the law back in college, which she had read the previous night while going through the Murder Book, had left her with a sense of unease. Maybe he had just been a dumb kid who did something very bad back then, or maybe he was a sexual predator who had gotten more careful after that. If nothing else, Patterson thought, it was worth digging a little deeper into Duane Snyder and his background, at least until they had another suspect to direct their attention on.

EIGHT

ESTHER CUTLER'S home was one of eight townhouses occupying a converted warehouse in East Dallas that once belonged to the Santa Fe Railroad. The company's name was still inscribed in stone across the front of the building between the second and third floors. Beyond this clue to the building's original purpose, little else was left to indicate that it had once housed meat, vegetables, and other items waiting to be shipped to all four corners of the United States and beyond.

Phoebe Cutler, the ASAC's administrative assistant and Bauer's might-or-might-not-be girlfriend, was sitting on the steps outside and browsing her cell phone when Patterson and Bauer pulled up to the curb. When she saw them, she jumped up and approached the car.

"Thank you so much for doing this," she said, beaming with gratitude.

"Our pleasure," Patterson said. "If our visit puts your grandmother's mind at rest, then we're happy to help."

"I'm still grateful. She's always been so sharp, but the last several months . . ." Phoebe sighed. "I'm worried about her."

"I'm sure you are." Patterson studied the petite administrative assistant. She could see why Bauer liked her. Dark hair, pulled tight at the back of her head by a hairband, fell to her waist in a lustrous cascade. Her hazel eyes sparkled in the late morning sun. She wore skinny jeans and a V-neck tee that highlighted her trim figure in all the best ways.

Phoebe stepped close to Bauer and pecked him on the cheek, then turned and started up the steps leading to her grandmother's front door. She motioned for them to follow her. "Come on, let's go meet her."

She tapped a code into a lock box hanging on the front door handle and removed a key, then turned back to Patterson and Bauer.

"I keep the key in this because it's easier than having multiple keys in the hands of the caregivers and anyone else who needs to enter," she said.

"Smart thinking," replied Patterson.

"Thanks." Phoebe unlocked the door and stepped inside, called out as she crossed the threshold. "Gran-gran, it's me, Phoebe. I'm here with some friends who can help you."

There was no reply from within the dwelling.

Phoebe waited for Patterson and Bauer to enter, then closed the door behind them. "She's a little hard of hearing, so you'll need to speak up."

"Got it." Bauer nodded.

Phoebe called out again, this time louder, and started down the hallway. To their left was a set of stairs that climbed up into the darkness, while ahead of them was a kitchen with a small island upon which were arranged coffee mugs, a stack of plates, and what looked like a collection of orange prescription pill containers. Phoebe led them to a door on the right side of the hallway, which opened into a large and airy room that had been knocked together at some point in the past. An archway separated the spaces. One side must have been the dining room, while the other, at the front of the house, was a comfy living room.

The first thing Patterson saw when they entered was a hospital style bed set up in the dining room. It had metal rails to prevent the occupant from falling out during the night. More pill containers were arranged on a table next to the bed, along with a bottle of soda and a glass. The bed was empty.

The old woman herself was sitting in a chair near the front window. When she saw her granddaughter, her face broke into a happy smile.

"Phoebe, my dear. How lovely of you to stop by," she said before her gaze shifted to Patterson and Bauer at Phoebe's rear. "Are these the people from work you told me about?"

"Yes," Patterson said, stepping around Phoebe and introducing herself and Bauer. "Your granddaughter told us you've been having some problems with an unwelcome visitor."

"He's unwelcome, alright. Been sneaking around the house in the middle of the night like a thief," the old lady said. "Sometimes, he stands in the doorway and watches me, but he doesn't say a word. Not even when I ask who he is."

"That must be very frightening for you," Patterson said, stepping close to Esther and kneeling so she wasn't towering over the old woman. "Can you tell me what he looks like?"

"Goodness no." Esther shook her head. "He never turns any lights on. All I can see is his outline. But it's a man, I can tell you that much."

"And has this man ever come into the room?" Patterson reached out and placed her hand over the old woman's, which was resting on the arm of the chair. "Has he ever done anything to you?"

"Like what, my dear?" Esther's eyebrows lifted.

"Hurt or threatened you?"

"Oh no. He just stands in the doorway watching me. Sometimes I wonder if it's my husband, Gill. He was always puttering around."

"Where's your husband now, Esther?" Patterson asked.

"Grandpa's been dead for twelve years," Phoebe said, motioning toward the chair occupied by her grandmother. "He fell asleep right there and never woke up."

"I see."

"Have you given anyone else a key to the house?" Bauer asked. "Apart from your caregivers."

"Nobody. I don't see many people these days. Most of my friends are long dead." Esther's gaze shifted from Patterson up to Bauer. "Are you the young man who's seeing my granddaughter?"

Bauer smiled, a flush tinging his cheeks. "We've been out a few times."

"If you're going to get married, you'd better do it soon. I'm not getting any younger, and I'd love to see Phoebe settled down before I go."

"I think it's a bit premature to talk about tying the knot," Bauer replied.

"I would rethink that, young man. She's not getting any younger, you know."

"Okay. I think that's enough, Gran-gran. Marcus and Patterson came here to talk about what you're seeing during the night, not to discuss my marital status."

"I'm just trying to help you along, dear." Esther smacked her lips together. "I'd been married for six years when I was your age. You need to find a good man before it's too late."

"I think we're getting off-topic here," Patterson said, releasing the old lady's hand and standing up. "I'm going to take a look around. See if there's any sign of an intruder."

"Good idea." Bauer shuffled from one foot to the other. "I'll come with you."

"And I'll make you a cup of coffee while they do that, Gran-

gran." Pheobe left the old woman sitting in her chair and escorted Patterson and Bauer back out into the hallway. When she was sure her grandmother couldn't hear, she turned to them. "I'm so sorry about what my grandmother said in there. She's not shy about speaking her mind, and her views are a little antiquated."

"It's fine," said Bauer with a grin. "But I think we should at least go on a third date before I propose."

"Cut it out." Phoebe slapped Bauer playfully. "I'm going to make the coffee. Which should give the two of you time to poke around and put Gran-gran's mind at rest, although I can't imagine you'll find anything."

"Probably not," said Patterson. "But if it makes her sleep easier at night . . ."

"Thank you." Phoebe looked relieved. "I really do appreciate this. She's been so difficult lately."

"Think nothing of it." Patterson nudged Bauer and nodded toward the stairs. "Come on, Casanova."

NINE

"WHAT DO you make of the old woman?" Patterson asked Bauer after they ascended the stairs and arrived at a short landing. Another flight of stairs covered by a threadbare runner continued up to the third floor. There were three doors on the second floor. One on each side and another ahead of them. All were closed.

"I think she's in pretty good condition for her age and probably bored to tears stuck in this house all day with no one to talk to for hours on end." Bauer opened the closest door and poked his head in. "Huh. A sewing room. Esther had a hobby. Shame she can't get up here to do it anymore."

Patterson stepped around Bauer into the room. There was a sewing machine near the window and a dressmaker's manikin standing off to one side. Several bolts of fabric were piled on top of an old dresser. Everything was dusty. She turned to leave. "Doesn't look like anyone's been inside this room recently."

"No creepy stranger lurking in the shadows?"

"Not unless you count the manikin," Patterson said, stepping back onto the landing.

The door opposite the sewing room was the master bedroom. A queen-sized bed with an elaborate carved dark wood headboard and footboard dominated the space. A wardrobe made of similar rich mahogany stood against one wall. A matching dresser stood between a pair of bay windows that looked out onto the street. One drawer was ajar, and Patterson could see what looked like neatly folded sheets and pillowcases inside. She walked over to the dresser and pulled the drawer further open. The bedding was outdated, just like the rest of the house. A faint smell of mildew rose from the drawer and wafted into the air.

"Guess no one's been in here for a while either," Bauer said, wrinkling his nose.

"Esther's confined to the ground floor, and I doubt anyone else has much reason to come up here." Patterson closed the drawer, gave the room a cursory inspection, and returned to the landing. The third door was a bathroom with an old clawfoot tub and sun-yellowed lace curtains draped in front of a frosted glass window that spilled weak light inside.

"Onward and upward?" Bauer said, glancing into the room before turning back toward the stairs.

"Sure." Patterson stepped out and closed the door.

The third floor contained two more bedrooms, only one of which was furnished, and a half bath. A wall-mounted cistern hung over the toilet, complete with a dangling pull chain.

"Haven't seen one of those in years," Bauer said, raising an eyebrow. "Doesn't look like Esther ever bothered to renovate."

"She probably has that 'if it ain't broke, don't fix it' attitude," Patterson replied. "My grandmother was the same way. A lot of people who lived through the Second World War were like that. They learned to make do."

"Makes sense." Bauer clapped his hands together. "I think we've done our duty here. Nothing has been disturbed so far as I can see, and there's no sign of forced entry. The only people with a key are the old lady's family and her caregivers so that rules out someone letting themselves into the building during the night."

"What would be the reason, anyway?" Patterson started back toward the stairs. "Nothing is missing, and Esther admits that her shadowy figure doesn't actually do anything to cause harm."

"If you want my opinion, she's dreaming it. And regardless of what she says about knowing every moan and groan in the old house, there are plenty of things that could sound like footsteps."

Patterson started down the stairs with Bauer at her back. "Agreed. But there may be even more to it than that. She admits to thinking the figure was her dead husband at one point. Esther could be experiencing false awakenings. The perception of waking up, but still being inside a dream state. It's remarkably common."

"A plausible explanation."

"It could also be hypnagogia."

"Never heard of it," Bauer said as they reached the second-floor landing.

"It's a transitional state between wakefulness and sleep. She could be hallucinating the silhouette man as she starts to doze off. That would also explain the footsteps."

"You think she's imagining those, too?"

"I think it's entirely likely she's either hallucinating as she falls asleep or thinking she's woken up when she hasn't."

"Is that what you want to tell her?"

"It might be worth suggesting, just to put her mind at ease."

"Works for me," Bauer said.

They were back on the ground floor.

Phoebe was waiting near the kitchen door. "Well?"

"All clear," Patterson told her. "I think your grandmother is probably dreaming her intruder."

"Either that, or it's a ghost," Bauer said with a grin.

"Is that your professional opinion?" Phoebe asked Bauer, laughing. "Because if so, I may have to suggest the ASAC schedules you for another psych eval."

"One was quite enough, thanks." Bauer glanced toward Patterson. "You want to take a gander in the basement, just to be thorough?"

"Why does this place even have a basement?" Bauer asked. "Isn't it unusual for a home in Texas because of the water table or something?"

"You're right. It is." Phoebe nodded. "But this building was originally a warehouse for the Santa Fe Railroad Company."

"We saw the sign on the outside of the building," Patterson said.

"Right. They also had four bigger buildings downtown. It was known as the Santa Fe Terminal Complex. A couple of those buildings are still there. One is now a hotel, another has been converted into lofts, and a third houses Federal offices. The fourth one was torn down."

"What does this have to do with basements?" Patterson asked.

"Because the four buildings of the complex were linked by an underground railroad. They used it to move freight between the warehouses and out of the city. Later it was used by bootleggers during prohibition to move and store their illegal hooch, and in the Second World War, they used it to move troops. This building was connected to that tunnel system by a branch line. Those tunnels are mostly still there, buried and forgotten under downtown. My grandmother's basement was part of the old station and branch line. The company that turned the building into townhouses walled it off to create cellars for the townhouses above. It was there, so why not?"

Bauer was enraptured. "Fascinating."

"Enough already with the history lesson," Patterson said.

She wanted to move it along. "How about you show me the basement now."

"Sure. It's through here," Phoebe said, motioning to the pantry next to the kitchen.

"Strange place to put the basement door," Patterson said as she stepped into the small room lined with shelves on both sides.

"It wasn't always a pantry. My grandfather converted it," Phoebe replied. "The original pantry in the kitchen was much smaller."

"That explains it." Patterson pushed the cellar door open. She fumbled around until she found a light switch. A bare bulb illuminated a set of rickety wooden stairs that descended into swirling gloom. "This looks like fun."

"You don't have to go down if you don't want to," Phoebe said. "I checked the basement last time I was here."

"Might as well finish the job." Patterson descended the stairs, keeping one hand firmly on the rail until she reached the bottom. There was another light switch here, too. She turned it on. The basement had concrete walls and floor. Sticks of old furniture lay here and there, including a tall cabinet pushed against one wall, a rocking chair with a torn fabric seat, and an iron bed frame. There was also a steamer trunk and several boxes. A homemade workbench occupied the far wall below a pegboard upon which hung rusty tools. These had probably belonged to Phoebe's grandfather.

There was nowhere for anyone to hide.

Patterson went back upstairs, brushing away a cobweb that caught in her hair.

"All done," she said, pushing the basement door closed and stepping back into the hallway. "Basement's clean."

"Good. let's go have another chat with Mrs. Cutler," Bauer said. "Let her know there's nothing to worry about."

"I realize I've said this already, but I appreciate you both taking the time out of your day," Phoebe said. "The two of you have been wonderful."

"Always happy to help a colleague," Patterson replied, stepping toward the door. She stopped and turned back to Phoebe and Bauer with mischief in her eyes. "Especially if that colleague is about to marry my partner."

"Hilarious," Bauer said with a half-suppressed smile. "I'm starting to see why you prefer to work on your own. I really am."

TEN

THEY LEFT Esther Cutler's house a little after noon and picked up lunch at a diner down the street. Afterward, they headed across town for the second time that day to speak with the family of Lauren Rigby, the second victim. But before they were even halfway there, Patterson's phone rang.

It was Gina, the medical examiner they had spoken to the previous day. Patterson answered without hesitation and put the call on speaker so Bauer could hear.

"Do you have some answers for us?" She asked.

"A few," Gina said. "We fast-tracked a DNA test and compared it to the swabs taken from the parents. Our victim is definitely Susie Tomlinson."

"Damn." Patterson wasn't sure how to feel. A small part of her had hoped it wouldn't be Susie. That they might still find her alive against all the odds. But at the same time, that would mean another unknown girl's life had been stolen from her in a gruesome manner. It was a no-win situation.

"There's more, but please keep in mind, the body was badly decomposed. There was only so much I could do."

"I understand," Patterson said, eager to hear the autopsy results.

"Very well. First off, I can confirm that Susie was not stabbed or shot. She also wasn't strangled, either manually or by ligature. The hyoid bone was not fractured, which would be the case if she had died by strangulation. I didn't find any other external signs of injury."

"Are you saying you couldn't confirm the cause of death?" Bauer asked.

"No. I have a tentative cause. Suffocation."

"Really?" Patterson sat up straight in her seat. This was news. The previous victims had been too badly decomposed to determine a cause of death.

"Yes. But like I said, it's mostly speculative. I found trace evidence around the victim's mouth and nose. It wasn't much. Just a few fibers, but given the lack of other indicators, I think she might have been smothered with something like a pillow or a towel. But here's the thing. Suffocation is hard to diagnose during postmortem examination, especially with a partially decomposed subject. I didn't see any sign of intraoral injuries like lacerations or bruising to the lips and cheeks that one might expect if the victim was struggling." Gina paused, and Patterson heard a slight exhalation of breath before she continued. "Keep in mind, these fibers might have come from somewhere else. I found nothing in Susie's lungs, such as inhaled fibers, to support my hypothesis. The transfer evidence could have come from a blanket, like if the body was wrapped to move it easier, or even an article of clothing worn by the killer."

"Then we don't have a cause of death so much as a guess."

"An educated guess." The medical examiner sounded weary. As if she had fought this battle before. "Unfortunately, it's not always possible to provide definitive conclusions in my job. The dead sometimes speak in riddles."

"I didn't intend to question your expertise," Patterson said in an effort to smooth the ME's ruffled feathers.

"It's fine." The weariness was still there, but Gina pressed on. "I have more bad news for you. We couldn't determine if Susie was assaulted, I'm sorry to say. Her remains were too badly decomposed."

"Which means we still don't know if the motive was sexual," Bauer said.

"Correct."

"Is there anything else you can share with us?" Patterson was feeling the start of a tension headache throbbing behind her eyes. She rubbed her temples, hoping to dissipate the uncomfortableness.

"I wish there was." Gina cleared her throat. "We're still waiting on the toxicology, so that might yield a clue, although I wouldn't hold your breath. I still think the most obvious cause of death is suffocation."

"Thank you," Patterson said. "I assume you'll let us know if anything changes?"

"Of course." The ME said her goodbyes, and the line went dead.

Patterson hung up and pushed the phone back into her pocket. "We're no closer now than we were two days ago, and the clock is ticking. Sooner or later, he'll snatch another girl."

"Let's hope we figure this out before that happens," Bauer said. "We still have time."

"Do we, though? The gap between abductions is getting shorter, just like the amount of time he keeps them."

"We can't assume our abductor is male," Bauer said.

"There's a fair chance he is." Patterson knew the statistics were in her favor. "Women rarely engage in this type of crime."

"I just don't want to jump to conclusions. Not when we know so little."

"Fair enough. What are your thoughts on our unsub

speeding things up?" Patterson asked. Unsub referred to the unidentified perpetrator of a crime. It was law enforcement shorthand for unknown subject.

"Simple. He's getting bolder." Bauer changed lanes and took a hard left into a residential area. According to their GPS, they would be at the second victim's house within a matter of minutes. "He's gotten away with his crime three times now, which means his abductions are becoming more routine. That could also explain why he's disposing of them quicker. He's not so hesitant to find a new victim or dispose of the old one."

"Maybe." Patterson wasn't convinced. She could understand why their unknown perpetrator wouldn't wait as long between abductions, but once he had a girl in his clutches, she couldn't see why he was becoming more eager to dispose of them. He clearly had a place to imprison his victims and take all the time he wanted with them, given the weeks and months he kept them, so why risk taking more girls than he needed to? She felt like she was overlooking some obvious detail. The answer lay in the pattern, she was sure, but without more information, she couldn't bring it into focus. It was frustrating. She stared out of the car's side window, lost in thought. It was only when Bauer spoke up again that she snapped back to reality.

"Here we are," he said, pulling up to their second ranch house of the day. "Do I need to remind you, these people are victims, too?"

"What's that supposed to mean?"

"You didn't exactly go easy on the family of the first victim," Bauer said, putting the car in park and turning the engine off. "I just think you might catch more flies with honey, as the saying goes."

"I'll be fine." Patterson pulled the door release and swung it open. She unclipped her seatbelt and climbed out, then strode toward the house without waiting for her partner.

ELEVEN

AT NINE O'CLOCK THAT NIGHT, Patterson sat cross-legged on the bed in her hotel room with her laptop open in front of her and browsed through the Murder Book entries relating to the second victim. She was looking for any discrepancy between the interviews originally conducted by Dallas PD and their own conversation with Lauren Rigby's parents earlier that afternoon. Unlike their first stop of the day, Bauer had called ahead to make sure they would both be there. Andrew Rigby, the victim's father, had made a point of leaving work early and was waiting along with his wife when they arrived. The interview lasted two hours but brought no new information to light. The Dallas PD files matched their own notes almost to the letter.

Patterson was disappointed. She had hoped that maybe the Rigby's would remember some previously unmentioned interaction with another family member, acquaintance, or even a stranger. But they hadn't. Their investigation was going nowhere, and she didn't know what to do next. They only had one person of interest. Duane Snyder, the stepfather of victim number one. His alibi for the period during which his stepdaughter disappeared was weak. There was a tight window of opportunity, even if no direct evidence pointed to him. Dallas police had felt the same because they brought him in for questioning again after the second victim went missing. As before, his alibi was not rock-solid. Lauren Rigby had disappeared on a Friday afternoon. It just so happened that Duane had left town that very morning to drive an hour and forty minutes to spend the weekend at a hunting cabin he owned southeast of Athens, Texas. Surveillance video from a gas station put him near there at noon. There was no indication he had returned to Dallas that day, and the police could find nothing to link him to the disappearance. But as before, there was a window of opportunity.

Patterson sighed. The lack of an airtight alibi wasn't enough to make an arrest, even if that person had a prior criminal record. Until more compelling evidence surfaced, or they could rule Duane Snyder out as a suspect, he would remain in the maybe column. In the meantime, the killer was still out there and would surely take another girl soon if they didn't stop him first.

Patterson closed the digital Murder Book file and pushed the laptop away. She had hoped for a speedy resolution to this case, which had been dropped on her by Walter Harris, Special Agent in Charge of the Dallas Field Office. She was itching to hit the road and follow her sister's trail to Amarillo, where the next piece of Julie's puzzle waited. Mark Davis, former bass player for the band Sunrise, with whom her sister had been traveling. But first, she must pay her dues and do as the Dallas SAC wanted.

Patterson swung her legs off the bed and stood up. She went to the window and looked out at the dark parking lot and industrial park beyond. Further away, close but out of sight, would be the Dallas FBI building. She was overcome by a sense of loneliness. Bauer had settled in here easily because it was his permanent assignment. But for Patterson, who was only in the city for a few weeks, it was harder to make connections. She would be gone before any permanent bonds were forged. She missed Special Agent Quinn back in Oklahoma City and her domestic partner, Leah. They were as close to friends as she had found in this part of the country and hoped to see them again when her quest to find Julie reached its conclusion.

Then there was Jonathan Grant back on the East Coast. She missed him the most. They hadn't talked in a few days, and she yearned to hear his voice. She went to the nightstand and picked up her phone. Dialed his number. After four rings, it went to voicemail. She waited a few minutes and tried again, but this time it only rang once before voicemail kicked in. She left a brief message and hung up, wondering where he was and why he wasn't answering. Was he involved in some big case and working late? It was a plausible, but he hadn't mentioned anything when they last spoke, so it must have come up quickly. Or maybe he just wasn't near his phone. Either way, she wouldn't be speaking to him unless he called back.

Patterson waited a few minutes to see if that would happen. When it didn't, she decided to head across the road to the bar where she had met Bauer the previous evening because the company of strangers was better than no company at all.

It only took her a few minutes to get ready and trek over to Pioneer Jacks. When she entered, Patterson was surprised to find it busier than she would have expected for a Thursday night. She made her way to the bar and ordered a drink, then looked around for somewhere to sit. Most of the tables close to the bar were occupied. She took her drink and weaved through a throng of patrons to the other end, where there might be a vacant stool.

But instead, she found a familiar face sitting alone with his elbows on the bar top and cradling a tumbler of whiskey. It was her partner, Marcus Bauer, and he looked the worse for wear.

TWELVE

"MARCUS?" Patterson approached her partner and pushed up to the bar next to him. "What are you doing here?"

At first, Bauer didn't respond, as if he hadn't heard her, but then he tilted his head in Patterson's direction. "Leave me alone."

Patterson placed her untouched drink on the bar and leaned close to her partner. "Not going to happen. What's going on?"

Bauer sighed and picked up his drink. He knocked it back in one gulp and motioned to the bartender. "Another one if you please."

"You sure that's a good idea?" Patterson could smell the liquor on his breath.

"Pretty sure." Bauer drummed his fingers on the bar while he waited for his drink.

"How about you get something a little less potent, like a beer, or maybe knock the hard stuff on the head altogether, and order a coffee," Patterson suggested. She wondered how long he'd been sitting there drinking and why. Her partner had been fine earlier that day. Had something happened with his new girlfriend?

"I'll stick with what I've been drinking, thanks."

"Everything good with Phoebe?" Patterson asked.

"Phoebe's great. We're peachy," Bauer replied as a fresh drink arrived. He sank half of it in one gulp and slammed the tumbler back on the bar a little too hard. Whiskey sloshed up the sides of the glass. "Why wouldn't we be?"

"I don't know, you tell me." Patterson leaned on the bar. "You're in here knocking back booze like prohibition is around the corner. I haven't seen you like this before."

"Maybe that's because you haven't really gotten to know me."

"That's not fair."

"Really?" Bauer turned to look at her with watery eyes. "The first day we met, you stormed up to the SAC's office to get me reassigned to someone else. You follow leads without me. You've made it clear that you find me irritating. You don't want a partner or a friend."

"Okay, maybe I didn't want to work with you in the beginning. I'm sorry for that." Patterson wondered why she was defending herself. "And *you are* my friend."

"That's not how it looks from my perspective. You can't wait to put Dallas and me in your rearview. Hell, you spend your evenings alone in a hotel room wallowing over Julie's disappearance and rereading old postcards."

"That's not fair. You know how much finding Julie matters to me." Patterson swallowed a sudden flash of anger. She realized it was the alcohol talking, not Bauer. "What's all this about, Marcus? What's really going on? Tell me."

"Go away, Patterson." Bauer scooped up the whiskey and finished it. "Get out of here."

He caught the bartender's eye for another drink.

Patterson considered asking the bartender to cut Bauer off, but she doubted he would take much notice unless she flashed her badge, which was not going to happen. It would get both herself and Bauer into hot water since the bar was a popular hangout for field office staff and agents. The last thing she wanted was a reprimand from SAC Harris for using her badge inappropriately or painting the FBI in a negative light, regardless of her well-intentioned motives. Instead, she left her unfinished drink on the bar and pushed back toward the door, leaving Bauer to his own devices.

When she reached the parking lot, Patterson stopped and took a deep breath. All she wanted was an hour away from the lonely hotel room. Instead, she had run into a bitter and mean Marcus Bauer who was well on his way to a crippling hangover the next morning. She started across the parking lot, intending to return to the hotel, take a hot shower, and climb into bed. But a couple of rows before the exit, she stopped. Parked in a bay between a dilapidated pickup truck with political stickers for elections long gone all over the bumper, and a red SUV, was a vehicle she recognized. Bauer's shiny new Dodge Charger Bureau car. She stared at it for a long second, wondering what to do. Bauer clearly didn't want her around, but there was no way she could let him drive. It might cost him his job, or worse. Not to mention that he wasn't supposed to be using the car for personal transportation. The Bucar, as agents referred to their Bureau assigned ride, was for official business only.

Patterson swore under her breath and looked back at the bar. The door opened, and a group of men stumbled out, laughing and joking among themselves, their voices a bit too loud, before heading off into the darkness.

"Dammit, Marcus," Patterson muttered and started back inside.

She found her partner right where she left him, propping up the bar and knocking back liquor. At her approach, he looked up, and a scowl crossed his face. But Patterson was in no mood to exchange barbs with him again.

She slapped the bar and waved down the bartender, then

nodded toward Bauer. "He's cashing out. I'm taking him home."

The bartender nodded and walked away to get the check.

"Hey. I'll say when I'm done," Bauer said in a slurred voice.

"Not tonight, you won't." Patterson pulled a credit card from her purse and handed it to the bartender when he returned. After settling the bill, she turned her attention back to Bauer. "Car keys. Now."

"No need to get snippy." Bauer reached into his pocket and almost fell backward off the stool. He caught himself in time, then came up with a set of keys.

Patterson snatched them from his hand. "You sober enough to remember where you live?"

"What kind of question is that?" Bauer glared at her and jumped down from the stool.

"The kind I shouldn't have to ask." Patterson grabbed Bauer's arm and led him toward the door. A few patrons gave them curious glances as they passed by, but quickly averted their gaze when they saw the look on Patterson's face.

Reaching the car, Patterson opened the door and told Bauer to climb into the passenger seat, then went around and got behind the wheel. "I'm going to drive you home now. Understand?"

Bauer nodded.

"Good. First I need your address," Patterson said. "And then you're going to tell me what the hell was going on in there."

THIRTEEN

NO SOONER HAD they left the parking lot than Bauer started to snore. Patterson wasn't going to get any sense out of him during the ride home. But at least he'd managed to give her his address before they left, which she typed into the GPS. Even at this time of night, it was a fifteen-minute drive, which made Patterson wonder why he had chosen to spend the night drinking at Pioneer Jacks. Was it just the closest bar to the field office after they returned from interviewing Lauren Rigby's family? That, along with many other answers, would probably have to wait until he sobered up.

Bauer's apartment occupied the top right quarter of a four-unit two-story building accessed by a set of metal steps that led up to an external balcony. Patterson pulled the Charger into a carport with the apartment's number stenciled on the back wall.

When she turned the engine off, Bauer stirred.

"Where are we?" He asked in a croaky voice, peering into the darkness beyond the windshield.

"Where do you think we are?" Patterson snapped, then

reined herself in. "This is your apartment building. I drove you home, remember?"

"I guess you must like me, after all." Bauer rubbed the bridge of his nose and winced.

"I wouldn't count on it," Patterson replied, opening her car door and coming around to the other side to help Bauer out of the vehicle. "Not after what you said to me tonight."

He waved a dismissive hand in the air and stumbled across the parking lot toward the apartments, weaving as he went. Patterson slammed the passenger door and locked the car, then hurried behind. She helped him up the stairs and opened the apartment door, then got him inside.

The apartment comprised a small galley kitchen and a living room dining combination. Beyond this, in a short corridor, was the bathroom and a single bedroom.

She steered Bauer toward the back of the apartment and waited outside the door while he used the toilet, then helped him into the bedroom.

He sat on the bed and kicked off his shoes, then struggled to undo the buttons of his shirt.

"Here, let me." Patterson unbuttoned the shirt. After he shucked it off, she laid the garment over the back of a chair sitting in the corner. When she turned around again, he was already out of his pants, which were crumpled on the floor. For a moment, she thought he was going to lose the boxers too and was about to intervene, but instead, he fell back onto the bed with a low grunt.

"Come on, let's get you under the covers," she said, maneuvering him into a more comfortable position with his head on the pillow before pulling a thin comforter up over him. "How's that?"

"You're an angel." Bauer reached out and took her hand, squeezing it.

"Who you don't deserve right now." Patterson placed his hand back on the bed.

"I know." Bauer offered her a weak smile, then rolled sideways and closed his eyes. "Thanks for bringing me home."

"It wasn't like I had much choice." Patterson sat on the edge of the bed and watched Bauer for a few moments before speaking again. "Want to tell me what was going on tonight?"

Bauer ignored the question. He sat up. "My throat is dry. Can you get me a glass of water?"

"Sure. Stay there." Patterson went to the kitchen and rummaged around in the cupboards until she found a glass, then filled it with water from the tap. She turned to head back into the bedroom, but then her gaze fell on the countertop and a pill bottle sitting there. Patterson placed the glass down and picked it up, reading the label. She didn't recognize the name of the drug, but a quick search on her phone revealed the answer. It was an antidepressant. The date on the label told her the drugs had been prescribed almost three years before. There were seven pills left. She put the bottle down, overcome by a sudden sense that she was snooping, but now she wondered about Bauer. He would have been required to disclose any mental health issues when he applied for the Academy and filled out the national security questionnaire. While a previous condition didn't prevent him from a career in federal law enforcement, there would certainly have been questions on his psych eval. The bottle of antidepressants sitting on his counter worried her. Was he taking them? And what motivated him to spend the evening in a bar getting drunk? Who knew what would've happened if she hadn't come along and taken control of the situation?

More than ever, Patterson needed a straight answer from Bauer. He was still a probationary agent and had been assigned to her so she could shadow and evaluate him. It wasn't her job to delve into his personal life, but she couldn't remain quiet if she knew he wasn't fit for duty.

"Dammit." Patterson snatched up the bottle and read the label one more time. It changed nothing. She put the bottle down and carried the glass of water back into the bedroom.

At first, she thought he was asleep, but he opened his eyes at her approach and took the water, drinking it in quick thirsty gulps. When he was done, he put the glass down on the nightstand. "Much better. Thank you."

"You're welcome." Patterson stood over the bed with her arms folded. "I have a question."

"Can it wait till morning?" Bauer slipped back down under the covers and turned onto his side, so he was facing away from her. "All I want to do now is sleep."

"I'd rather get an answer now."

"You want to know why I was in the bar tonight?"

"Yes. And why you have antidepressants on your kitchen counter."

"Those are old."

"I know. I read the label. Still doesn't explain why you have them."

"Tomorrow. I can barely think straight right now."

"Marcus—"

"I said tomorrow." Bauer shifted in the bed, still keeping his back to her. "Thanks for bringing me home, but I'll be fine now. See you in the morning. Go back to your hotel, Patterson."

"I'm not going anywhere tonight. You're in no condition to be here alone."

Bauer didn't respond.

"Ignoring it won't make my question go away. Sooner or later, you'll have to answer me."

There was still no reply from her inebriated partner.

Patterson waited a few moments more, then turned the

bedroom light off and headed toward the door. As she was about to step out, Bauer finally spoke again.

"You really want to know what's going on?"

"More than anything." Patterson turned back to find Bauer propped up on his elbows, looking at her.

"You might not like the answer."

"I'll take that chance."

Bauer hesitated, as if he wasn't sure he should say anything else, but then he sighed. "I shot someone," he said, meeting her gaze with eyes full of sorrow. "I murdered my best friend."

FOURTEEN

FOR A MOMENT, Patterson thought she had misheard Special Agent Bauer. She stood in the doorway staring at him, mouth agape. "What do you mean, you murdered your friend?"

"I think my answer speaks for itself." Bauer slid back down onto the mattress and rolled over again. "You asked me what was going on. I told you. I'm going to sleep now."

"You can't just drop a bombshell like that and then expect me to walk away without an explanation."

All she received from Bauer in reply was a low snore.

"You have got to be kidding me." Patterson watched her partner for another minute, but he was well and truly asleep. She retreated to the living room and went to the couch. It didn't look very comfortable. When she sat down her suspicions were confirmed. It was hard as a rock. But she had no intention of leaving Bauer to his own devices. She was determined to stay the night and ensure no further harm came to her partner. Which meant either sleeping on the sofa or on the floor.

She stood and hunted through the apartment, looking for

something to make her stay more comfortable. There was a closet in the hallway. Inside, she found a blanket and pillow. There wasn't a pillowcase, but it was better than nothing. She returned to the living room and settled down on the sofa after removing a pair of throw cushions. It was even more uncomfortable lying down. She pulled the blanket around herself and tried to fall asleep. It was one in the morning. A streetlamp in the parking lot outside cast a pale orange glow into the room. But she couldn't be bothered to get up and pull the curtains. From the bedroom, she heard Bauer snore. The only other sound in the apartment was a low rumble of cars from the interstate half a mile away.

Bauer's confession ran through her head on an endless replay. What had he done, and how had he passed the FBI background check, let alone the psych evaluation? Was he a danger to himself or others? Surely he was being dramatic when he said he murdered his friend. He couldn't mean that literally, could he? Patterson felt sick to her stomach. She might not have wanted Marcus Bauer as a partner when she arrived in Dallas, but he had proved to be an effective agent, and she liked him. Moreover, she trusted him. Now she wondered if that sentiment was misplaced. If they were to continue working together, she would need answers from the man who was currently passed out in the next room. But those answers would not come until morning at the earliest, and when they did, Patterson might have to report back to her superiors about what he told her. That meant Bauer could lose his job . . . or worse. She hated that he had put her in such a position. But there was nothing she could do tonight.

Patterson shifted on the uncomfortable sofa. Her back was already twinging. She missed the comfortable bed back in her hotel room and wondered if it would even be possible to fall asleep. At least until she did.

———

Patterson awoke to morning light streaming onto her face through the living room window. She groaned and sat up, wincing when a stab of pain shot from her neck down her spine. The sofa wasn't just uncomfortable. It was like sleeping on a bed of bricks.

She heard running water from the direction of the bathroom, followed by the pull of a flush. A few minutes later Bauer appeared with a towel wrapped around his midriff. His hair was wet, and he was clean-shaven, but she could see the hangover in his eyes.

"You look like crap," she said.

Bauer studied Patterson for a moment, taking in her wrinkled clothing and unbrushed hair. "I could say the same about you."

"You could . . . if you wanted to make the situation worse for yourself."

"Right." Bauer looked sheepish. His voice was gravelly. He cleared his throat. "What are you doing here, anyway?"

"You don't remember?"

"Bits and pieces."

"I drove you home. I put you to bed. You told me you murdered someone."

"Ah. I have a recollection of saying that."

"Yeah. Me too. Kind of hard to forget." Patterson stood and made her way toward the kitchen. "I assume you want coffee."

"That would be nice." Bauer nodded. "Just so you know, I didn't murder anyone. Not in the sense of committing an illegal act. I was being dramatic."

"Pleased to hear it."

"Right." Bauer looked uncertain of himself. "I had better get dressed."

Patterson nodded and watched him go, relieved that he wasn't actually a murderer, even if he hadn't provided much of an explanation. She was also pleased her partner had come out of the bathroom wearing a towel. The alternative would have made an already uncomfortable situation even worse. By the time he returned, now dressed in a pair of black pants and a white shirt, the coffee was ready. She poured a cup and handed it to him.

"You didn't go back to the hotel after you brought me home?" Bauer cradled the coffee in both hands.

"I was worried about you." Patterson scooped up the pill bottle and placed it on the counter in front of him. "Antidepressants?"

"It's a long story." Bauer eyed the bottle.

"Want to tell me about it?"

"Not really." Bauer sipped his coffee. "If you're worried about my mental state, there's no need. What happened last night was a one-off. Done and dusted."

"Is that all you have to say for yourself?"

"No. I'm sorry you saw me like that. It won't happen again."

"How do I know that?"

"You'll have to take my word for it."

"Not good enough. Tell me about the pills." Patterson observed Bauer over the rim of her own coffee mug. "Or do I need to have a chat with Walter Harris?"

"You'd really go to the SAC with this?" Bauer raised an eyebrow.

"Unless I get a satisfactory answer in the next few minutes." Patterson put the coffee mug down and folded her arms. "I need to know I can trust you. I need to know you've got my back if something goes down."

"Of course I do."

"Then explain about the bar. Put my mind at ease that you won't go off the rails when I need you."

"Patterson . . ."

"Or better yet, tell me why you confessed to killing a man last night."

FIFTEEN

THERE WAS a moment of uncomfortable silence, then Bauer put his coffee cup down and stepped around the counter into the kitchen.

"I'm going to make this easy for both of us," he said. "I was drunk last night, obviously. I'm sorry about all that murder baloney. It was the whiskey and my own self-pity talking. As for the pills . . . I disclosed everything necessary about my background when I applied to the FBI. There's nothing to hide. That prescription is old. Did I think about taking one yesterday? Yes. But I didn't do it. I shouldn't have gone to the bar either. That was a mistake and I'm sorry. If you feel it's necessary to report what happened to Walter Harris, I can't stop you. I'll even admit to having a few drinks if they ask me. But you know as well as I do . . . agents need to let off steam sometimes. The FBI aren't going to sideline me just because I went to a bar."

"There's more to it than that," Patterson said, frustrated. Bauer was clamming up and she didn't know how to make him tell her the truth.

"No. There isn't. Those medications were given to me for something that happened a long time ago, and I'm no longer taking them. I've been completely upfront with the FBI about the reason they were prescribed in the first place. Besides, there are no rules against an agent taking medication, even an antidepressant, so long as it doesn't affect their duties or impair their objectivity."

"And what about me?" Patterson asked.

"That's your decision. If you don't trust me, then make whatever report you need to and ask that I be reassigned to someone else. Otherwise, let the matter drop."

"I'm not sure I can do that."

Bauer shrugged. "Fair enough. But let me ask you one question."

"What?"

"How would you have felt if people treated you like this after the farm raid in upstate New York?"

"You know about that?"

"It's hardly a secret. You went to pieces in front of an entire team of agents. You almost found yourself on the receiving end of a pitchfork. And yet here you are, anyway. Basking in the spotlight of your accomplishments."

"That's hardly the same thing."

"I disagree. It's exactly the same. You want to know how you can trust me going forward when all I did was to have a few drinks and neglect to tell you I once took some antidepressants. You, on the other hand, put an entire raid team in jeopardy. Rumor around the office has it you thought your sister was being held in a buried shipping container when the truth was it was some other poor girl who fell afoul of a vicious serial killer who couldn't possibly have had contact with your sister. Want to tell me about that?"

"Not really." Patterson had been backed into a corner, and she didn't like it.

"Exactly." Bauer picked up his mug and took a long drink. "Coffee's good."

"That's it?" Patterson shook her head in disbelief. "You're really going to end this conversation with nothing but a compliment about my coffee-making skills?"

"Would you rather I said the coffee sucked?" Bauer glanced at his watch. "We should probably hit the road unless you want to add tardy to the list of transgressions you're itching to report me for."

"I'm not going to say anything . . . yet." Patterson finished her own coffee, rinsed the mug, and put it in the sink. "I'd like to stop by the hotel on the way. I need a change of clothes."

"Yeah. You look a little . . . unkempt."

"Wow. Whose fault is that?"

"Point taken. How was the couch, by the way?"

"I think you should invest in some better furniture."

"I'll take that under advisement just as soon as I'm sure you're not going to get me fired."

"Oh, for heaven's sake." Patterson picked up the car keys. "I'm driving."

"The hell you are," Bauer said. "It's my car."

"And you still smell like a distillery," Patterson shot back. "You have any mouthwash in that bathroom of yours?"

Bauer nodded.

"Good. Go use it." Patterson started for the door. "I'll meet you downstairs."

SIXTEEN

THE CALL from Detective Costa came as Patterson pulled into the field office parking lot. It was ten a.m., much later than they would normally have started their day, but Patterson didn't want to show up to work wearing clothes she had slept in, and Bauer clearly needed another cup of coffee to shake off the lingering effects of the previous night. To that end, they had stopped at the hotel, where Patterson showered and changed into more suitable attire. Afterward, they pulled through a Starbucks drive-through and picked up a latte for her and an iced coffee for Bauer.

"Detective," Patterson said, answering the phone with a sense of foreboding and switching to speaker. "Are you just checking in, or do you have news?"

"I have an active crime scene, is what I've got." Costa sounded weary. "A Fourteen-year-old girl named Amy Bowen went missing this morning."

"You think it's our killer?"

"Caucasian, similar age and build as the other girls, and snatched off a bicycle on the way to her part-time summer job cleaning rooms at a motel, so you tell me."

"It's only been two weeks since he disposed of the last victim," Bauer said.

"Yeah. Our killer is getting antsy." Costa was silent for a moment. "You okay there, buddy? You sound . . . off."

"I'm fine." Bauer pulled a face. "How long since she was taken?"

"Two and a half hours, give or take. When she didn't show up for work and couldn't be reached on her cell phone, the motel's manager called the emergency number on her job application—which was her mother's cell—to see what was up. Her parents spent the next forty-five minutes phoning Amy's friends looking for her before they decided to call us."

"You found the bike, I assume?" Patterson asked.

"U-huh. Uniform drove the route between the Amy's house and work. The bike was thrown into a ditch in a wooded area a quarter mile from her home. Found her broken phone at the side of the road, too. I'm already there. I'll send you the coordinates."

"Understood." Patterson was already reversing out of the parking space. "We're on our way."

———

Detective Costa was waiting when they arrived at the scene. He ducked under a string of yellow tape and approached the car with a grim look on his face.

The road was closed in both directions. They had encountered a cruiser diverting traffic a mile back. The officer present had tried to divert them, too, until Patterson flashed her badge.

Beyond the tape, she could see more cruisers, unmarked vehicles, and the obligatory forensics van. The activity was centered on a drainage ditch. Beyond this were pine trees and brush. It was desolate. The perfect place for an abduction.

"I was hoping we'd have more time before the killer struck

again," Patterson said, climbing out of the car. "Especially since school is out for the summer."

"Me too. Less opportunity."

"Yet here we are," Bauer said.

"Here we are indeed." Costa rubbed the back of his neck and swatted a mosquito. "And the clock's officially ticking on another murder. If our perp is true to form, he'll kill this one quicker than the others."

"Let's find him before that happens." Bauer slammed the passenger door and came around the vehicle. "I don't suppose you have any leads?"

"Actually, we do." Costa motioned toward the woods beside the road. "There's a house on the other side of the woods, about a mile distant. The woman who owns it takes a walk through the woods every morning. There are trails all through this area. She happened to be in the right spot at the right time to witness the abduction . . . or at least, the tail end of it."

"You're kidding me." Patterson could hardly believe their luck. "She saw the abductor?"

"Nah. We weren't that lucky. But she might have seen his vehicle. A white cargo van."

"License plate?" Patterson asked hopefully as they ducked under the crime scene tape and made their way toward the ditch.

"Again, no such luck. She was off in the trees and didn't have the best view, but she heard a screech of tires, and when she looked around a van was speeding down the road."

"And she didn't report it right away?"

"She didn't see the abduction . . . just thought it was some idiot driving too fast until the amber alert came through on her cell phone. When she saw police activity out on the road, she wondered if the speeding van might be relevant and made the call. I just got back from interviewing her."

"Our killer got careless," Bauer said with obvious satisfaction.

"I wouldn't go that far. He just got unlucky," Costa said. "The perpetrator chose this spot because it's remote, with little traffic. He'd probably been watching his victim and figured this was a great place to make the snatch. The one thing he didn't count on was our homeowner taking a morning constitutional because she hadn't been walking in the woods the last few days. She'd been out of town visiting her sister in Albuquerque. Got back late last night."

"There must be hundreds of cargo vans in the Dallas-Fort Worth metropolitan area, let alone the rest of Texas."

"More like thousands," Bauer said. "And the majority of the vans I see around are painted white."

"That's right." Patterson grimaced. "Could she provide any details about the vehicle that might help us narrow it down, like a make or model or some other distinguishing feature?"

"No make or model. Just like the license plate, she was too far away."

"Dammit." Patterson looked into the ditch. A yellow girl's bicycle lay on its side among the weeds and roadside trash. A forensics team was fussing over the discarded bike and picking through the closest garbage, most of which had probably been tossed from passing cars long before the abduction. Nearby was a photographer with a digital SLR camera slung around his neck. He looked bored. "We can't interview the owner of every white cargo van in the state."

"Not so fast. She gave us one tidbit," Costa said. "The van had a rack on top. The sort of thing tradesmen put water pipes or ladders on to transport them."

"Again, that doesn't really narrow it down," Bauer said. I probably saw six of those on the drive over here."

"I don't suppose there are any surveillance or traffic cams anywhere in the vicinity?" Patterson asked hopefully.

"Not close enough to do us any good."

"Figures." Bauer studied the road. "Did the van leave any tire tracks when it sped off? Any other trace evidence?"

"That would be nice, wouldn't it?" Costa chuckled, the sound hollow and mirthless. "But sorry, no tire tracks, discarded cigarette butts, or anything else that might help us unless a piece of trash in that ditch turns out to be a clue."

"I wouldn't hold your breath," said Patterson.

"My thoughts exactly," said Costa morosely as he watched a forensics tech tease a foil fast-food burrito wrapper from the weeds at the bottom of the ditch with a gloved hand and slip it into an evidence bag. "Which means the clock is ticking on another murder, and we're up the proverbial shit creek."

SEVENTEEN

BACK IN THE CAR, Patterson said, "I need to take another look through the Murder Book."

"Why? We've already gone over it so often we risk going cross-eyed."

"I have to check on something." Patterson put the car in gear and swung the wheel, doing a three-sixty in the road. She sped along, pushing the vehicle to fifteen miles over the speed limit as they headed back toward the field office.

"Whoa. Easy there." Bauer grabbed the side of the seat. "You trying to get us a speeding ticket?"

"No one is going to give us a ticket. Federal plates, remember?" Patterson weaved around a slower car blocking the lane ahead of her. "And if I'm right about this, we stand a chance of finding Amy Bowen before that bastard disappears into the woodwork."

"Right about what?" Bauer tensed as she blew through a yellow light without slowing down.

"You'll see."

"You could just tell me."

"I want to make sure I'm right first. Otherwise, you'll just shoot my theory down."

"You really don't have much faith in me, do you?"

"On the contrary, I think you're an excellent agent, the events of last night aside."

"Not going to let that be, are you?"

"Are you going to tell me what it was about?"

"We've been through this. It was a dumb mistake, that's all. I already told you it won't happen again." Bauer was irritated. "That's no reason to hold out on me."

"I'm doing no such thing," Patterson said as they merged onto the interstate and headed northwest through downtown. To their right was Dealey Plaza and the infamous Texas School Book Depository building, which was now a museum dedicated to the events of November 22, 1963.

Ten minutes later, after leaving downtown behind, she came off at the exit for Love Field, the smaller of the city's two major airports. But that wasn't her destination. Patterson steered them onto Justice Way and pulled around in front of the FBI building, where she found a parking space.

She hopped out of the car and raced toward the building without bothering to wait for Bauer, who ran to catch up. They entered the expansive lobby and made their way through the metal detectors and then up to the broom closet of an office assigned to them by Walter Harris the day after Patterson arrived in the city.

The office was as sparse now as it had been then. It contained two desks pushed together and a pair of chairs. There were no bookcases or other pieces of furniture. No personal items on the desks to give the office a semblance of warmth, save one. A silver-framed photograph of her sister that Patterson had placed on the furthest desk from the door to remind her of why she was an FBI agent and what was at stake.

The only other additions to the space were a pair of Bureau-issued laptops.

Patterson went to her desk and sat down, then pulled the laptop close. She typed her password and brought up the Murder Book.

"Now do you want to tell me what we're looking for?" Bauer asked, coming up behind her and peering over Patterson's shoulder.

"Give me a second," Patterson said, scrolling back through the digital pages until she came to the section relating to the first victim, Shawna Banks, and in particular, the Dallas PD interview with her stepfather, Duane Snyder. She pointed to a paragraph halfway through the interview and looked up at Bauer. "Here. Read this."

Bauer leaned over and read the paragraph, then straightened up with a surprised look on his face. "Well, I'll be damned. Duane Snyder uses a white cargo van for his air-conditioning business."

"I wonder where he was this morning between seven and eight a.m.?"

"Only one way to find out," Bauer said. "Let's ask him."

Patterson was already on her feet and heading toward the door. "Exactly what I was thinking."

EIGHTEEN

"DUANE'S NOT HERE," Jodi Banks said, standing in her half-open front door and blocking their access to the house. "What do you want to talk to him about, anyway?"

"We just have some follow-up questions," Patterson said. "Since we didn't talk to him when we were here before."

"And none of this has anything to do with that girl who went missing this morning, I suppose," Jodi replied. "I saw it on the news and wondered how long it would take for the cops to come sniffing around again. We're the victims here. Understand? You should be treating us with respect."

"We are treating you with respect, Mrs. Banks," Bauer said. "And we're sorry for your loss. However, we do have some questions that need to be answered, just so we can eliminate anyone who is not involved in the disappearance of your daughter and the other girls and catch the person or persons who committed these horrendous crimes."

"I'm sure you want that as much as we do, Mrs. Banks," Patterson said in the most soothing voice she could muster. "We aren't the enemy, I assure you, but to do our jobs effectively and provide the answers you need, we have to follow up on every piece of information, no matter where it leads."

"And where is your information leading you right now?" Jodi still sounded defensive, but the hard edge had dropped from her voice.

"There was a witness to the abduction this morning," Patterson said. "She didn't see the kidnapping, but the witness provided a description of the vehicle. A plain white cargo van with a roof rack."

"Duane drives a white cargo van like that." The color drained from Jodi's cheeks.

"We know," Patterson said. "We're not accusing Duane of being involved, but under the circumstances, we need to confirm that he isn't so that we can look further afield."

"It's standard procedure," Bauer added.

"What time was this?" Jodi chewed her bottom lip. She was close to tears. "When did your witness see that van?"

"Sometime around seven-thirty this morning."

Jodi was silent for a moment, then she stepped aside and held the door open. "We should talk inside. No point in giving the neighbors more reason to gossip."

"That would be for the best," Patterson said, stepping across the threshold with Bauer close behind.

As soon as the door was closed, Jodi turned to them. "You're absolutely sure a white van is involved in the latest abduction?"

"We're not sure of anything right now." Patterson could hear faint music coming from the kitchen where a radio was playing. An aroma of bacon wafted down the hallway, reminding her that they hadn't eaten yet. Her stomach rumbled a little too loudly. She ignored it. "As we said already, the witness did not actually see the abduction. Only a vehicle traveling away from the scene at a higher rate of speed than would be usual in that area. Until we find the white van and its driver, we can't definitively say one way or the other if they were involved or not."

"What time did your husband leave for work this morning, Mrs. Banks?" Bauer asked.

"Early. A little after six."

"Is that usual?" Patterson asked.

"Depends how far away he's working. He installs air-conditioning all over the metropolitan area and beyond. He might end up driving an hour or more to get to a job site."

"And today?"

"No. He was working locally. An office building on the east side of town. He wanted to finish the install yesterday but ran into issues with some old pipes that weren't up to code. Had to rip them out. Took him longer than he expected."

"Is that why he left so early this morning?" Patterson asked. "To finish up that job before whatever work he had scheduled for today?"

"No." Jodi looked down, avoiding Patterson's gaze. "He did leave early to finish it. That much is true. But it wasn't because he had another job on the roster. He was going to the cabin and didn't want to get held up."

"Tell me more about this cabin," Bauer said.

"It's a hunting cabin south of Athens. Been in Duane's family for decades. His grandfather bought it way back when. Sits on over five hundred acres of woodland. Duane said he was going to start a logging business but never did."

"And he was heading straight there after finishing up his install?" A tingle ran up Patterson's spine.

"Yup. Packed a bag last night and said he'd be gone until Monday."

"Does he go to the cabin often?"

"Depends on his mood. He's been going up there more the last few years. Mostly on weekends. Says he likes the solitude."

"And you don't go with him?"

"You must be kidding. I can't stand the place. He took me out there when we were first dating and once was enough. After that, I told him he was on his own if he wanted to spend weekends in a dank and smelly old cabin in the middle of nowhere. Honestly, I like the peace and quiet his trips give me. I can relax. Watch my shows on TV. Drink wine."

"Did he drive the van out to the cabin this morning, or did he bring it back and take another vehicle?" Patterson asked. She hadn't seen a van when they arrived, but that didn't mean much. He might have an industrial unit somewhere close that he worked from or a place to park it off the road.

"He took the van, which is unusual." Jodi looked uncomfortable. "He has a Jeep around back. He normally takes that. But the job was in the same direction as the cabin, and he didn't want to come back, so he told me he was taking the van."

"I see." Patterson sensed Bauer tense. He was thinking the same as her. "I don't suppose you could give us the address of this cabin?"

"Well . . ." Jodi sounded unsure. "You don't really think Duane is involved in this, do you?"

"I hope not," Patterson said. "But we need to find out."

"Of course. Hang on a moment." Jodi turned and disappeared into the kitchen. She returned, clutching a phone, which she browsed for a moment. "I have the address here. I can text it to you."

"That would be great." Patterson gave Jodi her cell phone number and waited until the text came through, then she reached out and gripped Jodi's arm. "We'll get to the bottom of this, I promise. And we'll find your daughter's killer, whoever that might be."

Jodi nodded and wiped moisture from her eyes. "I hope it's not Duane. God, I hope it's not him. I'm not sure I could handle it if a man I let through our front door killed my Shawna."

NINETEEN

THE DRIVE from Dallas to Duane Snyder's hunting cabin south of Athens—a small city of around twelve thousand residents—took a little over an hour and a half.

Along the way, Patterson called Detective Costa and filled him in. Costa had also made the connection with the white cargo van belonging to Snyder and was happy to let the federal agents follow up on the lead while he directed a search for the missing girl closer to home. Before hanging up the phone, he told them to keep him in the loop. Especially if the situation escalated and they needed backup, which would come from the Athens Police Department, whom he promised to appraise of the FBI agents' presence in their jurisdiction.

"You understand this trip could prove fruitless," Bauer said after Patterson finished talking to Costa. "Even if he has the girl, we don't have probable cause to enter any buildings or vehicles on the property unless we find evidence of an abduction. We won't even be able to search his land without permission, since we don't have a warrant."

"We would never secure a search warrant on such flimsy

evidence," Patterson replied. All we could go before a judge with is Duane Snyder's prior record dating back to his college years, and that he owns a similar van to the one seen speeding in the vicinity of the latest abduction. It's paper thin."

"My point exactly. And if he's guilty, Duane Snyder will never let us conduct a search. Even if he's innocent he might not. So why are we making this trip?"

"Because we might come across something that allows us to come back with a search warrant later," Patterson said. "And if the girl is there, I don't want to sit on this. Her life is at stake."

"Agreed. But we risk tipping him off to our investigation."

"The police already interviewed him after the first and second abductions. Duane Snyder has never been definitively ruled out as a person of interest, and he must know that. We gain nothing by tiptoeing around this."

"I hope you're right." Bauer settled back into the passenger seat and lapsed into silence until they passed through the city of Athens and wound their way through back roads into a woodland expanse dotted here and there with homesteads and an occasional roadside business.

Patterson slowed as she approached a narrow trail on their left marked by a green oblong street sign on a pole that read SNYDER WAY-PVT. Another sign affixed lower on the pole, this one larger with black lettering on a white background, informed anyone who cared to read it that everything beyond that point was private property and trespassers would be prosecuted . . . or shot.

"Duane Snyder knows how to roll out the welcome mat," Bauer said, studying the sign as Patterson turned onto the dirt trail. "Let's hope he's not as belligerent as that sign suggests."

"If he is, it won't end well for him." Patterson eased the car along the dirt trail, trying to avoid the worst of the ruts and potholes. Even so, it was rough going.

They continued along the trail for another half a mile until the trees parted to reveal a cleared area with a stone cabin sitting in the middle. To the cabin's left was a fire pit with thick logs around it to act as natural benches. A rudimentary lean-to carport had been built against the other side of the cabin. Nothing more than a roof held up by wooden posts at the corners. The white cargo van was parked underneath this.

"I guess he's here," Bauer said as Patterson pulled around in front of the cabin, brought the vehicle to a halt, and cut the engine.

"Let's go and see what he has to say for himself," Patterson replied, pushing open the driver's side door and jumping out.

Bauer climbed out of the passenger side and joined her.

They hadn't gone more than five steps when the cabin door opened, and a lean man in his mid-forties appeared. He had limp black hair that fell to his shoulders. A receding hairline made his forehead look too big. He wore blue jeans and a red checkered shirt, despite the summer heat.

"This is private property." He observed Patterson and Bauer with a mix of apprehension and indignation. "Who the hell are you?"

Patterson produced her badge and held it up, introducing herself and Bauer. "Are you Duane Snyder?" She asked.

"Depends on what you want."

"Your wife didn't call to warn you we were coming?" Patterson had assumed Jodi Banks would've been straight on the phone to her husband moments after they drove away from her house.

Duane shook his head. "Left my phone in the van."

"I see." Patterson kept her hand close to the Glock sitting snug in a shoulder holster under her light jacket. "Are you aware that another girl was abducted this morning, Mr. Snyder?" She asked, curious to see his reaction. "Snatched off her bike while she was riding to work."

"Just like Shawna," Bauer said.

"My daughter was taken on the way home from school," Snyder corrected them. "Maybe if you people had done your jobs instead of focusing on me, she would still be alive."

"The FBI wasn't involved in the investigation back then, Mr. Snyder," Patterson replied. "But I've read the case file. The Dallas Police Department did everything they could to find Shawna."

"Who wasn't actually your daughter," Bauer said.

"You're right, she was my stepdaughter." A curious look passed across Snyder's face. Patterson couldn't tell if it was anger or sadness. Maybe it was both. "Doesn't mean I loved her any less."

"We understand," said Patterson. Her eyes flicked to the cargo van. "You still haven't answered my question."

Snyder hesitated for a few moments. "You say another girl has been abducted? I don't know nothing about that. I've been on the road since early this morning."

"That's what your wife told us," Bauer said, then asked, "Why did you leave so early?"

"Needed to finish a job that took too long yesterday, then I decided to head straight out here in the van rather than waste the time going home to get the Jeep," Snyder answered, confirming his wife's earlier statement.

Patterson searched his face for any sign of deceit but saw none. That didn't mean he was telling the truth. He might just be a good liar. She threw her cards on the table. "Would you mind if we had a look around, Mr. Snyder?"

"Why?" Snyder's eyes narrowed.

"Just routine," Patterson said. "No big deal. Just a quick peek inside the cabin and van since we're here, and then we'll be on our way."

This time, there was no hesitation from Snyder. "You got a warrant?"

"We were hoping to keep this informal," Patterson replied. "Friendly."

"No warrant, then." Snyder shook his head. "I think I'll pass on that search if it's all the same with you. Don't like folk in my space." Then he turned and strode back to the cabin without looking back, stepped inside, and slammed the door.

TWENTY

"WELL, THAT WAS POINTLESS," Bauer said as they climbed back into the car.

"On the contrary, it provided us with some useful information," Patterson replied.

"Like?"

"We got eyes on the van, even if it was only from the outside, and confirmed that it matches the witness description." Patterson nodded toward the vehicle parked under the carport. "Look. It even has a roof rack."

"Granted. But we still don't know if Duane Snyder is involved in this morning's abduction, since he wouldn't let us look inside either the cabin or the van."

"Which could be an indication of guilt. He knew we didn't have a warrant because we would have served him with it the moment we rolled up. If he's hiding something, he's hardly likely to let us go where we please."

"Or it could be as the man says. He likes his privacy and doesn't see any need to cooperate, given how Dallas PD treated him." Bauer scratched his chin. "Now, if he does have Amy Bowen somewhere around here, he'll be itching to move her at the first opportunity just in case we do come back with a warrant."

"Seems likely."

"We overplayed our hand."

"Maybe." Patterson steered back down the trail, but as soon as they could no longer be seen from the cabin, she pulled over under the shade of a towering pine tree and killed the engine.

"What are you doing?"

"Seeing if we spooked Duane Snyder into doing something rash." Patterson exited the car and waited for Bauer to join her. Then she stepped off the trail into the woods and took off back in the general direction of the cabin.

They moved through the woods with ease. The trees were well spaced, and there was little undergrowth except for an occasional fallen limb. Tracking close to the trail, they saw a no trespassing sign nailed to a tree. Then, tacked to another tree, a second sign.

Bauer pointed one out as they passed by. "Let's not forget that Duane Snyder probably has guns in that cabin," he said in a soft voice.

"I'm sure he does," Patterson replied. "But I don't intend to let him see us."

It didn't take them long to reach the edge of the clearing within which Snyder's cabin was located. As they drew close, Patterson's movements became more cautious. When they reached an area with bushes that provided a line of sight to the cabin, Patterson came to a hold and kneeled.

Bauer dropped down beside her.

They waited and watched the cabin, but Snyder did not come back out. The shadows grew longer, and the temperature started to drop.

After a while, Bauer yawned. "I guess we didn't spook him."

"Let's give it a bit longer," Patterson whispered. "He might be waiting to be sure that we've left the area before he makes a move."

"Or he could be in there sipping a Manhattan and reading a good book because he's innocent."

"That too," Patterson said. She hated to think that Bauer might be right about Snyder. The man was an obvious suspect. He shared a house with the first victim and had easy access to her. His job allowed him the freedom to go where he wanted unsupervised. It also gave him an alibi, even if it wasn't perfect. He owned a cabin on secluded land far from prying eyes. And there was the white cargo van sitting in front of them like icing on the cake.

But until he made a move, they were powerless, and it didn't appear like he was going to do that anytime soon.

She leaned close to Bauer. "Maybe you're right and this is a waste of time."

"Hey, you wanted to give it a while longer, so let's just—"

The rumble of an engine interrupted him.

"Someone's coming." Patterson shrank down behind the bushes.

Moments later, a car tore into view. It was an old Honda with faded blue paint. The engine sounded ragged, like one of the cylinders was misfiring.

The car pulled up in front of the cabin and stopped. A skinny woman with bleach blond hair climbed out.

Patterson raised her phone and photographed the mystery visitor as she approached the cabin door and banged on it.

Snyder answered, and they exchanged words before he let her in and closed the door. Patterson couldn't hear what they said, but it didn't sound friendly.

"Who the hell is that?" Bauer whispered.

"Beats me." Patterson shrugged.

"You think he called an accomplice after we spoke to him?"

"I don't think so." Patterson shook her head. "She got here way too fast. And it didn't look like they were exactly friends."

"Right." Bauer paused. "She probably saw our car on the way up here."

"That thought crossed my mind," admitted Patterson. "But there's nothing we can do about it."

"If she mentions our car to Snyder, he'll know we're still around."

"From her demeanor, I got the impression she was in no mood to talk about a parked car."

"She sounded pissed." Bauer shifted to get a better view of the cabin. "I'd love to be a fly on the wall in there."

"Yeah."

"How do you want to play this?"

"I think we hang tight and see what happens."

"Or we could try to get closer so we can hear them," Bauer said as another muted exchange came from within the cabin.

Before Patterson could answer, the door flew open, and the woman stormed out. She strode back to the car and climbed in, slamming the door. The engine revved, and she peeled away from the cabin in a cloud of dust just as Snyder ran outside.

Patterson wondered if he was going to jump in the van and give chase. Instead, he watched her leave then turned and went back into the cabin with a shake of his head, slamming the door behind him.

"That was interesting," Bauer said. "You think we should hightail it back to the car and follow her?"

"We'd never make it in time. She'll be long gone. And if Snyder is our man, the victim is still here somewhere. Whoever that was, I got a strong sense he wasn't expecting her, and she left empty-handed. She's a distraction. We need to keep our focus on Snyder."

"Fair enough." Bauer rubbed his neck. "I sure hope he does something soon, then."

"Me too," Patterson replied. But unfortunately, Snyder appeared content to stay inside the cabin because another sixty minutes passed, bringing their unofficial surveillance to the two-hour mark. Patterson was growing restless. It was after six and they had a long drive back to the city. She stretched and nudged Bauer. "Want to knock this on the head?"

"About thirty minutes ago." Bauer kept his eyes on the cabin. "If Snyder has Amy Bowen in there, our visit didn't spook him into moving her."

"I know."

"And that's a big if. Honestly, our time would have been better spent pursuing other leads back in Dallas."

"Probably. but it's too late now," Patterson said, trying to hide her disappointment. There was something about Snyder that she didn't like. Her instincts told her he was hiding something. But that didn't mean it was an abducted teenager. She climbed to her feet and waited for Bauer to do the same.

It took them ten minutes to reach the Charger.

Patterson's stomach growled as she climbed behind the wheel, reminding her they had skipped lunch. Which was why, after they left the dirt trail and Duane Snyder's cabin in their rearview mirror, she asked Bauer to keep his eyes open for somewhere to pull off and grab a snack. On the outskirts of Athens, amid industrial units and dealerships that sold farm machinery, he found what she was looking for. And much more.

"Whoa. Hold up," he said excitedly, pointing toward a roadside diner off to their left. "Pull in here."

"Seriously?" Patterson said. "You want to eat in a greasy spoon on the side of a backwater highway?"

"No. But we're going to anyway."

"And why would that be?" Patterson asked, confused.

"Look." Bauer motioned toward a vehicle sitting alone in an

empty area off to the side of the building near a row of dump-sters. It was the same Honda with faded blue paint they had seen at Duane Snyder's cabin.

TWENTY-ONE

THE DINER WAS BUILT to look like an old railcar with chrome accents and oblong windows, but despite its outward appearance, the place had probably never ridden the rails for even a single day. Patterson's father was something of a train aficionado, having worked for the transit authority most of his life. He had given her a history lesson on diners like this more than once as they passed a sleek chrome embellished restaurant sitting aside one road or another. They were, in reality, the invention of a long-defunct company out of Massachusetts that sold prefabricated restaurant buildings in the early twentieth century. While the concept was based on the streamlined dining cars that zipped around the country in the golden age of rail, most were actually nothing more than a clever marketing ploy to draw the eye of passing motorists.

A sign attached to the roof blinked its name in green neon. *The Lonestar Skillet.* Patterson took her phone out and snapped a photo for her dad because he would get a kick out of the retro eatery.

"That is definitely the car we saw at Duane Snyder's cabin," Bauer said, studying the battered Honda.

After he spotted the vehicle as they drove by, Patterson had made a U-turn and pulled into the parking lot next to it.

"Let's see if we can find the driver," Patterson said, heading for the entrance. She held the door open for Bauer to enter, then stepped inside and looked around.

The diner's interior was well-maintained, if kitschy. Actually, it was a whole lot kitschy. There was as much chrome on the inside as on the outside. Red vinyl upholstered booths lined one side of the restaurant under windows with a view of the parking lot. A counter ran three-quarters of the diner on the other side, behind which several line cooks toiled over hot skillets, just like the name suggested. Each table came with its own personal jukebox. An aroma of grilled meats hung in the air.

A server in a uniform that looked like it had been plucked straight from the 40s appeared carrying plates of apple pie topped with vanilla ice cream. "Take a seat anywhere. Someone will be with you in a jiffy," she said, breezing by.

Before Patterson could reply, the woman bustled away, balancing the plates like a pro, and hurried toward the other end of the restaurant.

"I don't see the owner of that car," Bauer said, looking around at the restaurant's patrons.

"Me either," Patterson said. She considered chasing after the server to inquire about the car. But there was another employee standing behind a cash register near the end of the counter, taking payment from a family of four with a pair of raucous children who had clearly consumed too much sugar.

As soon as they stepped away, Patterson approached the cashier stand, pulled out her badge, and addressed the employee. "We're looking for the owner of a light blue Honda parked around the side of the building."

"That would be Darlene."

"She works here?" Patterson asked.

"Sure does." The cashier nodded. "Works the evening shift four nights a week. Did she do something wrong?"

"No." Bauer shook his head. "We want to ask her a few questions. That's all."

"Where is she now?" Patterson asked. The blond-haired woman who had stormed out of Duane Snyder's cabin was still nowhere in sight.

"She's here somewhere. Maybe out the back or taking a bathroom break. I can find her if you want."

"We'd appreciate that," Patterson replied. "Is there somewhere private we can talk to her?"

"Only the storeroom, and it would be mighty cramped with three of you in there."

"How about we take a booth instead," Bauer said, "and you can send her over to us."

"Sure thing, hon." The cashier offered them a couple of menus. "Y'all look hungry. Food's always free for members of local law enforcement. FBI ain't that but we'll make you honorary locals for the day."

"That's very kind." Patterson took the menus and handed one to Bauer.

"Think nothing of it. Our way of giving back."

Patterson thanked her and made for the nearest empty booth.

"You really want to eat here?" Bauer asked as they sat down.

"Sure. Why not?"

"I can think of a couple of reasons, not the least of which is wicked heartburn."

"I'll stop for a tub of antacids at the nearest drugstore after we leave."

"I'm holding you to that."

"Really?" Patterson laughed. "You eat junk food all the time. You have pizza practically every day."

"Exactly. If I'm going to get heartburn, I want it to be for something I really enjoy."

"Or are you trying to eat better because of a certain cute personal assistant you've been seeing?"

"Nothing of the sort." Bauer chuckled and glanced around. Most of the other booths were occupied. "This place is pretty busy considering."

"Means the food can't be half bad," Patterson said.

She studied the menu while they waited for the owner of the Honda to show up. All the diner favorites were there, including all-day breakfast, eggs cooked every possible way, and enough varieties of hamburgers to keep the most ardent fast-food junkie giddy for a month. But it was the corned beef hash that caught her attention. It was marked as a house specialty, highlighted in a red box near the top of the menu. Her grandmother had made the best hash, and the memories of that crispy fried potato laced with corned beef made Patterson's mouth water. At least until a skinny waitress holding a carafe of coffee approached the booth and pulled her back to the present.

The woman had shoulder-length straight bleached-blonde hair gathered into a ponytail. Her face was long and angular, although not unattractive. A rose tattoo graced the side of her neck. Patterson recognized her right away as the driver of the Honda.

"Y'all the FBI agents Maggie told me about?" She asked in a southern drawl while simultaneously pouring coffee into a pair of mugs sitting on the table.

"Yes." Patterson flashed her badge again, then slipped the credentials wallet back into her pocket. "Would you mind answering a few questions about Duane Snyder?"

"Never heard of him."

"We know that's not true, Darlene," Bauer said. "You were at his cabin earlier this afternoon. We saw you."

"Okay. Fine. I know him. So what?"

Patterson leaned on the table. "The pair of you got into a pretty heated argument. Mind telling us what that was about?"

"It was nothing. A stupid misunderstanding is all. He comes in here sometimes when he's staying at the cabin." Darlene wouldn't meet Patterson's gaze. "If you want something to eat, I'll give you a few minutes to look at the menu. Otherwise, I've got better things to do than stand here yakking."

With that said, Darlene turned on her heel and walked away at a brisk pace.

TWENTY-TWO

NO SOONER HAD Darlene walked away from the table than Patterson was on her feet. "Wait. We only have a few questions. Please, it won't take long."

Darlene was heading for the counter, but at Patterson's approach, she hesitated and turned back. "Look, I already told you, I don't want to talk about Duane."

"You're not in trouble if that's what you're worried about."

"Why would I be worried?"

"I don't know. You tell me."

"I'm not worried. Whatever you're looking for, I'm not your gal."

"Not even if it would help catch the person who took his stepdaughter?"

"What are you talking about?" Confusion flashed across Darlene's face. "He has a stepdaughter?"

"Had a stepdaughter," Patterson corrected her. "She was abducted and murdered. We're trying to find her killer."

"Oh my God. I had no idea." Darlene put the carafe down on the counter. Her face had turned pale.

"If you know something about Duane Snyder, you have to

tell us," Patterson prodded, pressing her advantage. "Put your-self in his wife's shoes. How would you feel if it was your daughter?"

"He's married?" Darlene's eyes flew wide.

Patterson nodded. "His wife's name is Jodi. Her daughter's name was Shawna. She's one of four girls abducted while riding their bikes. Three of those girls are dead. The most recent was taken just this morning."

"Sweet Jesus. That's horrible. You think Duane had some-thing to do with it?"

"We don't know who took these girls or why, but we would very much like to find out before the fourth victim ends up dead. Please, Darlene, if you know anything, you have to tell us."

"I really don't." Darlene had recovered her composure . . . mostly. She looked down at her apron and straightened it. When she looked up again, she kept her gaze fixed somewhere over Patterson's left shoulder.

"How about you tell me why you were at his cabin earlier?" Patterson said. "What was the argument about?"

Darlene hesitated. She tugged her bottom lip with her teeth. When she spoke again, her voice had lost much of its defen-siveness. "It was nothing to do with any missing girls or anything like that. He comes in here when he's at the cabin. He was here a couple of weeks ago and came in for dinner. Claimed he'd left his wallet behind. I spotted him the meal. Eighteen bucks plus tax and tip. He promised to pay me back when he came in next. When I called the diner earlier today to see when my shift started, one of the other waitresses told me he'd stopped by at lunchtime and hadn't left my money. I'm on a tight budget, and every penny counts. That's why I went to his cabin on my way to work. I wanted to get what he owes me."

"And did you?"

104

"No. I didn't get what I wanted." There was renewed anger in Darlene's voice.

"And you know nothing about his stepdaughter or the other missing girls?" Patterson asked.

"I didn't even know he had a stepdaughter until two minutes ago. And trust me, if I knew anything about missing or murdered girls, I'd be talking to the police, not serving coffee and pie to a bunch of cattle ranchers."

"You saw nothing unusual when you were at the cabin this afternoon?"

"No." Darlene's gaze shifted to the table where Bauer was still sitting in the booth, watching the exchange between the two women. "Look, I'm sorry for being so defensive. It's been a tough day, that's all."

"Don't worry about it." Patterson took an FBI business card from her pocket. She held it out to Darlene. "My cell number is on this card. If you remember anything after we leave, please call me."

Darlene took the card and looked at it for a moment, then slipped it into her apron. "I'll do that."

"Thank you."

"Are you and your partner hungry, or did you just stop in to ask questions?" Darlene gave Patterson a wan smile.

"A hot meal sounds pretty good right now," Patterson admitted.

"Good. We like to make sure law enforcement officers like yourselves don't leave here on an empty stomach. It's kind of our thing."

"Maggie already told us about your *feed the local cops for free* policy," Patterson said. "You must be all sorts of popular with law enforcement in this town."

"They like to come in, and we like to give back. It's a win-win."

Patterson smiled. "Which is why it would be rude of us to

skip out without eating." Her gaze fell to Darlene's apron pocket. "You won't forget that card I gave you, right?"

"I won't forget." Darlene patted her apron pocket. "Go join your friend. I'll come and take your order just as soon as I catch up on my other customers."

Patterson thanked her, then returned to the booth and sat down.

"Well?" Bauer asked. "Did you get anywhere?"

"I don't know." Patterson couldn't help but feel Darlene was holding out on her. Had the argument really been about nothing more than a stiffed check? "She has my cell number, so I guess we'll see what happens."

"I wouldn't hold your breath. The woman wasn't exactly friendly. You still want to eat here?"

"I can't imagine we're going to find anywhere better between here and Dallas. Besides, I'm starving."

"And it's free, too."

"Someone's changed their tune," Patterson laughed.

"Don't mock me. I'm still on a probationary pay rate. I need to save all the money I can."

"I remember. The first few years were tough." Patterson glanced over her shoulder toward the counter. Darlene was heading their way. She met Patterson's gaze briefly before dropping her eyes. Did she know more than she was letting on about Duane Snyder? Patterson had a suspicion the answer was yes, but they would have to wait and see if the waitress decided to talk.

TWENTY-THREE

BY THE TIME they left the restaurant and drove back to Dallas, it was getting dark. Even though Bauer had mostly returned to his old self, there was still an unspoken tension between them that Patterson wanted to resolve. She hoped Bauer would open up to her on the long drive back, but instead, he remained tight-lipped, willing to talk only about Duane Snyder and the case they were working on.

When they arrived back at her hotel, Patterson handed him the keys to the Dodge Charger, but not before she made sure there wouldn't be a repeat of the previous evening.

"You're going straight home tonight, right?" She asked while she still had possession of the keys.

"I told you already, it won't happen again."

"Scout's honor?"

"I wasn't in the Boy Scouts when I was a kid. Wasn't exactly an option. But if it makes you happy, then sure."

"That surprises me," Patterson said, dropping the keys onto his palm. "You look like the type."

"Yeah, well, looks can be deceptive." Bauer climbed into the driver's seat. "Don't worry. I'm not stopping off at any bars on the way home. I promise."

Patterson had no choice but to believe him. She watched Bauer drive off, pleased to see that he turned in the opposite direction to Pioneer Jacks, and then entered the hotel and went up to her room.

She sent the diner photo to her father and spent the next ten minutes texting back and forth with him. After that, she called Grant and spent a further hour chatting before once again finding herself at a loose end. Her thoughts turned to Bauer, and the events of the last twenty-four hours.

She grabbed her personal laptop and sat on the bed with it in front of her. Bauer had admitted to something terrible the previous night. He claimed to have killed his best friend. This was a stunning admission, especially coming from an FBI agent. Later, he had backtracked, claiming it was just the alcohol talking. But no one admitted to taking a life if they hadn't committed the act, did they? And if Special Agent Bauer really had shot and killed someone, it must have been in the line of duty. Nothing else made sense. His statement the previous evening sounded more like remorse than a confession of guilt to a previously concealed crime.

Patterson opened a search page, her fingers hovering over the laptop keyboard. Did she really want to do this? It felt like an invasion of privacy. Bauer clearly wanted to keep private whatever skeletons were lurking in his closet. Otherwise, he would have explained himself during the long hours they were stuck in a car together, driving back and forth from Duane Snyder's cabin.

But she had to know. Not just for the sake of curiosity, but also because they were partners, and trust was a big deal. She needed to confirm that Bauer would have her back in a tight situation.

With a heavy heart, she tapped away at the keyboard, entering a search term into the box on the screen.

Marcus Bauer. LAPD.

She hit the return key and then studied the list of results.

The first was an article in the Times about a rookie cop who had received a commendation for saving the life of a robbery victim stabbed by three unknown assailants in a back alley. Bauer's face stared back at her from the photograph accompanying the article. He looked like a kid in a uniform. So young and fresh-faced. It made her smile. But it was not what Patterson was looking for.

The next several results were generic hits about the Los Angeles Police Department that matched one or more keywords, but not all of them.

At the bottom of the page was another article that mentioned Bauer as part of a task force that had discovered over a million dollars' worth of drugs during a raid in East Hollywood.

There was still no mention of anything close to what Bauer had told her the previous night, even though she browsed three additional pages of search results.

Patterson second-guessed herself, wondering if she should be poking around in Marcus Bauer's past the way she was. But her reasons for doing so were as good now as they had been thirty minutes ago. Which was why she decided to try a more direct approach. She deleted the original search term and typed in a new one.

Marcus Bauer. LAPD. Officer-involved shooting.

This time, she found what she was looking for right away. The first six results all related to the same incident in South LA. A botched convenience store robbery. Patterson clicked on the first link and read the article.

• • •

LAPD officer shoots and kills suspect in convenience store heist.

Officers responded to the Dime-A-Dozen Value Mart twenty-four-hour convenience store on Imperial Highway in South-Central in the early hours of Tuesday morning around 1 a.m. after a passerby reported a robbery in progress.

Units arrived on the scene to find three masked assailants exiting the premises. All were armed—two with pistols and one with a shotgun. The suspects fled on foot into a residential neighborhood along Vermont Avenue. Two of the assailants were apprehended without incident after a short pursuit. The third attempted to evade capture by entering a dead-end alleyway and fired upon officers when it became clear there was no way out.

Veteran officer Marcus Bauer, who has been with the LAPD for almost a decade, returned fire, striking the gunman in the chest. The suspect was airlifted to Los Angeles General, where he succumbed to his injuries and was pronounced dead at 3:47 a.m.

Officer Bauer has been placed on administrative leave pending the outcome of an investigation, which is standard procedure for any officer-involved shooting. A source within the LAPD who was speaking off the record said that their preliminary findings indicated that Officer Bauer followed department policy when discharging his weapon.

Given the circumstances, it is not expected that Officer Bauer will face disciplinary action.

This story will be updated as more details become available.

Patterson read the article twice, then studied the accompanying photograph. It showed an alleyway cordoned off with crime scene tape being examined by a pair of forensic technicians. The article was dated three years before. Was this the incident Bauer had been referring to? She didn't see how it fitted what he told her. But at the same time, the article didn't mention any other shooting incidents in Bauer's past, which she would have expected if this was not his first fatal engagement. None of the other articles mentioned another shooting, either. Patterson didn't know what to think. But it didn't look like she would get any answers tonight.

She cleared the search bar and closed the laptop. If anyone knew more about Marcus Bauer's past, it would be the FBI. She briefly toyed with the idea of calling Jonathan Grant back and asking him to pull Bauer's Bureau application and any related records, including his psych eval.

But she didn't. Because Patterson already knew what her boyfriend come boss back in New York would say. It would be a hard no. If she wanted to know more, Patterson would just have to wait until Bauer was ready to tell her.

TWENTY-FOUR

AMY BOWEN HUDDLED in a corner of the small windowless room and strained her eyes to see through the darkness. She did not know where she was or why she was there. But Amy knew one thing: she wanted to go home.

She thought back to the previous morning, when the world was still a safe place. She had been riding her bike to the Rise and Shine Motel, where she had been working four days a week in housekeeping since school got out at the beginning of June. It was the first year Amy had been allowed to get a job. The legal age to work in Texas was fourteen, and even though vacuuming floors and changing bedsheets was hardly a fun way to spend the summer break, it also allowed her to save money. Which she desperately wanted to do, because her friend Madison was going skiing in Colorado with her family over the Christmas break and had invited Amy to go with her. And even though Amy's parents had said yes, there was a caveat. She needed to be responsible and pay her own way.

Except that instead of spending the day cleaning hotel rooms, Amy had ended up run off the road by a white van that showed up out of nowhere and veered in front of her. She lost control of the bike and went into a ditch, banging her knee and twisting her ankle. And then it got worse. The driver of the van jumped out. She thought he was going to help her, but instead, before she could react, he slapped a strip of tape over her mouth to stop her from screaming. Then he was dragging her into the van and binding her wrists and ankles with zip ties. He blindfolded her before climbing into the driver's seat and taking off.

They had driven for what felt like hours, and then the van had stopped. She heard the driver's door open, then slam closed again. She lay helpless in the back of the van, waiting for the man to come and get her, terrified of what he was going to do next.

Because Amy wasn't stupid. There were entire TV channels dedicated to what happened when strangers abducted young women. Murder-death-porn, her mother called it, even though she happily watched it. And most of the time, Amy was right by her side, sitting on the sofa with a big tub of popcorn.

But the man didn't come for her, at least not at first. As the day wore on, the van became unbearably hot. The sweat soaked through her clothes so that they stuck to her. She was beyond thirsty, too. She swallowed her own saliva in a vain attempt to quench the raging thirst, at least until there was no more saliva left. And all the while, Amy lay on her side, unable to move, and wondered if she had been left there to die.

But then, after what felt like an interminable amount of time, she finally heard the grind of the van's side door being opened and felt rough hands tugging at her. It was cooler by then. It was also night. She knew that because she could see a sliver of black starless sky above the blindfold as he dragged her outside. She also heard the hoot of a distant owl.

Her captor snipped the cable tie that cinched her ankles. Then he made her walk. Gravel and dead leaves crunched underfoot. She covered a short distance before her foot kicked a protrusion that she realized was a step. Her captor forced her up. She stumbled forward, trying to ignore the pain that flared in her injured ankle. When the steps ended unexpectedly, she put her foot down too hard and lost her balance, pitching forward with a muffled screech behind the tape. She tried to put her hands out to save herself, except her wrists were bound behind her back. A sudden jolt of panic gripped Amy before she felt her collar being grabbed and she was yanked back upright. Then she was hustled onward by a firm hand in the center of her back.

They were inside a building now. Even though she couldn't see, Amy sensed the walls close around her. She felt the flat and even floor beneath her feet. There were more steps. She was steered blindly down until her feet met even ground again. This was followed by more walking and even a moment where she was forced to crawl forward on her knees. She felt rough cold stone, or maybe it was bricks, digging into her back before she could stand again. The hand pushed her forward. Then her captor issued a terse command.

"Stop. Don't move."

She heard a sound like grating metal and then a squeal of unoiled hinges. She was thrust forward, careening into the unknown . . . At least until her captor pulled the blindfold off.

She looked up into the eyes of the man who had snatched her. She pleaded with him to let her go, even though the tape over her mouth made it impossible to talk in anything but a vague mumble.

Her captor ignored the muffled pleas. He backed up and pulled a metal door closed. The sort of thing she would have expected in a jail cell, with bars and a big lock. But this was no prison, at least not the traditional kind. The walls were lined with bricks, the mortar between them chalky and crumbling. The ceiling was curved, like a vault. The only source of light was a bare bulb hanging on the other side of the bars. And now, as Amy huddled in the darkness surveying her surroundings for the first time, she saw the photographs. There must have been a hundred of them arranged like some kind of sick collage on the wall behind her. And every picture was of the same person. A pretty girl who looked around the same age as Amy. And even though this unknown girl wore different dresses in many of the images, they all shared one thing in common. Butterflies. In every photograph, the girl smiling back at Amy was wearing butterflies.

TWENTY-FIVE

MORNING BROUGHT no answers to either Patterson's concerns about her partner or the current location of Amy Bowen, abducted as she rode to work the previous day. By midday, Patterson was about ready to climb the walls of their windowless office buried deep within the FBI's Dallas field office. They had checked in with the Police Department, who were leading the investigation, took another look into Duane Snyder's background, and pored over crime scene photos of the first three dump sites. All to no avail. All they were doing was retreading old ground.

Patterson was happy for the distraction when her phone rang. She saw it was Detective Costa calling her back. She had only spoken to him an hour before, and there had been no new leads. Maybe something had changed.

"Detective, tell me you have something," Patterson said, snatching up the phone and answering.

"Yes and no," Costa replied. He sounded tired. Patterson wondered if he had been losing sleep. A missing girl would do that. "We're still no closer to finding Amy Bowen than we were yesterday, and the longer we go, the closer we are to her showing up dead. But it's not all bad news. Forensics have been searching the previous victim's dump site for the past three days, combing through the area in an ever-widening circle. They've mostly found junk unlikely to be related to our killer or the victim. Old soda cans. A piece of abandoned farm machinery. Fast food wrappers. You know, the kind of thing you'd expect to uncover in a pristine wilderness maintained by the National Forest Service. But they found one item of interest."

"Hang on, let me put it on hands-free so Agent Bauer can hear." Patterson transferred the call to speaker. "Okay. Tell us."

"Sure." Costa cleared his throat. "Forensics were combing an area about a quarter of a mile from the scene, and they came across a pillowcase caught on a bush."

"A pillowcase?" Bauer frowned. "That's a strange thing to discard in the middle of the grasslands."

"That's what forensics thought. They bagged it and sent the pillowcase back to the lab for further examination. And it's a good thing they did. The fibers from the pillowcase match the fibers the ME found on Susie Tomlinson."

"You think it's the murder weapon?" Patterson's heartbeat quickened. Finally, a break in the case.

"That's what we're going with." Costa sounded hopeful. "We figure the killer either discarded the pillowcase somewhere near the body, and the wind blew it to where the forensics team found it, or maybe he took it with him and threw it from the car some ways distant after killing Susie. Probably figured it wouldn't ever be discovered, and even if it was, we couldn't connect it to her."

"Where's the pillowcase now?" Patterson wanted to look at it.

"Still at the lab. They're not done with it yet, but when they are, I'll send someone to pick it up. I'm as eager as you to examine it. In the meantime, I have plenty of photographs. I'll email them to you."

"I'd appreciate that," Patterson said. Their tedious and fruitless morning didn't feel so bad now. It was good to move the needle on the investigation. "Have you made progress anywhere else?"

"What, the pillowcase isn't enough?" Costa snorted.

"Just thought I'd ask. It has been a whole hour since we last spoke, after all."

"Yeah, well, maybe investigations move at the speed of light on the federal level, but in the world of local policing, we take it slow and steady, like snails."

"Nothing wrong with being a snail," Bauer said. "Don't forget to send those photos."

"Already doing it. You should have them momentarily," Costa said goodbye and hung up.

Patterson went straight to her email and refreshed it, hoping to see an email from the detective. There was nothing. She waited another five minutes, then checked again. This time, a message from Costa popped up.

"Got them," she said, opening the email.

"Me too," Bauer replied from over the top of his own laptop.

There were nine photos. Four of them showed the pillowcase snagged in the branches of a prickly bush. Two were wide-angle shots that showed the plant sitting on the edge of an expanse of green pastureland that rolled for miles toward a distant stand of trees. Two more were close-ups from different angles. The rest were lab photos. Patterson studied the images with a growing sense of good fortune. If it hadn't been for that shrub snagging the pillowcase, it could have ended up blown so far from the crime scene that they would never have found it.

She turned her attention to the photographs taken in the lab. The technicians had spread the pillowcase out on an examination table and photographed it, front and back, then taken more close-ups of a detail that hadn't been clear in the location photographs. An embroidered motif of roses growing from a thorn bush with green stylized leaves that ran down the short side near the pillow opening. It was intricately done and did not look modern. The lace edge lining the opening further cemented Patterson's hunch that the pillowcase was vintage. An odd choice of murder weapon.

Bauer thought the same. "Where do you think our killer got this? A thrift store?"

"Maybe." Patterson shrugged. "It's a good way of covering your tracks. If he bought a new pillowcase at a big box store, we could track the manufacturer and maybe even narrow it down to where the item was sold. Those stores all have surveillance cameras, which means our killer would be caught on tape."

"Not so much with a thrift or vintage store. They probably wouldn't even remember selling it. A lot of those places just take donations and put the stuff straight out. I can't imagine they keep detailed inventories."

"Right. And depending on the store, they might not even have surveillance."

"I'll bet you a thousand dollars that if our perpetrator purchased this in some thrift store or flea market, he chose one that didn't have cameras."

"I agree." Patterson flicked through the photos again. "And it doesn't look like there's a manufacturer's tag in the pillowcase that would help us date or otherwise determine its origin. If there were, they would have photographed it. Let's keep our fingers crossed that he left some trace evidence on the pillowcase."

"That would be beyond lucky," said Bauer.

"It's not outside the realm of possibility. If the pillowcase has a high enough thread count, a good forensics tech could pull a fingerprint."

"That's a big if. Prints rarely last more than a few days on a fabric like cotton, which this pillowcase probably is. And then you have to consider how long it's been exposed to the elements. And of course, our killer likely wore gloves, making this entire conversation moot."

"Hey, a girl can dream, can't she?" Patterson knew Bauer was right. It was unlikely the killer would be sloppy enough to leave fingerprints behind. She looked through the photographs one more time, then saved them to her hard drive before closing the email. "I don't know about you, but I could use a pick me up. Want to make a coffee run?"

"Why not?" Bauer stood and grabbed his jacket from the back of the chair.

At that moment, Patterson's phone rang again. It was a number she didn't recognize.

"Patterson Blake," she said, answering.

Bauer stopped in his tracks and turned to look at her.

"Special Agent Blake, this is Darlene Rourke. We met yesterday when you came into the diner. You gave me your card and said I could call you."

"That's right." Patterson exchanged a hopeful look with Bauer. "What can I do for you, Darlene?"

"Well . . ." Darlene took a faltering breath. "I'd like to file a complaint against Duane Snyder."

"What kind of complaint?" Patterson felt the hairs on the back of her neck stand up.

"Sexual assault," Darlene said. "He raped me."

TWENTY-SIX

TWO HOURS after Darlene Rourke called Patterson's phone, accusing Duane Snyder of rape, she and Bauer arrived at the City of Athens Police Department near downtown. No sooner had Darlene told them why she was calling than Patterson advised her not to say anything else over the phone and go straight to the local police, where she could file a formal complaint. She and Bauer would, Patterson assured her, be there as soon as possible.

After hanging up, they had wasted no time in making the drive southeast to Athens for the second time in two days. Their only concession was a couple of minutes spent pulling through the drive-through of a McDonald's on the way out of the city, where they picked up cheeseburgers and fries which they ate behind the wheel. Bauer also purchased a strawberry milkshake, which he claimed would give him energy since it looked like they were in for another long day.

They parked outside the police building in a space reserved for official vehicles and headed inside, where a female detective in a dark blue suit met them. She was African American, slim, and in her early forties with an attractive oval face.

"You must be the FBI agents we've been waiting for," she said.

"That's us," Patterson said, then introduced herself and Bauer.

"Pleased to meet you both. Detective Carol Voss. I'm what passes for a Special Victims Division around here. We've made Darlene Rourke comfortable in an interview room. I'll take you back to see her."

"Thank you," Patterson said as they left the lobby. "Have you taken a statement yet?"

"No. She wouldn't talk. Said she wanted to wait until y'all got here. We've already notified the Rape Crisis Center, and they sent over an advocate. She's with Darlene right now and will remain for the duration of the interview. I hope you don't mind."

"That's fine," Patterson said as they navigated a short corridor. "Whatever makes Darlene comfortable."

"What about a doctor?" Bauer asked. "Has she received any medical treatment?"

"No." Carol shook her head. "According to Darlene, the rape took place a couple of weeks ago, so any DNA or other evidence is long gone. Even so, we offered to have her checked out by a medical professional, but she refused." As they reached a closed door with a sign on it that read INTERVIEW IN PROGRESS, Carol stopped and turned to Patterson. "Do either of you have any prior experience interviewing victims of sexual assault?"

"No." Patterson shook her head.

"I do," said Bauer. "Spent over a decade with the LAPD. First as a beat cop, and then a detective. I investigated several cases involving sexual assault."

Carol nodded. "Then you understand how sensitive a matter this is. We need to tread softly. Make Darlene feel at ease."

"Understood." Patterson was eager to get into the room and see what Darlene had to say for herself. She wondered why the waitress had said nothing the previous day when she had the opportunity. Maybe she was ashamed or afraid. Or maybe she just didn't think anyone would believe her.

"When we get in there, me and Special Agent Blake will do most of the talking," Carol said. She looked at Bauer. "We'll be discussing some very intimate details of what happened to her. Darlene may not want you in the room. If that's the case, you will need to leave."

"I understand. As I already said, this isn't my first time dealing with a sexual assault allegation." Bauer pushed his hands into his pockets. He looked past the detective toward the interview room door. "Ready when you are."

TWENTY-SEVEN

DARLENE ROURKE WAS SITTING behind a wide desk and staring at a point up toward the ceiling on the opposite wall as if she were a million miles away when Detective Voss led Bauer and Patterson into the room.

Next to Darlene was a woman in her fifties with graying hair that fell below her shoulders. She rested her hands on the desk atop a closed notebook with a pen next to it. Patterson surmised this must be the Rape Crisis Center advocate.

Both women had mugs of coffee. One mug was empty, but the other, in front of Darlene, was still full, and she showed no interest in it.

"Hello, Darlene," Patterson said, approaching the desk and sitting down. "I understand you're not having a good day."

"You could say," Darlene answered, her gaze still somewhere over Patterson's shoulder.

"Is it okay if Special Agent Bauer stays in the room?" Patterson asked.

Darlene shrugged.

"Very well." Patterson waited for Detective Voss to take a seat next to her. Bauer remained near the door, leaning against the wall with his arms folded. After a few moments of silence, Patterson gave Darlene a gentle nudge. "Would you like to tell us what's on your mind?"

For a moment, Darlene didn't react, then her gaze slid down to Patterson. "I already told you on the phone. Duane Snyder raped me at his cabin."

"When did this happen, Darlene?"

"A couple of weeks ago. He came into the diner late on Friday evening. He had driven up from Dallas after work to spend the weekend at the cabin. At least that's what he said. He was the only person left when we closed for the night, nursing his fourth refill of coffee. Afterward, he was waiting in the parking lot. We chatted a while, then he asked if I'd like to go back to his cabin for a beer. Said he had a six-pack in the fridge. It was on my way home, so I said what the hell."

"You went to the cabin of a man you barely knew?" Patterson leaned forward.

"I knew him well enough. He's been coming into the diner for a couple of years, on and off. Whenever he's at the cabin. We were friends, and it wasn't the first time I'd been there, so I thought nothing of it."

"I see." Patterson folded her arms. "You acted like you only knew him in passing when we spoke last night. You also said you went up to his cabin because he owed you money. That when he came in a few weeks before, he didn't have his wallet, and you spotted his meal on the understanding he would pay you back. Did that really happen?"

Darlene didn't answer.

"You know, it's easy enough to check," Patterson said. "All we need to do is look at the receipts for the night in question. That would show us whether you paid for the meal."

"All right. I didn't tell the truth." Darlene glanced toward the Rape Crisis Center advocate, who gave her a nod of encouragement. "I was ashamed of what happened, so when you pressed me, I made up a story about why I was up there arguing with Snyder. I didn't want to admit what Duane Snyder did to me."

"So it wasn't about money. You went to the cabin to confront Duane Snyder about raping you." Patterson found that hard to believe. If Snyder was a rapist, would his victim really return to the scene of the crime to have it out with him? It made no sense. But then again, people did dumb things all the time. Especially when they were traumatized.

"I wanted to know why he did it. Why he forced himself on me like that? We were friends. I didn't go up there to have sex with him, but he wouldn't take no for an answer." Darlene took a shuddering breath. "Look, I know it was stupid, going back to that cabin. But I was angry with him. I felt betrayed."

"I can understand that," Patterson said in a soothing voice. "Had he ever made unwanted advances toward you before the night in question?"

"No. I mean, he's married, right?"

"Yes," Patterson said. "He has a wife in Dallas."

Detective Voss chimed in. "But that doesn't make him any more or less likely to commit a sexual assault."

"I know. I just didn't think . . ." Darlene sniffed and rubbed her nose with the back of her hand. "I thought I could trust him."

"Do you want to tell us what happened that night?" Patterson asked. "At the cabin."

"I guess. I've come this far, haven't I?"

"Just take your time, Darlene," Detective Voss said. "Whenever you're ready."

Darlene sat in silence for a while, then took a deep breath. "He was friendly at first. Brought the six-pack out and cracked a couple of beers. We sat on the sofa and drank them. It was nice, you know. Relaxing. Then he moved closer to me. Put an arm on my knee. Started touching me. Kissing me. I asked him to stop, but he didn't. That's when . . ."

"You don't need to go on if you find it too distressing," Patterson said. "We can take a statement later when you feel up to it."

"No. I'd rather get it over with." Darlene wiped tears from her eyes. Then she told them what had happened between herself and Snyder after they finished the beers. What he had done to her on the couch.

When she was finished, Patterson reached across the table and took Darlene's hand. "Thank you for telling us what happened. It took a lot of courage. You were very brave."

"Darlene nodded. "What happens now?"

"Well, we go have a chat with Duane Snyder," Patterson replied. "See what he has to say for himself."

"Are you going to arrest him?" Darlene asked. "Put him in jail?"

"I don't know yet," Patterson admitted.

"But he raped me."

"We need to hear both sides of the story and assess the situation," Detective Voss said. "I know it's hard to hear under the circumstances, but this might be a long process. The district attorney will decide whether to press charges based on the evidence we present, but right now, we need to collect that evidence and make our case. Do you understand?"

"I think so."

"Is there someone you can stay with this evening?" Patterson asked. "A friend or relative, maybe. You might not want to be alone, given the trauma you've been through."

"No, there's no one. Not around here, anyway. Besides, I have to work the evening shift at the diner."

"I'm not sure that's such a good idea," said Detective Voss.

"It doesn't matter. I can't afford to take the evening off. I need the money. And anyway, what would I tell them?"

"You could call in sick." Patterson was aware of Bauer's gaze behind her. He had stood silent and motionless throughout the interview.

"Don't make me laugh. I don't get sick days. At least not paid ones. If I call in sick, I might not have a job by tomorrow morning."

"We're just trying to do what's best for you, Darlene," Patterson said.

"I know," Darlene said. "If you really want to do what's best, how about you lock that asshole Duane Snyder in the darkest cell you can find and throw away the key!"

TWENTY-EIGHT

"WHAT DO you make of her story?" Bauer asked as they made their way back toward their car.

"I think Darlene Rourke suffered a trauma," Patterson said. "She's clearly upset. As for whether Duane Snyder raped her . . . I'd like to speak to him before I make up my mind."

"You think she's lying?"

"I don't know. She wasn't being truthful last night when we spoke to her at the diner. In fact, she came off as defensive and cagey."

"Which would make sense if Snyder raped her, and she was embarrassed about it." Bauer unlocked the car and waited for Patterson to climb in before heading around to the driver's side. "Victims often feel like it's their fault. That they somehow encouraged it. Sometimes they're afraid of their assailant and what might happen if they tell tales. That's why so many rapes go unreported."

"I'm aware of the statistics," Patterson said. "But we still have to follow the rule of law, which dictates that a person is innocent until proven guilty. I'm not willing to jump to conclusions after hearing one side of the story."

"Neither am I," Bauer replied. "But you have to admit, Darlene Rourke's crying rape has dropped a golden opportunity into our lap."

"Right." The opportunity that Darlene's accusation presented was not lost on Patterson, which was why she had asked Detective Voss to hold off on bringing Snyder in for questioning. At least until after she and Bauer had taken a crack at him. "We get to have another chat with Snyder. And this time, he won't be able to blow us off so easily."

"Even better . . . If we don't like what he has to say for himself, we might have sufficient evidence to go before a judge and get that search warrant. I'd say a credible accusation of rape gives us probable cause to believe he could have abducted and killed those girls."

"And that he took Amy Bowen as she rode to work yesterday morning."

"Exactly." Bauer pressed the Charger's ignition button and pulled away from the curb. "Want to go see if he's at home right now?"

"What do you think?"

"That's what I thought." Bauer pointed the car in the direction of Snyder's spread.

They made their way through town and out past the Lonestar Skillet. Twenty minutes later, they were driving up the narrow dirt trail that led to the cabin. Trees pressed in on both sides of them, mostly elm and cedar, interspersed with a few tall pines. The canopy above them blocked out the sun and cast dapple shadows across the hard-packed ground.

A few minutes later, the trees gave way to a clearing within which the cabin sat. Here, pine needles and the mulched remains of winter leaves covered the ground. The white cargo van hadn't moved since their last visit. It still sat under the lean-to at the side of the cabin.

"Looks like our man is still around," Bauer said, swinging the car around in front of the cabin and bringing it to a stop.

They climbed out and approached the building.

"Looks pretty quiet around here," Bauer said, his hand resting near the gun in a holster on his belt.

"Maybe he didn't see us pull up," Patterson said. Everything looked pretty much as it had the previous day, except that now a fresh pile of firewood was stacked against the far side of the cabin, as well as several logs waiting to be split. An axe head was buried into one of these, its handle sticking up as if it were waiting to go back to work.

"Looks like Snyder's been getting a good workout," Bauer said, following Patterson's gaze toward the woodpile. He hurried up the steps to the cabin door and banged on it with his fist. "Mr. Snyder? It's the FBI. Open up."

There was no answer from within the cabin.

Patterson stepped forward. "This is Special Agent Blake. We need to have another chat."

When there was still no response, Patterson went to the front window and peered in cautiously, then cupped her hands against the glass to get a better view.

"Looks like the cabin's empty," she said. "If Snyder's inside, he's lying low."

Bauer tried the door. "Locked."

"Even if it wasn't, we couldn't go in without a warrant."

"Unless we had reason to believe he was in distress."

"That's a stretch."

"Just saying. But I think you're right. He's not here." Bauer stepped back and glanced around before pointing toward the woods on the left side of the cabin and a narrow path that disappeared from view between the trees. "There are only a couple of easy ways out of this clearing. The trail we just drove up, or that track heading off into the forest."

"We know he's not on the main trail," Patterson said. "We would have seen him when we drove up."

"Which leaves the track." Bauer was already descending the steps and heading toward the trees.

Patterson took another look around and then followed.

It was cooler under the canopy of trees, where the sun struggled to reach the ground. Dead twigs and leaves crunched underfoot as they made their way into the forest and left the clearing behind.

After following the trail for ten minutes without sign of Snyder, Patterson began to think he had seen them coming and taken off on foot or that maybe he had another vehicle stashed somewhere around the property that he had used to make his escape.

At least until a sharp crack split the silence, sending several startled birds squawking out of the trees and into the sky above.

"That sounded like a gunshot," Patterson said, turning toward the noise.

"You think it's Snyder?" Bauer said, slipping his gun from its holster.

"I think it's a fair bet." Patterson slid her own gun out, just as a second shot sent a bullet whizzing between them and into a tree trunk at their rear with a splintering thud.

TWENTY-NINE

PATTERSON DOVE to the ground and rolled, coming to rest near the edge of the path and sheltering behind the trunk of a pine tree. When she looked over, Bauer had done the same and was now crouched behind a tree several feet away.

She motioned in the direction of the gunshot and risked a glance around the tree trunk into the woods with her gun at the ready.

Bauer aimed his own gun in the same direction.

"Armed federal agents," he shouted in the general direction of their assailant. "Cease fire and show yourself."

"Don't shoot," a voice said from off in the trees. A moment later, a figure appeared. It was Duane Snyder with a .22 rifle in his hands.

"Put the gun on the ground," Patterson instructed him, standing up and making sure to keep the tree between herself and the shooter. "Put it down right now."

"Okay." Snyder bent and laid the rifle on the ground, then straightened again.

"You have any other weapons about your person?" Bauer stepped out from cover with his Glock trained on Snyder.

"Just the rifle," Snyder said quickly. "And a hunting knife." He slipped a four-inch blade from a sheath on his belt and threw it on the ground. "Now I'm unarmed."

"Why did you shoot at us?" Patterson said, stepping out from behind the tree with her own gun still raised.

"I wasn't shooting at you." Snyder looked panicked. "I came out into the woods to hunt. I heard movement and thought it was a target."

"You always shoot in the direction of noises before you find out what they are?" Bauer looked angry, but he kept his voice under control.

"No . . . I mean . . ." Snyder was getting more flustered by the second. "It was just instinct. I own this land, so I wasn't expecting anyone else to be out here."

"You didn't hear us calling your name back at the cabin?"

Snyder shook his head.

"You realize we could arrest you right now for assault on a federal agent," Patterson said, stepping closer to Snyder. "Maybe even attempted murder."

"What? It was an accident. I swear."

"Accident or not, you're in deep trouble." Bauer motioned for Snyder to leave his weapons behind and step onto the trail.

"Why? I haven't done anything. I said already, I didn't mean to shoot at you."

"That's not what I was talking about," Patterson said as Snyder approached them. "Would you mind accompanying us back to the cabin so we can ask you some questions?"

"Look, if this is about that missing girl again, I had nothing to do with it. Just like I had nothing to do with Shawna."

"This is something else." Bauer pointed in the direction of the cabin. "Move."

With Snyder walking ahead of them, they returned to the cabin. When they got there, he turned to them at the foot of the steps leading up to the covered front porch and door.

"I suppose you want to come inside," he said.

"It's either that or we arrest you right now and take you in for questioning." Patterson felt an uncharacteristic surge of satisfaction in saying those words. Snyder rubbed her the wrong way, and the more she looked at him, the more she was convinced that he was a snake.

"Fine. Come in." Snyder ascended the steps and unlocked the door, then let them inside. "Happy now?"

"What were you hunting out there, Mr. Snyder?" Patterson asked, looking around the cabin. It was cramped, with a rustic kitchen and living room on the ground floor and what looked like a loft area above that served as a bedroom. There was a door under the stairs. She wondered where it went.

"Why? It's my land. I can hunt whatever I want."

"That's not strictly true. You need a permit to hunt, even on your own land. You have one of those, right?" Bauer said.

"Yes. I have a permit."

"And we're out of hunting season. Depending on what you're going after, you might be breaking the law."

"Feral hogs," Snyder said, glowering at Bauer. "I'm allowed to hunt those anytime. They're considered a pest."

"That's correct." Bauer nodded. "If you're telling the truth."

"You didn't come all the way out here to see what I was up to in the woods." Snyder put his hands on his hips. "Why don't you tell me what the hell this is really about?"

"Mind if I take a look upstairs," Patterson said, glancing up toward the loft.

"Knock yourself out." Snyder shrugged. "Since you already forced your way in here."

"We didn't force our way in, you let us in." Patterson started up the stairs. A railing at the top separated the loft from the rest of the cabin. There was a queen-sized bed with a headboard constructed from rough pine planks. Cut logs with varnished tops sat on each side, serving as nightstands. Above the headboard was a small window. The ceiling sloped like the sides of a tent following the roof line, making the space feel smaller than it looked from below. It was also empty of anything that might help them in either their murder investigation or the alleged rape.

Patterson returned to the ground floor. "Nothing. It's clean."

"What's that?" Bauer asked Snyder, nodding toward the door under the stairs. "Storage or something else?"

"An old root cellar. The cabin dates from 1900. They stored provisions down there back in the day before there were modern conveniences like refrigerators."

Patterson walked over to it and tried the handle. "Locked."

"Mind opening it for us?" Bauer asked.

"Can't." Snyder pushed his hands in his pockets. "Don't have the key. It's back in Dallas."

"That's convenient." Patterson stepped away from the door.

"It's the truth." Snyder frowned. "You got inside my cabin without a warrant. You snooped around. Now I'd like to know why you're here."

"You want to tell him?" Bauer asked, shooting a look at Patterson.

"Sure. Why not." Patterson crossed the distance between them, stepping around an old sofa with a colorful blanket thrown across it. The scene of the crime? "Darlene Rourke says you raped her."

THIRTY

"WHAT THE HELL? I didn't rape anyone, let alone Darlene." Snyder took a step back and held his hands up. "Why would she say something like that?"

"I don't know. You tell us." Patterson studied Snyder's face, looking for any signs of deceit. All she saw was surprise.

"I have no idea." Snyder sounded panicked.

"Is it true that you invited her back to your place a couple of weeks ago to split a six-pack?" Bauer asked.

"What?" Snyder rubbed his forehead as if he had a headache. "Sure. I drove to the cabin late and stopped at the diner for food. It was almost closing time. After that, I asked if she wanted to stop by and have a beer with me. You know, since it's on her way home."

"Is that all you wanted?"

"Look. We're friends. That's all. I'm a married man, in case you hadn't noticed."

"Oh, we noticed." Patterson smelled blood in the water. "Doesn't mean you didn't decide to have some fun on the side."

"I didn't rape Darlene," Snyder shouted. He paced back and

137

forth, his breaths coming in short, sharp exhalations. "I've been coming out to the cabin for years. Always stop off at the diner for food on the way through. I know her, sure. But I didn't hurt her. Never would."

"Can you prove that?"

"How could I . . ." Snyder looked baffled. "It's her word against mine, right?"

"At the moment."

"That's what I thought. I don't know what's gotten into that stupid blonde head of hers, but she's making it up."

"You have a history with rape allegations," Patterson said. "How many other women have you tried it on with who didn't report you?"

"None. And I didn't touch that girl in college, at least not like that. I was drunk, and I went a little too far. When she said no, I stopped. That's it."

"Yet they still charged you with assault," Bauer said.

"Like I said, it was a stupid mistake. Everyone makes them. Doesn't make me a rapist."

"Still, two allegations are a couple more than most men have in their lifetimes." Patterson took a step toward the door, just in case Snyder decided he fancied his chances at running. "Some might say where there's smoke, there's fire."

"Then they'd be wrong." Snyder shook his head. "I can't believe she said I raped her."

"Is there something you're not telling us, Mr. Snyder?" asked Bauer.

"Like what?"

"I don't know. Seems a little suspicious . . . your inviting Darlene back here so late at night just so the pair of you could drink beer. Don't you think?" Bauer rubbed his chin. "Especially since, as you pointed out, you're a married man."

"I already told you we're friends."

"Does Jodi know about her?" Patterson asked.

"I don't know. I might have mentioned her."

"And your wife has no problem with you hanging out with other women in the middle of the night."

"She trusts me."

"In that case, you won't mind if we ask her about Darlene."

"Okay. Fine. I might have forgotten to mention her to Jodi. But if I did, it was an innocent omission. It's no big deal."

"Doesn't look that way from where I'm standing," Patterson said. "I can't imagine your wife is going to be happy when she finds out about the rape allegation."

"Oh my God. You're right. She left her last husband because he cheated. This could ruin us."

"Maybe you should've thought about that before you started bringing other women back to the cabin," Bauer said.

"It wasn't other women. It was one woman."

"And that was all it took to drop you in hot water." Patterson was still trying to figure out if Snyder was genuinely outraged at the rape allegation, or if he was doing a good job of covering up his crime.

"Also makes me wonder about Shawna and the other girls." Bauer circled Snyder, never taking his eyes off him. "You sure you had nothing to do with those abductions and murders?"

"We're back on that again?" Snyder shook his head in disbelief. "Look. Even if something did happen between Darlene and me—and I'm not saying it did—that's a world away from raping and killing teenage girls."

"No one mentioned anything about them being raped," Patterson said.

"I just assumed—"

"You'd make this a lot easier for yourself if you just told the truth," Bauer said.

"Jesus. This is going to ruin my life," Snyder wailed. He sat down on the couch and buried his head in his hands. "I can't believe this is happening." He looked up at Patterson. "Please don't tell Jodi. She's been through so much. What with Shawna going missing, and then the police finding the body like that? This would end her."

"Maybe you should have thought of that before you got involved with Darlene Rourke," Patterson said, sitting down on the sofa next to Snyder. She leaned forward with her elbows on her knees. "There's no good way out of this situation, at least for you and Jodi. You might as well tell us everything."

"Do you want to go to prison?" Bauer asked. "Because with the previous allegation against you already, the DA might just decide this is worth taking to trial."

Snyder sat back and folded his arms, then unfolded them again. He stared glumly at the cabin floor, and for a moment, Patterson thought that whatever secrets Duane Snyder was keeping were going to come tumbling out. But then he took a measured breath and stood up. "I don't think I want to say anything else without a lawyer present."

"Fair enough." Patterson took out her phone and dialed a number. She lifted the phone to her ear and said, "He's all yours."

"What are you doing?" Snyder asked in a panic.

Patterson didn't need to respond because the wail of a police siren told Snyder everything he needed to know.

He went to the window and looked out. A cruiser was pulling into the clearing, followed by an unmarked unit from which Carol Voss stepped out.

Snyder turned back to the two FBI agents. "You told me you wouldn't arrest me if I answered your questions."

"And we kept our word," Patterson said, standing and going to the door to let the detective in. "We aren't going to arrest you. Athens PD will do that."

THIRTY-ONE

PATTERSON AND BAUER waited until the Athens police department had taken Duane Snyder away before they left the cabin. But not before Patterson made one more attempt to get the cellar door open. When that didn't work, she pressed her ear to it, hoping to hear some sound from the other side that would give her cause to bust the lock. But everything was quiet. Even so, she couldn't help but worry that Duane Snyder might have Amy Bowen restrained down there.

Bauer must have felt the same way because he stepped outside and returned a moment later carrying a small pry bar from his trunk, which he inserted between the door and the frame. After a couple of attempts to force the door, which were accompanied by a good amount of huffing and puffing, and at least a few choice swear words, the door popped open with a splinter of wood.

"Would you like to do the honors?" He said, gesturing towards the dark staircase that disappeared down under the cabin.

"I can't believe you did that," Patterson said. "What happened to needing a warrant?"

"We'll still need a warrant to turn this place over from top to bottom," Bauer replied. "But I have no intention of walking away and leaving Amy Bowen alone and scared if that man has her in this cabin somewhere."

"Wow. You never cease to amaze." Patterson stepped past the door and started down the stairs. The wooden steps creaked underfoot, and she felt a sudden panic that they might collapse under her. But then she was at the bottom.

The root cellar was just like Duane Snyder claimed. It was small and dank, with a dirt floor and brick walls. A bunch of rotten shelves lined one wall, looking like they might fall apart at any moment. A tall cabinet stood against another wall, its wood dark and stained with age. An odor of rot permeated the space. Spiderwebs hung from the low ceiling, and at one point, Patterson saw something with more legs than she was comfortable with scuttle away along a joist. What she didn't see was Amy Bowen. The cellar was empty.

She went back upstairs and pushed the door closed, noting how it didn't sit straight in the frame anymore.

"Duane Snyder is sure to notice this," she said to Bauer.

"Meh." Bauer didn't look concerned. "I have a feeling he has bigger concerns than a busted lock. Besides, like he said about Darlene, it's our word against his. Even if Snyder files a complaint, who are they going to believe?"

"Fair point." Patterson made her way through the living room and stepped out onto the porch. It was early evening, and the sun was sinking toward the horizon, but it wouldn't set for at least a couple more hours. There was still time to make it back to Dallas before dark.

She glanced over her shoulder toward Bauer. "You want me to drive?"

"Sure." Bauer tossed her the keys. "I can catch some shuteye on the way back."

"Hang on." Patterson strolled around the side of the cabin and approached the white van. It was locked, as she expected. She stood on tiptoe and stretched herself tall to peer into the cab through the driver's side window. It gave her just enough field-of-view to see the cargo area behind if she craned her neck. Empty except for a couple of toolboxes and some lengths of pipe. Not that she expected anything else.

Satisfied, she returned to the car and climbed in.

"Nothing?" Bauer asked as she put her seatbelt on.

"Clean. Just like the basement."

"You think we're wrong about Snyder?"

"I'm not sure what to think." Patterson swung the steering wheel and pointed the car toward the trail. "But I'm not ready to rule him out as a suspect. Just because the girl isn't here doesn't mean he's not keeping her somewhere else."

"And it doesn't mean he is," Bauer pointed out.

"Which is why I'm fifty-fifty."

"And it's not like we have any other suspects right now."

"That too." Patterson steered the car along the trail, avoiding the worst ruts and potholes until they reached the road where she turned left toward Athens and Dallas, a good way beyond. She figured they would arrive back in the city by nine at the latest. She looked forward to a hot shower to soothe away the aches of the day. Patterson still had not fully recovered from her encounter with Ryan Gilder, the crazed boyfriend who had killed his fiancée years before in Seattle and almost killed Claire Wright. Not to mention Patterson herself. She still had the knife wound and bruises to prove it. Claire was also on the way to recovery and had provided new information about Julie that Patterson was eager to pursue just as soon as she put this current case behind her. As for Gilder, he was still in a coma, and the doctors weren't sure he would recover. If he did, he would spend the rest of his life in prison.

"Hey," Bauer said, nudging Patterson. "You okay?"

"Sure. Why wouldn't I be?"

"You looked like you were a million miles away."

"Just thinking about Claire Wright and what she told me."

"Eager to continue the search for Julie, huh?"

"There are answers waiting for me in Amarillo. Julie went there with some of the band members after TexFest. The bass player still lives there."

"Mark Davis."

"That's right." Patterson fell silent for a moment. She was itching to head north and follow her sister's trail wherever that might lead. "He must know where Julie went next."

"I hope he does, for your sake," Bauer said. "And for Julie. She deserves to come home."

"Yes, she does." Patterson's throat tightened. She swallowed a sob.

"Sorry. I didn't mean to upset you." Bauer peered down the road toward the distant lights of Athens, where Detective Voss was probably grilling Duane Snyder in an interview room at that very moment. "The Lonestar Skillet is still open a while longer. Fancy grabbing a burger?"

"You want to go back to that place?" Patterson asked, grateful that Bauer had changed the subject. "I thought you didn't like it."

"It grew on me." Bauer grinned. At that moment, his cell phone rang. He took it from his pocket. "Phoebe."

"Aren't you going to answer?" Patterson asked. "Don't worry, I'll do my best not to listen."

"And how are you going to do that, sitting right next to me?"

"Just take the call before the poor woman gives up."

Bauer did as he was told, then raised the phone to his ear. After a brief conversation, he hung up.

Patterson glanced sideways at him. "That sounded serious. Something wrong?"

"She asked if we could find time to drop by and speak with her grandmother again tomorrow," Bauer said. "The old lady isn't any better. Claims her unwelcome house guest paid her another visit last night."

THIRTY-TWO

LATER THAT NIGHT, back in the hotel room, Patterson took a long shower and then sat propped up on the bed with pillows behind her back and flicked through the cable TV channels, pausing on a local news network that was in the middle of a story about the latest abduction. They hadn't named Amy Bowen, or any of the other victims, which pleased Patterson, but they had come up with a frightening and ratings worthy moniker for the perpetrator.

The Butterfly Killer.

Someone must have leaked details of the investigation to the press, and in particular, the butterfly dresses the three victims were wearing when they were found, because this information had not been officially released. Maybe it was an employee at the Medical Examiner's Office or even someone within the police department. No matter how the information got out, it was frustrating. Giving the killer a catchy name might be good for the network, but it also created a bogeyman. It solidified the idea of a monster stalking the streets and heightened fear. It also ran the risk of egging the killer on. Stoking his ego. But there was nothing Patterson could do about it.

Disappointed, she continued flicking through the channels until she found a rerun of Friends, which she watched mostly to take her mind off the newly minted Butterfly Killer, and also to distract herself from thinking about Julie, who might have fallen victim to a similar predator.

A couple of hours later, after four more episodes, she turned the TV off and got ready for bed. She was about to climb under the sheets when her phone rang. She hurried to pick it up, expecting Grant to be on the other end, but it was Detective Voss from the Athens Police Department.

"Sorry to call so late, Special Agent Blake. I hope I'm not disturbing you."

"I was just about to climb into bed."

"I'll make this brief, then. We released Duane Snyder about an hour ago. These types of cases can be tricky. They have a habit of turning into a 'he said she said' kind of thing, and because Darlene waited so long to report the rape, we have no physical evidence to corroborate her version of events."

"What story did Snyder give you?"

"He agreed she was telling the truth about going back to his place to split a six-pack, but after that, their recollections diverge. She claims he assaulted her. He says nothing untoward happened. That they finished the beers, and she left."

"That's pretty much the same as he told us," Patterson said.

"I'll keep you in the loop with our progress, but unless something more turns up, this complaint is likely to go nowhere. We'll keep an eye on him just in case, but as of now, Snyder's walking free. Just thought you should know."

"Thanks. I appreciate that." Patterson had expected as much, but at least Darlene's accusation had given them an excuse to search Snyder's cabin for evidence that he was Amy Bowen's abductor and the person who killed the previous three girls. But they had found nothing. If Snyder was the Butterfly Killer, he was doing a good job of covering his tracks.

She ended the call and sat for a long moment with the phone clutched in her hand. More than anything, she wished Grant were here. The longer she was on the road, the lonelier she became. She dialed his number. It rang four times, then went to voicemail.

She waited for the beep and left a message.

"Hey. It's me. Just calling to say good night. Love you and miss you."

After hanging up, she sat for a couple of minutes more, expecting Grant to listen to the voicemail and call her back or at least send her a text. When nothing came through, she put the phone on the nightstand and slid down under the covers before turning off the bedside lamp.

THIRTY-THREE

AMY BOWEN SAT in the darkness and waited. She had only seen the man who abducted her twice since she was taken and thrown into this place. The first time was a couple of hours after he put her in the brick room with the metal bars. He had stood on the other side of the bars and watched her. Then he turned and left, disappearing along the narrow corridor made of the same bricks as her cell.

The second time was many hours later. He brought her a paper plate with bread and cheese on it, which he folded to slide through the bars. He told her to come close and removed the tape on her mouth so she could eat.

"Don't even think about screaming or shouting for help," he said. "Not that it would matter if you did. This is a special place. A secret place. No one can hear you down here. Even if someone comes looking, they'll never find you."

Those words sent an icy chill racing up her spine. As did the way he looked at her, which convinced Amy not to cry out.

Her abductor pointed to the plate of food. "Eat."

"I can't. My hands are tied," Amy said in a small voice.

"Too bad. Do the best you can."

She wasn't sure how that would work but dropped to her knees and tried to eat the food anyway because she was starving. She lowered her head to the plate and grabbed at the food with her mouth. It was hard going, but she soon developed a technique that was, if not elegant, enough to let her consume the meager offering.

As she ate, her captor sat on a wooden chair in the corridor against the far wall and watched. When she was finished, he stood and told her to come close to the bars. When she did, he put the tape back over her mouth, then plucked the paper plate back out of the cell before leaving without another word.

That must have been at least eight hours ago, maybe more, and she had seen nothing of him since.

Until now.

Because there was movement in the narrow corridor outside her cell. Soon her captor appeared with a bucket in one hand and a fabric bag in the other. He pushed the bag through the bars and told her to put it over her head. She hadn't wanted to, but one look at him convinced her that disobeying was not a smart thing to do, so she did as he asked and waited, blind and vulnerable, to see what would happen next.

It didn't take long to find out.

The sound of a key turning in a lock was followed by the sense of her abductor standing next to her. A moment later, she felt a tug at her wrists as he cut the zip tie binding them.

She moved her arms, grateful for the freedom. Her shoulders ached, and her wrists were chafed where the zip tie had dug into them.

"Don't move," her captor said.

She heard footsteps and then the sound of the cell door being closed and locked.

"You can take the bag off now."

Amy reached up and removed the bag.

"The tape too. But don't scream. You hear me?"

Amy nodded and pulled the tape off her mouth. It hurt and she let out a small mewling sound.

"Good." Her captor folded his arms. "How do you feel?"

"Okay." Amy stuttered even though she felt anything but. Especially when she saw the bucket of water sitting on the floor next to her. Inside was a sponge.

"Your clothes are filthy. You stink of sweat. Undress and bathe yourself." Her captor retreated to the same chair he had sat on before and sank down.

Amy shook her head, mortified. She had no intention of undressing in front of this man.

He must have read her thoughts, or perhaps it wasn't the first time he'd done this. "You don't need to worry. I won't watch. But I'm not going to leave you alone, either."

"Please, I can't," she said, on the verge of tears.

"Do it, or I'll come in there and remove your clothes for you."

Amy's gut tightened. Better to do as he said than have a stranger do it for her. She reached up and pulled her sweat-soaked polo with the motel logo below the right lapel up over her head and off, then dropped it on the floor.

"Good girl. Now the rest of them and wash your body. Clean it good." He reached down under the chair and came back up with a dog-eared paperback, which he opened to a page marked with a slip of paper. He lowered his head and started to read.

Amy watched him for a while, wondering if he was peeking over the paperback, but she saw no sign that he was watching her. She removed the rest of her clothes, shivering now, and used the sponge to clean the dirt and stale sweat from her body. She dried herself with a thin cotton towel sitting next to the bucket, then reached down to dress herself.

"Don't." Her captor had closed the book and stood up. He approached the bars even as her hands flew to cover herself.

This is it, she thought. He's going to do the same to me as men do to girls in the murder porn shows on reality TV.

Instead, he issued a terse command. "Push your clothes through the bars. Give them to me."

She kicked the pile of clothes with her foot, unwilling to remove her hands from her naked body. She nudged the clothes between the bars.

"Put the bucket by the door."

This time, Amy couldn't keep herself covered. She dropped a hand from her breasts and picked up the bucket, then put it next to the cell door as quickly as she could before returning her arm to cover her chest.

"Stand back."

She did as she was told.

He took a key from his pocket and slipped it into the door lock, turning it with a metallic squeal. He opened the door just enough to drag the bucket back through to his side, watching her all the while.

He closed the door and locked it again then scooping up the clothes and bucket, he started down the corridor—no not a corridor . . . it was more like a tunnel—toward a metal door at the end. He pulled it open and stepped out.

Amy was confused. Scared, too. He had taken her clothes, and now she was trapped in this place with nothing to wear. Was this all part of some sick game he was playing with her?

But then the metal door opened again, and the man reappeared. In his arms were fresh clothes. He stopped at the bars and held out the topmost garment, offering it to her.

"Put this on."

When she didn't move to take it, he let the garment flutter to the floor, and Amy saw that it was a butterfly print dress, just like the ones in the photographs on the back wall.

"Put it on," he repeated, then turned his back and waited.

Amy finally dropped her hands and scooped up the dress. She dropped it down over her head and wriggled into it.

"I'm wearing it," she said in a small voice, trying not to cry. She didn't want him to have the satisfaction of seeing her like that.

Her abductor turned around again. He made a small noise that sounded like pleasure as he looked at her wearing the butterfly dress.

"You're perfect," he breathed. "Just like always."

"I don't understand," Amy said, confused.

The man stood there a while longer, ignoring Amy's confusion. Then he sighed. "Take it back off and fold it up."

"What?" A new tremble of panic flared inside her. "Please don't make me get undressed again."

"Take it off." He turned to face away from her again.

Amy hesitated, then slipped the dress back over her head, folded it, and walked to the bars before placing it between them on the other side.

At this, the man turned, just as Amy covered herself and took a step backward. He was carrying more clothes. A pair of jeans and a T-shirt. He laid them on the floor outside the bars, close enough for her to reach.

"Are you going to be a good girl, or do I have to put the zip ties and tape back on?"

"I'll be good," Amy said quickly. "I promise."

The last thing she wanted was that tape over her mouth again. During the hours she was alone in the basement room, it was so hard to breathe. She thought she might suffocate.

"Make sure you are." Then the man scooped up the dress, turned away, and headed toward the metal door. "Get dressed. I'll be down soon with supper."

THIRTY-FOUR

BAUER PARKED at the curb and peered toward Esther Cutler's townhouse. He said, "Looks like Phoebe isn't here yet."

It was ten in the morning, and they were doing a favor for Bauer's girlfriend. Despite their chat with the old lady on their previous visit, Phoebe's grandmother still insisted a stranger was visiting her home in the middle of the night.

They climbed out of the car and made their way up the steps to the front door. As they reached the top, the neighbors' door opened. A man in his early forties appeared with a boy of about eight years old at his side. The boy held a plate of cookies.

"You're not Jesse," the kid said, squinting up at Patterson and Bauer in the bright morning sunlight.

"No, we're not," Patterson said, smiling down at the young man. "Those cookies look delicious."

"Thank you. Mom made them because they're Samantha's favorite. Chocolate chip peanut butter."

"Yum." Patterson grinned. "Who's Samantha?"

"My big sister," Danny said. "But these are for Mrs. Cutler, but you can have one if you like."

"We always bring some next door on Sunday mornings when Jesse stops in. He's Mrs. Cutler's caregiver," the man said. He held his hand out. "Hi, I'm Benjamin. My son's name is Danny."

Patterson shook hands with the neighbor and introduced herself and Bauer.

"I saw you here the other day with Phoebe," Benjamin said. "Are you family?"

"No. We're FBI agents."

"Oh." Benjamin looked taken aback. "I hope everything's okay."

"Are you going to arrest Mrs. Cutler?" His son asked, wide eyed.

"No, Danny, were not. Her granddaughter works with us at the FBI. We just came around to visit Mrs. Cutler because she's all alone," Patterson said, not wishing to mention the real reason for their visit because she didn't want to embarrass the old woman or spread gossip in the neighborhood. She nodded toward the plate. "Is your offer of a cookie still good?"

Danny nodded, a wide grin spreading across his face. "I bet you'll like them. Everyone does."

"I'm sure I will." Patterson took a cookie.

When the boy offered the plate up to Bauer, he took one too.

Benjamin watched the exchange with a bemused expression. "I'd offer to let you in, but we don't have a key. I've told Phoebe before she should give us the lockbox code, in case of emergencies, but . . ."

"That's okay." Patterson looked down to see a lockbox hanging from Esther Cutler's front door. An easy way to let the caregivers in without having keys floating around unaccounted for.

"You can wait in our house if you want," Danny offered. He looked up at his father. "Can't they."

"That won't be necessary. We're meeting Phoebe here at any moment," said Patterson in between mouthfuls of soft chewy cookie. She looked down at Danny and gave him a thumbs up. "These are really good."

"Delicious," Bauer agreed, polishing off his cookie so quickly that Patterson wondered if he had inhaled it. "Your mother should sell these."

"Thank you," Benjamin said. "I'll tell her you said that. She'll be so happy. It's an old family recipe."

"I'd ask her to share it with me, but I can't imagine she would," Patterson said, finishing her own cookie and dusting the crumbs from the front of her shirt.

"You wouldn't be the first to try and pry the secret ingredient out of her," Benjamin said with a laugh. "She won't even tell me."

"That's okay," Patterson said. "My baking skills are somewhere between terrible to nonexistent. I'd probably end up burning them."

"They're not hard to make," Danny piped up. "I made a batch with her last week."

"Then you must be a better baker than me," Patterson said. "I don't suppose you know the secret ingredient?"

Danny gave his head a vigorous shake. "She made me look the other way when she put it in."

"Smart woman." Patterson laughed. She looked down at the plate, which still had six cookies on it. "We can take those and give them to Mrs. Cutler if you want."

"Well . . ." Danny looked unsure. "How do I know you won't eat them yourselves instead?"

"They're FBI agents, son." Benjamin tasseled Danny's mop of blond hair. "If we can't trust them, who can we trust?"

"Okay then." Danny offered the plate for Patterson to take.

"But I'll ask Mrs. Cutler how many cookies you gave her the next time I see her. Just to make sure."

Bauer snorted. "I think this kid has a future with the Bureau."

"I promise we won't steal any cookies," Patterson said, accepting the plate.

"Hey, you're early," a female voice said from behind them.

Patterson glanced around to see Phoebe climbing the steps. "We got here a few minutes ago."

"I see you've met Benjamin and Danny," Phoebe said, nodding toward the neighbors.

"They brought cookies for Esther."

"You're too kind, as always," Phoebe said to Benjamin. "Tell Helen I said thank you. Esther looks forward to her Sunday morning cookies."

"I'll do that," Benjamin replied. "We should probably get going. I have to make a run to the hardware store. I'm fixing up the basement as a man cave. My wife hates football, so she told me to find somewhere else to watch it. Half the basement was just sitting there unused, and DIY is kind of my thing, so . . . "

"I'm with Helen on that one," Phoebe said. "Good luck."

"I'll need it. Been working on the project for almost a year and still don't have it finished."

"In that case, we won't keep you." Phoebe thanked Benjamin and his son again and stepped past Patterson and Bauer. She typed a code into the lockbox, removed the key, and let them inside, calling out to her grandmother as she did so.

The townhouse looked like it had on their last visit. They followed Phoebe into the living room, where Esther was sitting propped up in bed.

When she saw Phoebe, her eyes lit up. "You came."

"Of course," Phoebe said. "I told you I would, didn't I?"

"And you brought those nice people you work with back."

"They came to have a chat with you about your mystery

visitor." Phoebe sat on the edge of the bed and gave her grand-mother a kiss on the forehead. "They want to put your mind at rest. Let you know that there's nothing to worry about."

"Tell me it's all in my head, you mean." The old woman looked past her granddaughter toward Patterson and Bauer. "Phoebe doesn't believe me. No one does. Not even my care-givers. But I'm not senile. I know what I'm seeing and hearing. Someone is sneaking around my house in the middle of the night. I don't know why, but they are. And I want it to stop."

THIRTY-FIVE

"NO ONE THINKS you're making it up," Patterson said, walking over to the bed and kneeling so she was on eye level with the old woman. "When was the last time your unwelcome visitor made an appearance?"

"Night before last around midnight. I'd just fallen asleep, and I heard the door creak. I knew it was him. It's always the same when he comes."

"Did you see him?" Patterson asked.

"No. Not that time. Sometimes he stands in the living room doorway and looks at me but not always. I could hear him walking around the house, though. After living here so long, I know every squeaky board. He was in the kitchen first, then the hallway. Probably came in the back door."

Patterson exchanged a look with Bauer. "Are you sure he entered through the back door?"

"Oh yes, my dear. It makes a very distinctive sound when it opens. Has done for years. Tom always said he'd fix it, but he wasn't really a handyman, God rest his soul."

"Tom was my grandfather," Phoebe interjected. "Goodness knows what he would have made of this."

"Let's take a look at that door," Patterson said to Bauer.

She stood and motioned for Bauer to accompany her. When they were in the hallway, she turned to him. "What do you make of it all?"

"Beats me," Bauer said, keeping his voice low. "She's ninety-eight years old. I only hope I'm that sharp at her age."

"Come on." Patterson walked into the kitchen. She made her way to the back door and turned the knob. It didn't open.

"There's a deadlock," said Bauer.

"Right." Patterson unlocked the door and tried again. This time, it opened with a groan. She closed then opened it again, with the same result. "Distinctive noise just like Esther said."

"Except . . ."

"You would need a key to get in from the outside," Patterson said, completing Bauer's thought.

"Phoebe said no one has access to the key except her family and the caregivers."

"Let's double check that with her. Just to be sure."

"You think someone really is sneaking around in the dead of night?" Bauer looked puzzled. "Why would they bother?"

"Beats me." Patterson stepped back into the hallway. "Esther's pretty sure of herself."

"Doesn't mean she isn't dreaming the whole thing."

"Agreed." Patterson poked her head into the living room and beckoned for Phoebe to join them.

"Did you find something?" Phoebe said, looking worried.

"No. Other than a creaky door, just like your grandmother said." Patterson reached around Phoebe and pulled the living room door closed so that they wouldn't be overheard. "Can you think of a reason anyone would want to come in here during the night?"

Phoebe shook her head. "No. I can't."

"And you're sure no one has key access outside of the family and caregivers?"

"Absolutely." A look of panic flashed across Phoebe's face. "You don't think someone really is coming in here, do you?"

"I don't know what to think," Patterson told her. "On the one hand, we're dealing with a ninety-eight-year-old woman who could easily be imagining this . . . And I say that with all due respect."

Phoebe nodded. "I know."

"On the other hand, she's adamant about what she's experiencing."

"And that door makes a very distinctive sound when it opens," Bauer said.

"So, where does that leave us?" Phoebe asked.

"I'm not sure." Patterson took a moment to gather her thoughts. "I know this is a longshot, but I don't suppose your grandmother has internet?"

"What do you think?"

"I'll take that as a no."

"What are you thinking?" Bauer asked.

"Cameras," Patterson replied. "I'd like to install some surveillance cameras in the hallway and other areas where Esther doesn't go. That way, we can see who's coming and going."

"That's a great idea," Phoebe said. "It would give us peace of mind. I know she's probably imagining it all, but I have to say, it's been stressful."

"You want to use Bureau resources to do this?" Bauer asked. "Because that's going to take some doing. You'll need to get a sign-off from a senior agent at the least. Probably the ASAC. Not an easy task under the circumstances."

"I agree." Patterson had no intention of involving the FBI. "We can't make this an official investigation, which means we'll have to do it ourselves. Get a cable company out here to install Wi-Fi." Patterson shifted her attention to Phoebe. "Are you up for that?"

"Sure." The relief on Phoebe's face was clear. "Anything to get an answer."

"That'll take a while," Bauer said. "When I tried to get internet installed in my apartment, they didn't show up for two weeks."

"It's the best we can do," Patterson said.

"I'll call the cable company this afternoon," Phoebe said.

"Good. Let us know what they say."

"I'll swing by your place and help you pick out some cameras this evening if you like," Bauer said to Phoebe. "It will give me an excuse to see you."

"I can't. Not tonight." Phoebe shook her head. "It's my dad's birthday, and I promised to video chat with him. How about sometime later this week?"

"Sure." If Bauer was disappointed, he didn't show it.

"If we're settled, I'd like to take another look around the house," Patterson said. "Just to be sure."

"I'd appreciate that." Phoebe's hand rested on the living room door handle. "I'll go say goodbye before we leave."

When Phoebe was gone, Patterson turned to Bauer. "Want to take a peek around with me?"

"Sure." Bauer headed for the stairs.

They made their way up to the second floor and poked around, then climbed to the third. Everything looked just as it had on their previous visit.

On the way back down, Patterson asked Bauer a question. "How serious is it between you and Phoebe?"

He shrugged. "Not sure. We've only been seeing each other for a few weeks. It's not 'meet the parents' serious, if that's what you're asking."

"It wasn't. Take it slow, okay? Workplace romances can be tricky. Trust me, I know."

"Trouble between you and Jonathon Grant?"

"No. Not as such, it's just . . ." Patterson thought back to the previous night. Grant hadn't returned her call. In fact, their phone conversations were becoming less frequent. He was always busy, it seemed. Were they drifting apart? She hoped not. "Never mind. You know what, I'm sure it's all this time away from home getting to me, that's all."

"If you need someone to talk to . . ."

"I appreciate that." Patterson reached the bottom of the stairs. "But I'll be fine."

"Offer's there."

"I'll keep it in mind." Patterson turned toward the living room. "Come on. Let's go and say goodbye to Mrs. Cutler. Then we can get back to finding the Butterfly Killer."

THIRTY-SIX

AS THEY WERE LEAVING Esther Cutler's townhouse, Patterson's phone rang. It was Detective Costa. When Patterson picked up, his greeting was less than enthusiastic.

"Just thought you'd want to know, uniform just responded to a domestic on Cranston Avenue," he said wearily.

"Cranston Avenue." For a moment, Patterson couldn't remember why the address sounded familiar, then it snapped into place. "That's where Jodi Banks and Duane Snyder live."

"Give the woman a cigar," Costa said. "Apparently, they were going at it for at least thirty minutes before a neighbor called when the argument spilled into the street."

"I guess Jodi must have found out about the rape allegation." Patterson reached the car and leaned against it.

"That would be my guess," Costa replied. "It got pretty heated by all accounts. Snyder might have been better off staying at the cabin instead of going home."

"Where is he now?" Patterson asked.

"Beats me. He wasn't there when our officers arrived on the scene, which was probably just as well, or one of them might have ended up in jail for domestic battery. Possibly both of them. Jodi was pretty upset. Poor woman. First, she loses her daughter like that, and now this. You can't blame her for going off on him."

"Not in the least." Patterson couldn't imagine how it would feel to discover that about your partner out of the blue. A person you trusted. She must be wondering about other things. Like Shawna's abduction and murder. After all, Duane had been accused of rape twice now. "Would you mind if we stopped by and spoke to her, Detective Costa? I don't want to step on any toes, especially since this isn't directly related to the Butterfly Killer investigation."

"Feel free. Actually, I was kind of hoping you would. Maybe she'll let something slip. She wasn't exactly pleased we were sniffing around Snyder after her daughter disappeared, but this changes the dynamic."

"Great. We'll keep you informed." Patterson ended the call and turned to Bauer. "Cat's out of the bag. Jodi Banks knows about the rape allegation."

"I figured as much," Bauer said. "I would not have wanted to be in Duane Snyder's shoes when he went home."

"Sounds like she gave him a pretty good ear full." Patterson waited for Bauer to unlock the car and climbed in. "You remember where she lives?"

"I think I can find it." Bauer started the engine and pulled away from the curb.

———

When they turned onto Cranston Avenue and pulled up outside the Banks' residence, Patterson couldn't help but notice the curious stares of neighbors lingering in their front yards or at their windows. The drama earlier that day had piqued the interest of pretty much the entire street.

"We're being watched," Bauer said as they climbed from the

car and made their way toward Jodi's front door. "This should keep the rumor mill churning for days."

"Everyone loves a good scandal," Patterson said as she pressed the doorbell. "And given what this family have been through over the last few months, it's a doozy."

"Poor woman," Bauer said seconds before the door opened to reveal a haggard-looking Jodi Banks with tear streaks down her cheeks.

"If you're here to say I told you so, don't bother." Jodi turned and retreated back into the house, leaving the door open.

"That's not why we came," Patterson said, following her into the house with Bauer close behind. "We came to see how you are doing."

"How do you think I'm doing?" Jodi turned on them, her face a picture of anguish. "My husband is a rapist, and for all I know, he killed Shawna."

"You don't know that," Patterson said.

"Are you married Special Agent Blake?" Jodi asked.

"No." Patterson shook her head.

"How about you, Special Agent Bauer?"

"No, ma'am."

"Then neither of you can understand." Jodi led them into the living room and sank down onto the couch. "I know Duane. Probably better than anyone else on the planet. When he said nothing happened between him and that woman, he was lying. I don't expect you to believe me, but I could see it on his face. God, I want him to be innocent of this, but . . ."

"How did you find out about the allegation?" Patterson asked.

"She phoned me. Told me what he'd done."

"Darlene?"

Jodi nodded. "At first I thought it was some kind of sick joke. Someone trying to wind me up. But then I called the police department in Athens. They put me on to some detective. I think her name was Voss. She didn't want to tell me at first, but when she found out who I was, she confirmed the allegation." Jodi rubbed her eyes. "I can't believe this is happening. It's like I'm living a nightmare."

"How long afterward did Duane show up?"

"Thirty minutes. He came strolling in like nothing was wrong even though he never comes home on a Sunday when he's at the cabin."

"What happened next?"

"What do you think happened?"

"According to the police, you got into a fight. It spilled into the street."

"That about covers it. I told him to get the hell away from me. I don't want him anywhere near this house."

"And then he left?" Patterson asked.

"You better believe it. He hightailed it out of here so quick you could barely see him for dust. Climbed back into that van of his and took off." Jodi swallowed hard. "Good riddance. I don't need that in my life."

"I'm sorry," Patterson said. "I really am."

"Yeah." Jodi sighed. "That ain't gonna bring Shawna back, is it?"

"No." Patterson wished she could say something, anything, to make Jodi feel better.

"And it's not going to stop my husband from being a rapist, is it, Special Agent Blake?"

"We don't know that he is," Patterson said. "Yet."

Jodi fixed her with a withering stare. "You spend eight years married to someone, Special Agent Blake, and then you come back in here and tell me that."

THIRTY-SEVEN

ON THEIR WAY back to the field office, Patterson voiced her concerns about Duane Snyder. "You think he went back to the cabin?"

"Where else would he go?" Bauer was driving. He pulled into a Starbucks and drove around to the drive-through lane and stopped behind a line of cars waiting to order drinks. "Thought we could use a pick-me-up."

"You read my mind." Patterson fell silent as they inched forward and placed their order. Afterward, she returned to the subject of Duane Snyder. "He must be pretty steamed that Darlene phoned his wife to say he raped her. If I was Darlene I'd be keeping a low profile right about now. Who knows what Snyder will do if he runs into her?"

"Or goes looking for her."

"Right. We should warn Detective Voss. I'd hate for something bad to befall Darlene, even if she did poke the bear by phoning Jodi."

"I was thinking we go one step further," Bauer said. "Put a body on Snyder."

"You mean like surveillance?"

"That's exactly what I mean." Bauer nodded. "They won't be able to legally enter his property, but a car parked on the road at the end of the trail leading up to his cabin could be beneficial."

"And could also result in a police harassment complaint."

"Not if that unit was there to catch speeders. Rural stretch without any traffic lights or intersections . . . I bet the cars just zip along there."

"Devious."

"Thank you."

They pulled up to the window and collected their coffees, then swung back onto the road.

"It would certainly put a chilling effect on any designs Snyder has with regard to Darlene," Patterson said as she sipped the hot beverage. "I'm not sure how it helps us with Amy Bowen, though. We already searched his cabin and she's not there."

"That we know of." Bauer steered them onto the interstate, which was still the quickest way to get across town despite the heavy traffic. "It's a big property. Over five hundred acres. He could have another building somewhere out in the woods, and we'd never find it without a coordinated search."

"Not going to happen unless we have a solid lead that she's there, rape allegation or not."

"Which is why a cop at the end of his driveway might not be a bad thing. The window of time between abduction and murder is shortening with each victim. If Snyder is the killer, he won't risk murdering Amy while he's under scrutiny. This allegation from Darlene might have bought us more time. And a police cruiser so close to his cabin will only make him more cautious."

"That's assuming Snyder is even our man."

"If he isn't, we haven't lost anything." Bauer left the highway. A couple of minutes later he pulled into the field office parking lot.

As he was about to climb out of the car, Patterson caught his arm. "Hold up a moment."

"What?" Bauer moved his hand from the door.

"I need to ask you something." Patterson had not been able to stop thinking about what Bauer had said about killing his friend. The online article she had found only compounded her concern. "I came across a news story from several years ago . . . An officer involved shooting after a convenience store robbery in LA."

Bauer was silent for a while, then he turned to Patterson. "I thought you were going to give me time on this."

"I'm worried about you," Patterson said.

"So you thought some snooping would be in order?" Bauer looked at her with narrowed eyes.

"I wasn't snooping."

"Right. You know what, Patterson. Sometimes you can be too inquisitive for your own good. You had no right—"

"I had every right. We're partners. I have to trust you." Patterson wished she hadn't brought the matter up at that moment. The chill between them the morning after Bauer's admission had thawed and he was back to his old self. It was like he had decided to ignore what happened at Pioneer Jacks. Forget it ever happened. But Patterson could not forget, and sooner or later, the subject had to be broached. But, she thought, now might not have been the right time.

Bauer rubbed his neck with a scowl. "Trust is a two-way street."

"I know."

"You shouldn't have gone digging into my background without asking me first."

"I didn't. It was a web search, that's all. The article was out there already. I just read it."

"Semantics. Just because something is easy to find, doesn't make you any less a snoop."

"Marcus, tell me what happened. What you said the other night . . . it was related to the convenience store robbery, wasn't it?"

"I don't want to have this conversation." Bauer pushed the driver's door open and got out of the car. He started toward the field office without looking back.

Patterson cursed. Bauer could be stubborn. Infuriatingly so. She wished he would tell her the truth, but it wasn't her decision to make. She climbed out and slammed the door, then followed him.

When she reached the portico in front of the building, she placed a call to Detective Voss down the road in Athens. Ten minutes later, having secured the detective's agreement that a cruiser would be placed at the end of the trail leading to Snyder's woodland cabin-just to catch speeders of course-Patterson hung up and made her way inside.

THIRTY-EIGHT

THE REST of the afternoon passed in an uneasy silence broken only by the conversation necessary to do their jobs. Patterson wanted to shake him by the lapels. She couldn't understand what the big deal was. Something was clearly going on with Bauer, and it would be better for both of them if he just told her what it was. But her partner didn't share Patterson's pragmatic outlook on the matter and kept his demeanor courteous but frosty.

At five-thirty, Patterson stretched and stood up, intending to head back to the hotel for the evening. She grabbed her jacket from the back of the seat and was about to slip it on when her phone rang.

It was Detective Voss.

"You aren't going to believe this," the detective said. "But we have Duane Snyder in a holding cell."

"What happened?" Patterson asked, switching the phone to speaker. "Did you find evidence to support Darlene's accusation?"

"Not yet. But that cruiser we sat at the end of the trail near his cabin paid off. I decided to use an unmarked vehicle because it would be less obvious. The last thing we want is an accusation of harassment. It hadn't been there more than a couple of hours when Snyder took off in his van. The officer followed him from a distance and guess where Snyder went?"

"Darlene Rourke's apartment?" Said Bauer.

"Very good, Special Agent Bauer." Voss sounded impressed. "Give yourself a pat on the back."

"Nothing to it," Bauer told her. "Just putting myself in his place. If I'd just been accused of rape, and the woman who accused me made a call to my wife and got me kicked out of my own home, that's where I would go. I'd be mad as hell, even if I really were a scumbag rapist."

"He was mad, all right," Voss agreed. "Practically kicked in the door when she wouldn't answer. Stormed inside and confronted her. If we hadn't tasked an officer with trailing him, who knows what Snyder would have done."

"Was Darlene hurt?" Asked Patterson.

"A little shaken up maybe, but other than that, she's fine."

"And she's sticking to her story that Duane raped her?"

"She's more adamant than ever."

"Can you hold on to him until we get there?" All thought of returning to the hotel had evaporated from Patterson's mind. What she now saw was an opportunity to pressure Snyder into slipping up. And not just about Darlene's rape accusation but also about the three dead girls and the one who was still missing. "This might be our best chance to get some straight answers out of the man."

"Don't worry, Special Agent Blake. He's not going anywhere, anytime soon," Detective Voss said on the other end of the line. "You get yourselves down here, and we'll provide a nice comfy interview room for y'all to have a chat."

"Thank you," Patterson said.

"No thanks necessary. There's something about Snyder that rubs me all wrong."

"Me too," admitted Patterson. "See you in a couple of hours?"

"I'll be here with a pot of hot coffee," Detective Voss said before hanging up.

Patterson looked at Bauer. "Ready for another drive?"

Bauer nodded. "Try and stop me."

THIRTY-NINE

THEY ARRIVED in Athens with Patterson feeling more hopeful than she had all day. Duane Snyder going off on Darleen was a stroke of luck. It gave them an opportunity to pile the pressure on and see if he slipped up, not just about the rape but also about Shawna and the other victims of the Butterfly Killer.

But when they entered police headquarters, Detective Voss was waiting for them with a sour look on her face.

"Hate to be the bearer of bad news, but your trip was in vain," she said. "We released Snyder fifteen minutes ago."

"What?" Patterson could hardly believe what she was hearing. "Why?"

"In a word, Jameson Screed."

"That's two words," Bauer pointed out.

"And not a nice pair of words either," Voss replied. "Snyder refused to talk and then lawyered up. He called Screed, who ran right down here with all the glee of a puppy poking its nose in shit. Pardon my crude language."

"We've heard worse," Patterson said. "Who is this Screed guy, anyway?"

175

"I'm sure you've seen his billboards on the highway outside of town. Can't miss them. Calls himself 'the people's attorney.' Specializes in representing lowlifes. No client is too slimy or dirty."

"Is he the guy with the motto, 'keeping the cops in line, so you won't do time'?" Bauer asked.

"Oh yeah. That's him." The detective's dour look turned to one of disgust. "I'm all for fair representation, but that man is something else. His mantra is innocent even when proven guilty. If you believed Jameson Screed, no one has ever actually committed a real crime. It's all a big conspiracy by law enforcement to fill up the jails. Pretty much says so on his infomercial that plays on Channel 6 from midnight to six A.M."

"Gotta love a lawyer with an infomercial," Patterson mused. "Where's Snyder now?"

"Your guess is as good as mine. Screed had him out of here so fast it would make you dizzy."

"What about Darleen Rourke?" Bauer asked. "Couldn't you hold him on the basis of her safety?"

"We tried that one. Didn't fly. Screed claimed entrapment. Said Darleen called Snyder and asked him to come over there so they could talk, then refused to answer the door. Antagonized him into busting into her apartment so she would have a stronger case for rape."

"If that's true, it could have backfired in spectacular fashion," Bauer said. "Darleen couldn't have known you had an officer trailing Snyder."

"That's right. But Snyder's phone shows an incoming call from her thirty minutes before the incident. And Darleen placed a panicked call to 911 right around the same time Snyder arrived there before he even put a shoulder to her door. Then there's the unofficial surveillance. He raised the question of police harassment just as we feared. Bottom line. Screed has our backs to the wall, and he knows it."

"And you let him walk." Patterson cursed under her breath.

"Nothing else we could do. And on top of that, if Darleen did invite Snyder over there, she may have shot her case all to shit rather than helped it. Screed will eviscerate her on the stand."

"This is going from bad to worse."

"Tell me about it. Not sure where that leaves you with the Butterfly Killer."

"Same place we were before," Patterson said. "He's our only suspect so far and we have no firm evidence of wrongdoing other than a decades old assault charge, shaky alibis, and this mess."

"Sorry." Voss pulled her best sympathetic face.

"Yeah." Patterson thanked the detective, and they left the station.

As they were about to climb into their car, a man in a double-breasted charcoal suit approached. He was tall and burly, over six feet, with thinning salt and pepper hair and beady eyes that looked too small for his face.

"Special Agent Blake, I assume?" he said, closing the distance between them.

"Yes?" For a moment, Patterson was taken aback, but then she saw Duane Snyder lingering next to a late-model silver Cadillac parked at the curb some distance down the street.

"Allow me to introduce myself. Jameson Screed."

"I figured as much," said Patterson without bothering to hide the disdain in her voice. "Can I help you with something?"

"You most surely can," Screed said in a silky Texan drawl. "I hear that you and your partner have been harassing my client regarding the heinous abduction and murder of his step-daughter, whom he loved very much, and other unfortunate girls."

"We've done no such thing," Patterson countered. "We simply asked him some questions about his movements."

"I would advise you to be careful before pursuing my client

further. You have no basis for your unconscionable harassment of an innocent man."

"Again. Not true." Patterson knew she should turn and walk away, refuse to take the bait, but her hackles were up. "For a start, he owns a van similar to one witnessed at the scene of the most recent abduction."

"As do many other people, Miss Blake."

"*Special Agent* Blake."

"Indeed." Screed smiled. "How many white cargo vans do you think there are within a hundred miles of where we're currently standing, *Special Agent* Blake?"

Patterson didn't answer.

"That's what I thought." Screed's smile widened into a leering grin. "Stay away from my client from now on, if you please."

"Or what?" Patterson met Screed's gaze with a defiant stare.

"Or we shall have another little chat, and next time it won't be so informal." Screed paused a moment for dramatic effect before speaking again. "Good day to you both."

Then Screed turned on his heel and strode back toward the Cadillac and his waiting client.

FORTY

"THAT LAWYER WAS A MOST UNPLEASANT MAN," Bauer said as he pulled away from the curb and headed through town. "I can see why Detective Voss doesn't like him."

"And why Duane Snyder does." Patterson yawned. She was exhausted after a long day, but there was still more work to do. As they left downtown behind on their way toward US-175, which would take them back to Dallas, Patterson told Bauer to head in the opposite direction toward Snyder's cabin instead.

He shot her a quizzical look. "You really want to tangle with Duane Snyder again after our run-in with his rat of a lawyer?"

"Not Snyder." Patterson shook her head. "The Lonestar Skillet. Darlene Rourke isn't exactly an angel. If she really is crying wolf with that rape allegation, as Snyder claims, I want to know."

"You think one of the other workers might dish the dirt on her?"

"Worth a try. Nothing spreads faster than workplace gossip. I'm sure they've all heard about the allegation by now. Someone might be willing to provide a little context."

"Okay." When they reached 175, Bauer swung the wheel left to head south instead of north toward Dallas. "But answer me this. What reason does Darlene Rourke have to make a false accusation?"

"I don't know. But that doesn't mean she's telling the truth. Wouldn't be the first time someone cried rape against an innocent man."

"And that's why rape cases can be so tricky," Bauer said. "Unless there's corroborating evidence, it turns into one person's word against another, even though the vast majority of reported cases are probably genuine. The statistics back it up. Only fifty percent of those accused of rape are ever arrested. And while the chances of prosecution are high if you're in that percentile, there's less than a sixty percent chance of conviction by a jury. Add to that the thirty percent of convicted rapists who never spend a day in jail, and you have an uphill battle."

"And that's on top of the estimated sixty percent that are never reported," said Patterson. "Even if Duane Snyder did rape Darlene Rourke at his cabin, there's less than a twenty percent chance he'll end up in prison for it. Which is why we need to make sure the allegation is genuine and do everything possible to nail him to the wall if that proves to be the case."

"Let's not forget Amy Bowen and the three dead girls. He's still our only lead on the Butterfly Killer. Even if Darlene isn't being truthful, it might not mean he's innocent in a broader sense."

"I know," Patterson said as they pulled into the diner parking lot. "But we have to investigate each case separately and to the best of our ability to see where the facts take us."

"You're an excellent investigator, Patterson Blake," Bauer said, complimenting her as he climbed from the car and slammed the door. "If I were accused of a crime, I'd want you on my case."

"Unless you were guilty." Patterson made her way toward the diner entrance.

"Touché." Bauer held the door open for Patterson to enter.

She paused, her gaze sweeping the parking lot. Darlene's car was not there so far as she could see. With any luck, she wasn't working. Satisfied, Patterson stepped inside and approached the cashier stand. The woman they had spoken to on their previous visit was there, tending to a customer. Patterson remembered her name was Maggie.

When she was done, Maggie looked their way and smiled. "Couldn't stay away, huh? You must have liked the hash and eggs."

"Very much," Patterson acknowledged. "But that's not why we're back. We have some questions about one of your employees, Darlene Rourke."

"Ah." The look on Maggie's face told Patterson that word of Darlene's accusation against Snyder had indeed spread fast. "I really don't know Darlene very well myself. We don't exactly have much in common. Your best bet would be Brooke. They work a lot the same shifts."

"Is Brooke working tonight?"

"Sure is." Maggie pointed to a thin woman of about thirty-five on the far side of the diner. She was delivering food to a family of four.

"Would you mind if we speak to her?"

"Sure. It would be a bit hypocritical to say we love law enforcement around here if we didn't let you do your job just because it involves one of our employees." Maggie motioned toward an empty booth with no other diners around it. "Why don't you guys take a seat, and I'll fetch Brooke just as soon as she's finished with that table."

"Thank you." Patterson turned toward the booth.

"Here, take these." Maggie held out a couple of menus. "We

might as well feed you since you're here. You both look hungry."

"That obvious, huh?" Bauer said.

"I've seen my fair share of weary cops come through here. The pair of you look wearier than most right now."

"It's been a long couple of weeks," Patterson admitted, taking the menus. She went to the booth and sat down.

Bauer slid in next to her, leaving the other side of the booth open.

Less than a minute later, Brooke appeared. She was scrawny, with mousy brown hair that fell below her shoulders. There were bags under her eyes. A tattoo of a coiling snake weaved its way up one arm and under her sleeve. There was another tattoo barely visible above her left breast in the V of her shirt, but Patterson could not tell what it was. She folded her arms. "Maggie said you had some questions about Darlene Rourke."

"We do." Patterson motioned to the empty bench seat opposite. "Please, sit down. I know you're busy, so we won't keep you long."

"Honestly, feels good to take a load off," Brooke said, sinking onto the bench seat and sliding over to the middle. "Six hours into an eight-hour shift, and my dogs are barking like you wouldn't believe."

"We get it," said Patterson. She wasn't immune to aching feet herself. "How well do you know Darlene?"

Brooke frowned. "Better than I want to." She leaned forward and whispered. "Between you and me, the woman is trailer trash."

"Why do you say that?" Bauer asked.

"Because I work with her almost every evening. Have done for years. I mean, she's friendly enough, but the things she comes out with." Brooke rolled her eyes. "She's had a string of boyfriends, most of them trash like her, and it never ends well.

Can't say that what's going on with this latest one comes as much of a surprise."

"You mean Duane Snyder?" Patterson asked. She sensed a revelation coming.

"Yeah. That's the guy. Been coming in here for a while. Recently it seems like almost every weekend. Can't say I like him much either, but Darlene sure took a shine to the guy. Even asks for his table whenever he comes in, so she gets to serve him."

"You think he's more than just a customer to her?" Bauer asked, leaning forward.

Darlene shrugged. "I know they're friendly. Even saw the pair of them necking out in the parking lot one time when I was leaving work. She always works the last shift on weekends. He comes in late and then hangs around outside until she leaves so they can drive off together."

"You've witnessed this with your own eyes?" Patterson asked.

Brooke nodded. "U-huh."

"Do they leave in one car or two?"

"Two. He drives away, and she follows. He has a cabin out in the woods, and I bet that's where they go." Brooke pursed her lips. "That's why I was surprised when I heard about the rape. Not that she's been in work since to ask, but if they were screwing, she was all into it given how she talks about him."

"Why didn't you come forward with this information?" Patterson asked.

Again, a shrug. "Not my business. Besides, Darlene has a mean streak. I don't want to get on the wrong side of that, thank you very much."

"What kind of mean streak?"

"I don't know. Sharp tongue. Not averse to getting up in your face if you piss her off. Saw her go off at a new waitress once because she cashed out one of Darlene's checks. Accused the woman of trying to steal her tips when she was just trying to be helpful."

"Is that so?" Bauer said thoughtfully.

Patterson's mind was going a mile a minute. "Is there anything else you can tell us about Darlene?"

Brooke shook her head and glanced over her shoulder. "Looks like my table back there needs a coffee refill. I should probably go take care of it before they decide I'm not worth a full twenty."

"Twenty?"

"My tip," Brooke said. "Twenty percent. Need all the money I can get, what with a new baby at home and my husband on disability. He works construction and fell off a ladder."

"In that case, we won't keep you any longer," Patterson said. She watched Brooke slide from the booth and hurry away. Then she turned to Bauer. "What do you think?"

"I think we should bring Darlene Rourke in for another chat tomorrow," Bauer replied, picking up his menu. "But right now, I think we should sample the bacon cheeseburger."

FORTY-ONE

AFTER THEY FINISHED EATING, Patterson settled the bill and took a copy of the check for her expenses, then stepped toward the door. But she turned back and reached for her wallet again, pulling out a twenty-dollar bill. She extended it toward Maggie.

"Here. This is for Brooke."

"She wasn't your server and you've already tipped," Maggie said. "You don't need to do this."

"I know. But she took time out of her busy evening to talk with us, and it sounds like she could use the money."

Maggie smiled and took the cash. "I'll make sure she gets it."

"Thanks." Patterson turned back toward the door.

"You come back anytime. You hear?" Maggie called after them. "Folk like you are always welcome at the Lonestar."

"We'll keep that in mind," Patterson said, stepping outside into the evening air. As they climbed into the car, Patterson suppressed a yawn. "I'm not sure I'm up for a ninety-minute drive back to Dallas tonight and then another long drive first thing in the morning to come back and speak to Darlene.

Unless you have hot plans, I'm going to suggest we find a motel somewhere around here to bed down."

"What hot plans am I likely to have at this time of night?" Bauer asked, raising an eyebrow.

"You tell me." Patterson gave him a halfhearted grin as she muffled another yawn with the back of her hand. "Maybe Phoebe was planning to drop by and keep you warm."

"Yeah. Not sure we're quite at that stage of our relationship yet." Bauer drove through the parking lot toward the road. "And even if we were, I'd ask for a raincheck. I'm not sure I can keep my eyes open long enough to drive back."

"Great." Patterson hopped on her phone and sat in silence for a few moments as they cruised back toward Athens. Then she looked up. "There's a motel about three miles ahead. Rooms are only seventy bucks a night."

"Sounds wonderful," Bauer replied. "I hope you like bedbugs."

"I've stayed in cheaper places."

"That's not an endorsement."

"Never said it was." Patterson scrolled through the online reviews. "Doesn't sound awful, but doesn't sound great, either. No mention of bedbugs. Besides, I'm blowing all my per diem on the hotel in Dallas, so this is coming out of my pocket. Luxury is not an option, at least for me."

"In that case, seventy bucks a night will do the trick. Want to give me some directions?"

Patterson nodded and let the phone guide Bauer to the hotel. When they arrived, he pulled up under the portico and hopped out. "I'll get us a couple of rooms. Stay there."

Patterson watched him head into the lobby, then stared out through the windshield at the dark parking lot while she churned over the evening's events in her mind. It was looking more and more like Darlene had made up the rape accusation. The question was why. If she was seeing Snyder, what reason would she have? Then again, he was a married man. Maybe Darlene got mad because he wouldn't leave Jodi and decided to get even. Patterson sighed. The answers would have to wait until tomorrow when they could talk to her.

At that moment, Bauer returned with a pair of key cards. He jumped behind the wheel and handed one to Patterson.

"Room 103." He pulled the car forward and around the side of the building, then parked up outside of a two-story motel block. "I'm next door in 104."

"Great." It hadn't occurred to Patterson until now, but she didn't have an overnight bag. She said as much.

"On it." Bauer hopped out of the car and went to the trunk.

She followed him. "Don't tell me you have a makeup kit and a nightgown stashed in there."

"Sadly, no. But I have my go bag," he replied, referring to the overnight bag that all agents were required to keep in their cars for instances such as this. Patterson had one, too. But like everything else, it was back in New York because she hadn't expected to be reinstated and working cases while following her sister's trail.

"How does that help me?" Patterson asked.

"Patience." Bauer plucked Patterson's key from her hand and went to her room. He opened it and stepped inside, then placed the go bag on the bed and unzipped it. Rummaging around, he pulled out an extra-large-sized T-shirt. He tossed it to her. "Here. Makeshift nightgown."

"My hero," Patterson said.

"There's more." He made another dive into the bag and came out with a travel-sized toothbrush and toothpaste in a small clear pouch. He handed them to her, then dove back in and produced a bottle of spring water which he put on the bed. "Probably best not to drink the tap water."

"Yeah." Patterson held up the toothbrush and toothpaste. "What about you?"

"Got my own," he said, lifting a similar kit from the bag to show her.

"You think of everything." Patterson dropped the pouch on the bed along with the T-shirt.

"I try." Bauer scooped up his go bag and stepped toward the door. "Good night, Special Agent Blake. I'll see you in the morning."

"Good night." Patterson closed the door behind him and engaged the deadbolt. She turned and surveyed the room. It was outdated, with furniture that looked like it had been purchased in the 80s, and a floral pattern bedspread. Brass wall lamps hung above a pair of fake wood nightstands. A refrigerator made faint gurgling noises in an alcove under a woefully small TV. She picked up the bottle of water and opened the fridge, noting that it didn't feel very cold inside. But at least the room looked clean enough.

She pulled the curtains, then peeled off her clothes and laid them over a chair in the corner, then wiggled into the T-shirt. The cotton felt cool and soft against her bare skin. She was about to pick up the toothpaste kit and head to the bathroom, when there was a light knock at the door.

She crossed the room and pressed her eye against the peephole to see Bauer standing on the other side. She pulled back the deadbolt and opened the door. "Forget something?"

"No." Bauer shook his head. "After I went to my room, I couldn't help thinking about us, and the way I've treated you recently. I've been acting like a jerk, and I'd like to set the record straight."

"You mean, tell me about what happened at Pioneer Jacks the other night, and the shooting in LA? What you said about killing your friend?"

Bauer nodded. "I'd like to clear the air."

Patterson hesitated. She was tired, and it was late. She was also undressed and ready for bed. But if she put him off, Bauer might change his mind by morning. "Give me a moment?"

Bauer nodded.

Patterson closed the door and found her jeans, pulled them on quickly, then opened it again and stepped aside. "Come on in."

FORTY-TWO

BAUER HESITATED, taking in the sight of Patterson wearing the oversized T-shirt and jeans. She felt her cheeks redden under his gaze and briefly wondered if this was a good idea. But before she could change her mind, a look of resolve came over his face and he stepped past her into the room.

He went to a spindly office chair under a narrow desk next to the TV stand and pulled it out, sitting down.

Patterson closed the door and retreated to the bed. She sat on the edge. There was a minute of silence between them before Patterson gave him a verbal prod. "If you have something to say, you'd better say it."

"Right." He took a deep breath. "I'm not sure where to begin."

"Why don't you start with the bar. What were you doing there getting drunk like that?" The air-conditioning kicked on as Patterson spoke. The low rumble of the unit underneath the window forced her to talk louder. It was already chilly in the room. She wondered what the thermostat was set on but didn't want to distract Bauer from his confession.

"The bar. Yes." Bauer gathered his thoughts for a moment.

"I didn't intend for you to see me. I went there to be alone. It was the anniversary of my friend's death, and I was drowning my sorrows. I haven't handled it very well, as you probably noticed."

"Who was he?" Patterson asked, leaning forward with her elbows on her knees.

"His name was Simon. We grew up together in Central City East. Skid Row. It was tough. Gang activity was rampant and by the time he was twelve years old, Simon had joined one." Bauer trailed off. He looked unsure of himself, but then pulled it together. "I wasn't far behind him. I was on track for a much different life than the one I have now."

"I can't imagine you running with a gang." Patterson couldn't believe what she was hearing. Bauer was every bit the strait-laced Fed.

"Not back then. Crappy home life. No money. Alcoholic mother and a jerk of a father. I was angry at the world and looking for someone to take it out on."

"What changed?"

"We were fourteen years old. Still kids, but thought we were men. We decided to rob a liquor store in Koreatown. Simon had gotten us a couple of guns—don't ask me where he found them because I still don't know—and we thought we were invincible. The pair of us bust into that place and started waving those pistols around even though they weren't even loaded. The proprietor saw through our act. He was an old Korean guy and had probably been robbed a hundred times already. He pulled out the biggest gun I'd ever seen and told us to get the hell out of his store. Before we knew it, we were running for our lives with nothing to show for our efforts but wounded egos. The store owner must've had a panic button because the police showed up when we were less than a block away. They gave chase and we split up. I got away and Simon got caught."

"What happened next?" Patterson was struggling to believe

that this teenaged hoodlum Bauer was describing could be the same person sitting in front of her.

"Nothing. At least for me. I ditched the gun on some waste-land and went home. Jumped into bed and spent the entire night waiting for the cops to come and kick the door in. It was terrifying. All I could think of was what would happen when my mother found out I'd tried to rob a liquor store."

"And Simon?"

"He wasn't so lucky. They knew he wasn't the only person involved in the robbery, but he kept his mouth shut. For his efforts he ended up in juvy. After that, we only spoke a few times. That liquor store robbery scared me straight. I wanted to be part of the solution, not the problem. The next time I saw him, I'd already applied for the police academy. He'd gone right back to the gangs the minute he got out. We were on opposite sides of the law despite my best efforts to show him the error of his ways. It broke my heart."

"I can't imagine," Patterson said. "But what does that have to do with the convenience store robbery and the guy you shot?"

"Everything." Bauer looked heartbroken. "I'd responded to a hundred calls like that one over the course of my career with LAPD. Goes with the territory. This one was different. I'd only ever fired my gun outside the range a couple of times before that, and I'd never killed anyone. But this guy just would not back down. He came at me. Left me no choice. I put two slugs into him because I truly believed that if I hadn't, he would have killed me."

"It was Simon, wasn't it?"

Bauer lowered his head. He studied the patch of motel carpet between his feet. "When I pulled the trigger, I didn't know it was him. I swear. He was wearing a ski mask."

"It wouldn't have made a difference." Patterson's throat tightened.

"I don't know if it would have made a difference or not," Bauer said. "He was wearing a mask. I wasn't. Even though it was dark, I still wonder if he recognized me. We were so close growing up. Like brothers. He might've thought I wouldn't actually pull the trigger. But I did. I shot him dead."

"That's not your fault. Like you said, he was wearing a mask. You couldn't have known. Even if you did, you had a job to do."

"Doesn't make it any easier."

"None of what happened is on you." Patterson leaned over and grabbed Bauer's hand. She pulled him from the chair toward the bed. "Simon chose to rob that store. He chose to flee. He chose to come at you."

Bauer looked defeated. "Simon was my best friend, and I let him down. I failed him."

"No. You didn't." Patterson put her hand under Bauer's chin. She lifted his head. "You did the right thing, even if it doesn't feel like that."

Bauer didn't answer. Instead, he stared into her eyes, and in that moment, Patterson's breath caught in her throat.

"I've never told anyone about this," Bauer said. "The truth of my past died with Simon. Not even my family knows everything. You're the only person I've ever truly confided in."

Patterson didn't know what to say. She reached out and touched Bauer's cheek. "The fact that you overcame such an awful start is testament to the good within you."

"Even if I let my best friend take the rap for a robbery we both committed?"

"Even then. You were a kid growing up in a dreadful situation surrounded by influences you couldn't control."

"Doesn't help."

"It wasn't meant to. It was simply an observation." Patterson couldn't explain why, but in that moment, she felt closer to Bauer than she ever had to Grant. She leaned in, aware of the thin veil of fabric between them. Of her breasts pushing against his chest and the smell if his musky aftershave.

Their lips brushed.

He hesitated as if waiting for permission to go further. Then she felt his hand on her back, bunching the fabric of the T-shirt he'd lent her. His other hand found her leg, pushed up under the loose shirt to her hip.

She fell into the moment, pressing her lips against his. Time stopped, and it was just the two of them caught in a lover's embrace.

Then reality crashed down.

Patterson pulled away, overcome with a sudden sense of remorse. She was with Grant, and Bauer was dating Phoebe. No matter the feelings between them in the heat of the moment, this could not go any further.

She took a deep breath and ignored the heat racing through her body. "You should go."

Bauer didn't argue. His hand lingered a moment longer on her back, then he stood and cleared his throat. "This didn't happen."

"Agreed."

He met Patterson's gaze, and she sensed the longing in his eyes, before he took a deep breath, turned, and left. She heard him enter the room next door, and then nothing but silence. Patterson sat and looked at her own motel room door for a long while, wondering what might have been, then slipped off the jeans and folded them over the chair, brushed her teeth, climbed into bed, and turned off the light.

FORTY-THREE

AMY BOWEN SAT cross-legged in the darkness. Hours before, she had cried; the tears coming in waves as she thought about home, and her parents, who would be worried sick. They would also be looking for her, but Amy didn't think they would find her. Her captor had said this place was a secret. That even if she screamed, no one would come. And she believed him. But at least he hadn't done anything awful to her yet. At least, nothing too awful.

Then there was the wall of photos. It was hard to see them because the only light came from a bare bulb hanging in the tunnel beyond the bars. But she could see well enough to know they were all the same girl. A teenager about her own age with a pretty face not unlike Amy's. And then there were the dresses. They were cute. Amy could see her mother buying something like that for her as Sunday best. A knee-length dress printed with butterflies. This girl must have loved butterflies because every dress featured them. Amy wondered who the girl was. Another captive like herself, perhaps? But that made no sense. This wall felt like a shrine. The photographs were arranged neatly and placed with care. And it was obvious they had been there a long time. The corners of some photos were curling. The tape used to hold them to the wall and to each other had yellowed. Some photos had fallen off and been reattached with fresh tape that looked newer.

None of this convinced Amy she would remain safe. And when her captor appeared unexpectedly, carrying a metal folding chair and what looked like a cosmetics bag, her alarm only increased.

He came through the metal door at the end of the tunnel and approached the bars, then stood looking at her in silence for a while. She squirmed under his gaze and thought about begging him to set her free, but she didn't. They were beyond that.

"Stand up and turn with your back to me," he said eventually.

Amy did as she was told, unable to stifle a whimper of fear. If her captor heard it, he made no comment. Instead, the sound of a key being inserted into an old lock reached her ears. It turned with a metallic clunk, and then the cell door opened on protesting hinges before closing again.

"You can turn back around now."

Amy did so to find that her captor had set the metal chair in the middle of the cramped space. She glanced past it to the cell door.

"Don't even think about running," her captor said, reading the look. "Even if you got out of your room, the tunnel door is locked."

"I wasn't going to—" Amy started to say. But her captor interrupted.

"I know exactly what was going through your head. You always were smart." His eyes lifted briefly to the wall of photos before settling back upon Amy.

She stood in silence, confused by the strange statement, but didn't ask about it. What was the point? Her captor was clearly deranged, and she was more concerned about what was going to happen next.

She soon found out.

"Sit on the chair," her captor commanded.

Amy followed his instructions, unable to stop herself from shaking.

Her captor unzipped the cosmetics bag and removed a pair of small sharp scissors, then placed the bag on the ground next to the chair.

Amy's breath caught in her throat. Overcome with panic, she tried to rise, but a firm hand landed on her shoulder and pushed her back down.

"Stay where you are. Keep still or I'll hurt you."

Amy nodded.

The scissors flashed toward her face. She flinched despite herself, but then her captor's free hand grabbed at her long hair —the same hair her mother said made her look like a princess —and pulled it into a tight bunch. She felt a tug at the back of her head, followed by the sound of scissors closing.

The pressure was momentarily released, and Amy saw a wad of hair fall to the floor before her captor took hold of another handful and repeated the process.

This went on for another ten minutes while Amy tried to sit still despite the panic that closed her throat. When she cried, her captor leaned down.

Hot breath tickled her ear. "Don't cry. I'm fixing you."

That only made Amy cry all the more.

At least until the ordeal was over and her captor stepped away, pushing the scissors back into the cosmetics bag and letting her stand up.

He folded the chair and made her walk to the opposite wall and stand there while he left the cell and locked the door. Taking the chair with him, her captor went back to the metal door at the end of the tunnel and stepped through it.

Amy breathed a sigh of relief. He was gone. For now.

Except he wasn't. After a couple of minutes, she heard the metal door open again and her captor reappeared. He was holding the same bucket he'd made her wash with before. In his other hand was a folded dress.

He opened the cell door and put the bucket down, followed by the dress, then retreated to the same chair he'd sat on before.

"Wash yourself and put that dress on," he said.

Amy complied, even though the last thing she wanted was to repeat the humiliating experience. She took off the jeans and T-shirt he had given her and used the sponge to clean away the sweat and grime that had accumulated since the last time he'd made her wash.

Her captor sat reading the same book as before, paying her no attention. At least until she pulled the dress over her head and wriggled into it.

Now he stood up and stepped into the cell, looking at her as if he were seeing a ghost. He came close enough that she could smell garlic on his breath. She wrinkled her nose at the unpleasant odor and tried not to gag.

"You're perfect," he said, running a light finger down her neck and smoothing her newly cut hair. Then he stepped back and took a compact digital camera from his pocket. He snapped a picture, the flash temporarily blinding her. After returning the camera to his pocket, he picked up the bucket and backed away through the door, then went to lock it.

At that moment, a sudden sense overcame Amy that if she didn't act now, she would never leave this place alive.

She bolted forward and turned her shoulder to the door a moment before he could fully close it. Red-hot pain shot down her arm as her shoulder connected with the bars. The door swung back against her captor, causing him to stumble and providing enough of a gap for her to squeeze through.

She surged ahead, making for the metal door at the end of

the tunnel. Only now did it occur to her that the door would probably be locked. In her blind panic, she hadn't considered this possibility despite her captor's earlier statement. But when she gripped the handle and pulled, it opened.

She felt a surge of adrenaline mixed with a heady sense of elation. She was going to escape, after all. But at that moment a pair of powerful arms circled her waist and dragged her back. Her feet scuffed the floor. She squirmed and cried out, beating at her captor with clenched fists even as he pulled her inexorably back toward the cell.

He threw her back inside, and she stumbled, then fell, landing on the dirt floor so hard that it knocked the wind from her lungs.

Her captor bore down upon her, his face twisted into an angry mask. "I should put you over my knee for that."

Amy scrambled backward, horrified at the thought of a spanking from this man. He reached down, grabbed her hair, and yanked her head up painfully so she was forced to look into his eyes.

"I don't know what's gotten into you," he growled. "You were always so good."

"Please," Amy begged. "Don't hurt me."

"You don't deserve the dress," her captor replied, grabbing at the collar and yanking it upward.

Amy squealed and tried to pull it back down, even as the garment slid over her head and off.

Amy fell backward, her bare rump hitting the ground and sending a jolt of pain up her spine. She coiled into a tight ball and lay there, crying softly.

This is it, she thought. He's going to rape and kill me for sure.

But he didn't.

Dress in hand, her captor strode from the cell, slammed the door, and locked it behind him. When he turned to look at her again, the anger had fallen from his face to be replaced by a look of disappointment.

"When you've had time to reflect on your actions, we'll talk about your future in this household."

Then he retreated down the tunnel and through the metal door, leaving her curled on the floor.

FORTY-FOUR

THE WALL between them was back up, only now for a different reason. Patterson sat silently in the passenger seat of Bauer's car as they left the hotel at nine a.m. and drove toward Darlene Rourke's apartment. After enduring the uneasy atmosphere for a few long minutes, Patterson placed a call to Detective Voss and filled her in on the previous evening's conversation with Brooke at the diner.

Voss listened without interrupting and only spoke when Patterson was finished. "Looks like our case against Duane Snyder is on the rocks," she said at length.

Patterson agreed. "Even if Brooke's statement isn't accurate, it will introduce enough uncertainty to make the DA think twice about prosecuting. Not to mention that slimy lawyer, who's going to be all over this the minute he finds out."

"You think Darlene really was seeing Snyder and made a false accusation against him?"

"That's what I intend to find out," Patterson said. "We're on our way to Darlene's apartment now to see what she has to say for herself."

"I'd like to be present for that conversation," Voss said. "How about I meet you there?"

"Absolutely. You're the investigating detective. We're just the hired help."

"And doing a good job of it," Voss said. "Not that I wouldn't have gone out to the Lonestar to question her coworkers myself."

"Now you don't need to," Patterson said. She agreed to meet the detective in the parking lot of Darlene Rourke's apartment at ten. That gave them almost three-quarters of an hour to kill since the apartment was only fifteen minutes away. Patterson put the phone back in her pocket and looked sideways at Bauer. "Want to grab some breakfast and talk about last night?"

"Nope."

"Then how about we just grab breakfast and ignore each other instead?"

"Sounds good to me." Bauer lapsed back into silence until they came across an IHOP further down the road.

They parked and headed inside. After placing their order, Patterson tried again.

"We can't ignore what happened between us last night," she said. "Unless you want to spend the rest of my time in Dallas giving me the cold shoulder."

"That's not what I'm doing," Bauer said after the server filled their mugs with coffee and stepped away. "I'm ashamed of myself. I shouldn't have kissed you."

"I didn't exactly stop you," Patterson pointed out. "We're equally to blame."

"You have a boyfriend. And one who could get me fired, at that."

"And you're with Phoebe." Patterson ripped the top off the sugar packet and dropped it into her coffee, then stirred the steaming liquid. "We got caught up in the moment and almost made a terrible mistake. But we stopped ourselves and that's what matters. How about we chalk it up to an error of judgment brought about by too little sleep and move on?"

"Except that isn't true."

"It has to be."

"Under different circumstances . . ." Bauer trailed off.

"I know," Patterson said. Their eyes met, and she felt an echo of the same desire that had almost driven her into his arms the previous night. She pushed the sensation away. "Why don't we focus on the job at hand and forget this ever happened?"

"I'd like that." Bauer agreed.

A minute later, the server arrived back at their table with two stacks of pancakes drenched in syrup and topped with bacon. Fifteen minutes after that, they were back in the car and driving toward Darlene Rourke's apartment to meet Detective Voss.

FORTY-FIVE

WHEN THEY ARRIVED at Darlene's apartment complex, Detective Voss was waiting. She was leaning against the side of a plain Crown Victoria that still managed to look like a cop car despite its lack of markings.

Together, the three of them climbed a set of steps in the breezeway between two buildings and knocked on Darlene's second-floor apartment door.

She answered looking bleary-eyed and tired, dressed in a pair of sweatpants and a loose tank top. She wore no makeup.

"Huh. Detective Voss and the FBI agents from Dallas." Darlene whetted her lips with her tongue. "You stop by to say Duane Snyder is in jail for what he did to me?"

"Not quite," Patterson said. "Can we come inside?"

"What for?" Darlene kept the door partially closed between herself and the three law enforcement officers.

"We'd like to have a chat. Make sure we're all on the same page regarding what happened between you and Duane," Patterson replied.

"Not a good time." Darlene went to push the door closed.

"We understand," Voss said, placing a hand on the door and

pushing back. "I can always come back later with a couple of deputies, and we'll have our conversation in a more formal location."

"You can't arrest me. Done nothing wrong. I'm the victim."

"Not according to your coworkers at the diner," Patterson said. "They paint a much different picture of your relationship with Snyder."

"You went to my work?" Darlene drew in a sharp breath. "You had no right to do that."

"Sure we did," Bauer said. "It's called investigating the crime."

"Except in this case there wasn't a crime, was there Darlene?" Patterson said. "At least, not one committed by Duane Snyder."

"Dammit." Darlene glanced toward the other apartment doors, then opened her own door wider. "You'd better come in."

They stepped across the threshold and followed her to a cramped living room. A laundry basket sat on the floor full of unwashed clothes. There was a coffee table in front of a sagging fabric couch. An ashtray full of cigarette butts and piles of tabloid magazines on the coffee table completed the tableau. A faint odor of cigarette smoke hung in the air.

"I don't know what those girls at the diner have been telling you, but it's not true. None of it," Darlene said, after picking up a remote from the side of the couch and turning off the TV sitting on a cheap stand. "Duane Snyder raped me, and I'm sticking to that."

"Are you denying that the pair of you were in an intimate relationship?" Bauer asked. "Because your coworker told us you and Snyder have been friendly for months. Claimed he even waited for your shift to end so the pair of you could take off together."

"Who was it said that?" Darlene pressed her lips together.

"We're not at liberty to divulge," Patterson replied. "But they claimed to witness you and Snyder kissing in the parking lot one night after the diner closed. If that's true, it would refute your claim that the two of you were just friends."

"And it should be pretty easy to verify." Bauer folded his arms. "Did you know the diner has cameras covering the parking lot? If you and Snyder were getting a little too close, one of those cameras would have recorded it."

"What?"

"That's right." Patterson didn't know where Bauer had gotten the information about cameras, but it didn't matter. Darlene looked nervous. "We haven't requested the footage yet, but it shouldn't be hard to get. These modern surveillance systems upload everything to the cloud and store the footage for a year or more."

"Look, maybe Duane and me had something going for a while. That isn't a crime, even if he's married."

"No, it's not." Voss fixed Darlene with an icy gaze. "But making a false accusation of rape most certainly is."

"Tell me, Darlene, did you know that Duane Snyder was married before a couple of days ago when I questioned you about him?" Patterson asked, remembering the look on Darlene's face the first time they met in the diner when she mentioned Snyder's wife in Dallas and his recently abducted and murdered stepdaughter.

Darlene hesitated. She clasped her hands together and glanced toward the door as if she wanted to be anywhere else but there. Then the air seemed to deflate from her. "No. I didn't."

"Is that why you made the rape allegation?" Voss asked. "To get even after you found out he'd been lying to you?"

Darlene nodded mutely.

"Anything else you'd like to tell us?"

Darlene stifled a sob. There were tears in her eyes. "I

thought I'd finally found a good man. He had his own business and a house in Dallas. He made me feel loved. Told me that his cabin in the woods was our special place."

"And you didn't suspect he was married?" Patterson asked.

"Why would I?"

"Because you only ever saw him on weekends when he came to the cabin. Didn't you ever wonder why he didn't invite you to his home in Dallas?"

"I did. That's why we were arguing that day you came into the diner." Darlene sniffed and wiped tears from her eyes. "I wanted to go to Dallas. Spend the week with him there. But every time I asked, he claimed to be too busy. Said he had too much work. He kept putting me off until I gave him an ultimatum. Either let me into his life full-time, not just for a weekend here and there, or we were through. That's what the argument was about."

"How did you get his wife's number to tell her he'd raped you?"

"His address in Dallas was listed on the paperwork for the rape. Once I had that, it was easy to find a cell phone number. I'd looked him up online before when we first got together— you know, to make sure he wasn't married or anything—but I didn't know his exact address back then. When I didn't find anyone else with his surname, like a wife, I thought it was okay."

"His wife didn't take Duane's surname when they got married," Patterson said. "She kept the name of her previous husband to make it easier for her kids. That's why you couldn't find her so easily."

"I know that now."

"Tell me about yesterday," Patterson said. "When Duane forced himself into your apartment. You called to lure him here, didn't you?"

Darleen dropped her head. "I thought that if he was caught

harassing me, it would make him look more guilty, so I told him to come here and then refused to let him in. Goaded him into pushing his way into the apartment."

"After you called 911 to report him trying to break in," said Voss.

"It was stupid. I realize that." Darlene looked between the FBI agents and Voss. "Are you going to arrest me?"

"Not at the moment," Voss said. "But I will have more questions. Lots of them. Depending on those answers . . ."

Darlene nodded.

"I'm going to ask you not to leave the area without my permission until we settle this. Understand?"

Darlene nodded again. "I'm sorry for the trouble I caused. I was just so angry. He made me feel like such a fool."

FORTY-SIX

AS THEY DROVE AWAY from Darlene's apartment, Bauer voiced what Patterson was thinking. "Maybe we're just chasing our tails with Duane Snyder. I'm not so sure he's the Butterfly Killer. He's coming across more as a sleazebag cheating husband."

"I agree," Patterson said halfheartedly. "You think we should give him the good news that he's probably off the hook for rape?"

"That's where I'm heading right now." Bauer had already turned onto the road leading to Duane Snyder's property. "If nothing else, it will give us one last chance to have a poke around that cabin before we end up back at square one with no suspects or leads on the Butterfly Killer."

Patterson settled back and took out her phone as they drove. She sent a text message to Grant back in New York. A few seconds later, she got one in return.

'Good morning to you, too.'

'Busy day?' she asked.

'Always.'

'Call me tonight?' Patterson typed.

For the better part of two minutes, there was no reply. Patterson stared at the screen, overcome with the sudden notion that Grant somehow knew what had happened the previous night between herself and Bauer in the hotel room. That was crazy, of course. But yet . . .

The phone screen lit up again as three animated dots appeared on her screen, swiftly followed by a curt reply.

'Sure. Call you later. Have a meeting now.'

Patterson breathed a sigh of relief. She slipped the phone into her pocket and looked back up just as Bauer swung a hard right onto the trail leading up to Duane Snyder's cabin.

Soon the cabin itself came into view. The first thing Patterson noticed was the absence of a vehicle. The lean-to carport was empty.

"Doesn't look like anybody's home," Bauer said, getting out of the car and glancing around the clearing.

Patterson made for the cabin and climbed the steps to the covered porch. She went to the window and cupped her hands against the glass to peer inside. All the lights were off and there was no sign of movement. Unlike the last time they came here looking for Snyder, there were no gunshots in the woods.

She descended the steps and took a quick tour around the clearing to make sure he hadn't parked his Jeep or the cargo van somewhere else. There were no vehicles to be found. Snyder was gone.

"What do you think?" Bauer asked, leaning against the side of the car. "Went back to Dallas with his tail between his legs?"

"That would be my guess," Patterson said. "Either that or he took off thinking he was going to get a rape charge pinned on him."

"I don't think he's on the run." Bauer shook his head. "Don't forget about that sleazy lawyer he hired. For all we know, Screed has already heard that Darlene recanted."

"If he hasn't, it won't be long." Patterson rubbed the back of her neck. The sun was beating down, and she had put no sunscreen on that morning. If she wasn't careful, she would burn. "Can't see any reason to stay around here. Want to head back to Dallas?"

"Might as well." Bauer climbed back into the car and waited for Patterson before he continued. "We can swing by the Banks' residence and see if he's there. Use the excuse that we're giving him the good news. With that lawyer sniffing around, it might be our last chance to talk to him unless we get some compelling new evidence."

"It's not like we have anything else to do." Patterson checked her phone again as Bauer pulled down the dirt trail and out onto the road. There were no more text messages from Grant.

They rode most of the way back lost in their own thoughts. The events of the previous evening had left them both feeling unsure of where things stood, despite the short conversation over breakfast. For her part, Patterson was feeling guilty and suspected the same of Bauer. It wasn't just that they had kissed, almost slept together, but that she had wanted it. A part of her still did. What did that say about her relationship with Grant? Sure, she'd been feeling that they were drifting apart, but that was probably a side effect of her dogged pursuit of Julie. She was as guilty of not making time as he was. And it was not an excuse for kissing another man.

She was still pondering this when Bauer pulled up at the curb outside of the home Duane Snyder shared with Jodi Banks.

The cargo van was parked at the side of the house behind a green Kia that Patterson assumed must belong to Jodi. The Jeep Duane often took up to the cabin was nowhere in sight, but that meant nothing because Jodi said he often parked it around the back.

"Looks like we're in luck," Bauer said, hitching a thumb toward the cargo van.

"We'll see." Patterson walked to the front door and rang the bell.

Jodi answered.

"What do you want?" she asked in a snippy voice.

"Is your husband here?" Patterson asked in return.

"Yeah. Duane's here."

"Guess you forgave him, huh?" Bauer craned his neck to see past Jodi, but she moved sideways to block his field of vision.

"None of your business."

"Can we talk to him?" Patterson asked.

"Why?" Jodi stood with one foot wedged against the back of the door as if she were afraid they would push their way in.

"It's fine. Let them talk," said a voice at Jodi's rear. It was Snyder. "It's just more fodder for my lawyer."

"You'd better come in then," Jodi said, removing her foot from behind the door.

"Thank you." Patterson followed Bauer inside and they all went to the living room where Snyder turned on them with a look that reminded her of a snake that was about to eat a mouse.

"You realize the harassment complaint my lawyer is filing will mean you won't be able to come within a hundred miles of me pretty soon." Snyder smirked. "So go ahead, say your piece. I'm not worried because I know I didn't do it."

"We agree on that." Bauer couldn't help a small smile of his own. "That's why we came to see you."

"What?"

"Can we talk in private?" Patterson asked, glancing toward Jodi.

"Anything you have to say to my husband you can say in front of me," Jodi said, stepping up to Duane and slipping her hand into his. "We had a long talk last night after the police released him."

"Kissed and made up, huh?" Bauer asked.

"something like that."

"I still think we should talk in private," Patterson said to Snyder.

"No. I want my wife to hear you say I didn't rape that woman. Whatever you have to say, you can say it right here and now."

"Fair enough." Patterson had done her best to save him from the humiliation of what was about to come. And honestly, Jodi Banks deserved to know what type of man she had married. "Darlene Rourke admitted she made up the rape allegation."

"See. That wasn't so hard." Snyder was practically gleeful. He turned to his wife. "I told you I was innocent."

"Not quite innocent," Patterson said, stepping forward. "She also told us you've been having an affair with her for the better part of a year."

FORTY-SEVEN

JODI BANKS SNATCHED her hand back like she'd been burned and stepped away from her husband. "Is this true?"

Duane was temporarily speechless, then he reached out to his wife. "Baby, come on. It's just more bullshit. The woman is clearly a pathological liar. She can't help herself."

"Are you sleeping with her?" Jodi was trembling. "Answer me."

"I told you already. We were friends. When I stop in at the diner we chat sometimes. That's all. I can't help it if she lives in a fantasy world."

"Is he telling the truth?" Jodi asked, looking at Patterson and Bauer. "Is that woman making this up like she did everything else?"

"We don't believe so, ma'am," Bauer said.

Jodi spun around and focused back on her husband. "Were you with her the day Shawna was taken?"

"I was doing a job. You know that." All the arrogance had disappeared from Snyder's voice. Now he sounded more like a school kid who'd been caught smoking behind the gym.

"I don't know what to believe. All those weekends when

you went to that cabin . . ." Jodi glared at her husband. "All that time, you were sleeping with some tramp who works in a diner."

"Baby. Jodi. I swear you have it wrong."

"All right. How do I have it wrong?" Jodi's voice had risen half an octave. There were tears in her eyes. "Tell me."

Snyder said nothing.

"Fuck." Jodi stormed from the room and slammed the door.

Snyder didn't move. Nor did he speak. He just looked straight ahead as if he were in a daze.

Less than a minute later, Jodi returned carrying a hard-shell suitcase. Patterson saw the arm of a white shirt caught under the lid.

"Get out." Jodi threw the suitcase across the room. Snyder jumped aside to avoid it hitting him. "Just get the hell out."

"Where am I going to go?" Snyder looked bereft.

"Anywhere but here. Why don't you go back to that cabin of yours and have another romp between the sheets with Darlene the skanky waitress. She can have you."

"This isn't over," Snyder growled. He snatched the suitcase and headed toward the door before turning back toward his wife. "I'll call you later when you've calmed down."

"Like hell, you will."

Snyder hesitated as if he hoped the last ten minutes would somehow fade from existence, then he turned and left the room. The sound of the front door slamming followed. Soon after, Snyder's van roared to life and Patterson saw it peel away from the curb through the front window.

"You should probably go as well," Jodi said, focusing her attention back on Patterson and Bauer.

"Will you be okay?" Patterson asked.

"Probably not." Jodi sank onto the couch. She picked up a framed photo of Shawna that was sitting on the coffee table. "What am I going to do?" She looked at Patterson with wide eyes. "I've lost my little girl. The man I loved is nothing but a cheating liar. Where do I go from here?"

"I can reach out to Detective Costa if you want. Have him arrange for a victim advocate to drop by and see you. It might help you move past this."

"Easy for you to say." Jodi stared at the photo. "You never lost anyone like this."

Patterson kneeled next to her. "Actually, I did. My big sister, Julie. She disappeared on a cross-country road trip sixteen years ago and was never seen again."

Jodi glanced up. "I'm sorry to hear that. Did the pain get any better?"

"No, it didn't. We learned to live with the loss."

Jodi nodded and looked back down at the photo of Shawna. "That's what I thought."

FORTY-EIGHT

AS THEY DROVE across town on the way back from the Banks' residence, Patterson mulled over the events of the last few days. She felt sorry for Jodi Banks. After everything she had gone through with Shawna, from the abduction to the discovery of her daughter's body four months later, she now had to deal with the knowledge that her husband had been lying to her the entire time. It was heartbreaking. Even if Duane Snyder wasn't the Butterfly Killer, he was still a creep.

She was so lost in thought that she didn't notice where they were going until Bauer stopped the car and she looked up, surprised to see they were at Esther Cutler's townhouse, and not the field office.

"What are we doing here?" She asked.

"Just thought I'd stop by and check on Esther. Phoebe said she loves to get visitors." Bauer was already getting out of the car. "Her caregiver comes in around this time of day. Don't worry. I texted Phoebe and cleared it with her while you were talking to Jodi."

"Aw. That's sweet of you," Patterson said, wondering if her partner's sudden desire to check in with his girlfriend's grandmother had something to do with lingering guilt from the kiss she and Bauer had shared the previous evening. Like her, he might be wondering how far the encounter in that hotel room would have gone if they hadn't come to their senses.

As they made their way toward the townhouse, Patterson saw a woman in her late thirties struggling to unload the back of a car parked outside the townhouse next door. She had trays of plants that she balanced while she tried to close the trunk. More trays sat at the curb.

"You need some help there?" Bauer asked, stepping up to the woman.

"Is it that obvious?" She turned to Bauer and smiled. "I saw the pair of you through the window the other day talking to Benjamin. You're friends of Phoebe's, right?"

Bauer nodded. "We were in the area and stopped by to see her grandmother because her caregiver comes in around this time. Phoebe says she gets lonely with no one to talk to all day."

"I'm sure she does. Poor woman. She'll be happy to see you. Jesse should be here soon. He runs late sometimes if he gets held up at his previous visit."

"Which gives us enough time to help you in with those plants," Bauer said, picking up a couple of trays from the sidewalk. "They look awkward."

"They are. I wouldn't normally buy this many at once, but they were on sale, so I thought I'd take advantage". The woman smiled. "I'm Helen, by the way."

"Marcus." Bauer nodded toward Patterson as she picked up the last two trays from the sidewalk and introduced her.

"Pleased to meet you both." Helen mounted the steps to her townhouse. She juggled her trays on one arm and pulled a set of keys from her pocket, then unlocked the front door and stepped inside. She waited for Patterson and Bauer to follow before leading them down a hallway that looked just like the one next door, except the layout was flipped.

They followed Helen from the hallway and through a kitchen that looked as modern as Esther Cutler's kitchen next door looked stuck in the past.

"You have such a nice home," Patterson said, looking around the kitchen.

"Thank you." Helen reached the back door and opened it. "We completely renovated after we moved in. That was a while ago now, though."

"What type of plants are these?" Bauer asked as they descended a set of stone steps into a backyard surrounded by a high brick wall.

"Milkweed." Helen set her trays down on a low wall surrounding a garden area bursting with flowers. "But don't let the name fool you. It produces glorious purple flowers that are something to behold."

"I'm sure these plants will look great out here," Patterson said, taking in the copious flower beds lining the backyard and the paved area between them with a sitting area around a stone fire pit.

"That's the plan. Now all I have to do is put them in the ground." Helen wiped her hands on her jeans.

"I don't envy you that chore." Patterson was not a gardener. She could barely keep a houseplant alive, let alone flower beds like those surrounding her at that moment.

"It really isn't a chore." Helen started back toward the house. "More a labor of love."

"In that case, I'm pleased we could help," Bauer said as they walked back through the house to the front.

"Which I'm grateful for." Helen opened the front door to let them out. "I'd love to stay and chat some more, but I have to collect Danny from school, and then once Ben gets home, I'm off to work."

"So late?" Patterson had assumed Helen was a stay-at-home mom.

"U-huh. I'm a nurse. Third shift four evenings a week, Sunday through Wednesday. Honestly, with Ben's job and charity work keeping him away all day every day, sometimes it feels like we're ships in the night. We barely see each other."

"I'm sorry to hear that," Patterson said.

"We're used to it," Helen replied. "Of course, it was easier when Ben wasn't volunteering so much. He's gotten involved in this charitable foundation through our church. They're working on a low-income housing project. They hire contractors to do some of the stuff like plumbing and wiring, but they do a lot themselves to save money."

"Makes sense," Bauer said. "What does Ben do for a living, if you don't mind me asking?"

"He's an accountant, just like his dad. Helps out three days a week at his father's office, which is why he can spend so much time working with the church."

"If only everyone was so charitable," Bauer said as he stepped out onto the stoop.

"Indeed." Helen smiled.

"Say hello to Ben from us," Patterson added, following Bauer outside.

"Sure." Helen nodded and watched them descend the steps to the sidewalk before closing the door.

As they turned toward the townhouse next door, Patterson saw a man in blue scrubs walking toward them, who she assumed must be Jesse, Esther Cutler's caregiver.

FORTY-NINE

"YOU MUST BE MARCUS AND PATTERSON," the caregiver said as he approached the townhouse. "Phoebe said I should expect you this afternoon."

"That's us," Bauer said. "I hope you don't mind the intrusion."

"Not at all." Jesse mounted the steps, removed the key from the lockbox, and opened the front door. "Esther gets so few visitors. She'll be thrilled to see you."

"That's what we thought."

Bauer and Patterson followed Jesse into the living room where the old lady was sitting up in a chair near the front window.

At their appearance, she beamed. "Three visitors at the same time. How wonderful."

"Hello there, Esther," Bauer said. "How are you doing today?"

"Can't grumble. Arthritis is playing up like you wouldn't believe and I'm always chilly, but other than that . . ."

"We'll make sure you aren't cold tonight," Jesse said, before disappearing from the room and returning with a pile of fresh sheets in his arms. He went to the bed and stripped it down, peeling back the thick comforter and replacing the old sheets with new ones before pulling the comforter back up and fluffing up the pillows.

Patterson watched this while Bauer sat in a chair next to the old woman and talked to her. Esther must have had the bedding for a long time. The floral patterns looked dated and old. But the sheets themselves were still in good condition. The flower print on the comforter reminded Patterson of one her own grandmother had owned years before except she only brought it out in the winter when the temperature plunged below zero and the ground was covered in snow. This one looked too heavy for the time of year, and Patterson wondered how uncomfortable Esther must be that she needed such thick bedding in the middle of summer.

Jesse finished with the bed and turned to the old woman. "Are you ready for your dinner yet?"

"Starving," Esther said with a glint in her eye. "What's on the menu?"

"I have pork with scalloped potatoes or chicken and rice." Jesse pushed his hands into the pockets of his scrubs. "What do you fancy?"

"Definitely the pork." Esther wet her lips and looked at Bauer. "There won't be enough for everyone, I'm afraid."

"That's quite all right," Bauer replied. "We can fend for ourselves."

"Doesn't look like you're doing a very good job of it." Esther gave Bauer the once over before her gaze shifted to Patterson. "You both look too thin."

"We work off a lot of calories in our job," Patterson replied, bemused. "Don't worry, we'll eat just as soon as we leave here."

"You make sure that you do."

"Okay, Mrs. Cutler. How about we just worry about keeping

you fed," said Jesse with a grin. He looked to Patterson and Bauer. "I'll be in the kitchen."

When he turned to leave, Patterson followed. Bauer was doing a good job of entertaining the old woman, and she had some questions for the caregiver.

When she entered the kitchen, Jesse was removing a pre-prepared frozen meal from the freezer. It looked a bit like a TV dinner, except the packaging was plain and she didn't recognize the brand.

Or her approach, Jesse glanced up. "These meals are a godsend. We have them delivered weekly so she always has food in the house. She can pick what she wants from a menu specially formulated for people like her, and then Phoebe orders them online."

"Which is why you were able to give her a choice of meals tonight," Patterson said.

"Exactly." Jesse pulled the lid off the container and moved the contents onto a plate which he put into a countertop microwave. "Is there something I can help you with?"

"Maybe," Patterson said. "You see Esther every day. How do you think she's doing?"

"For a ninety-eight-year-old woman, I'd say she's doing remarkably well. She has trouble walking so I help her into her chair in the morning and put her to bed at night, but other than that, she's sharp as a tack. I wish all my clients were so easy."

"What about her mystery visitor?" Patterson asked. "Has she complained about that recently?"

"Ah. The phantom in the night. All has been quiet on that front the last few evenings. He doesn't visit her all the time." Jesse leaned on the countertop and looked at Patterson. "If you want my opinion, she's dreaming it. I'm here five days out of seven, and I've never seen anything to suggest that someone is creeping around in the dead of night."

"Doesn't mean they aren't," Patterson said.

"Except that Phoebe keeps a tight rein on who has access to Esther. Apart from her, the only people who know the lock box code are myself and the woman who comes in on the days when I'm not working."

"Does the agency you work for keep the code on file?"

"Sure. Just in case another caregiver needs to cover for one of us. But they keep that information confidential, and besides, Phoebe changes the code monthly. I guess working for the FBI makes you security conscious."

"It has a tendency to do that," Patterson said. "Do any of Esther's neighbors know the code?"

Jesse shook his head. "Not so far as I know, but I'm sure they could call her if they ever needed quick access."

"Interesting."

"So you see, it's unlikely anyone is letting themselves in and walking around at night." The microwave dinged and Jesse opened the door. He pulled out the food and checked its temperature. "We'll know soon enough, anyway, when Phoebe gets those cameras put in."

"Right. The cameras." Patterson remembered the conversation a few days before about installing Internet so that Phoebe could keep an eye on the place when she wasn't there. "Do you know when that's going to happen?"

"End of next week," Jesse replied. "I guess the cable company is backed up on installations. After that, Phoebe will still have to install the cameras, of course."

"I'm sure Special Agent Bauer can help her."

Jesse nodded. "Honestly, I think it's a good thing Phoebe's putting cameras in. Some of my other clients have twenty-four-hour monitoring and it's worth every penny. Eases some of the stress."

"I can imagine."

Jesse opened the fridge and grabbed a can of cola, then picked up the plate of food along with a clean knife and fork.

"I'd better get this to Esther. If she goes too long without meals she gets grumpy, and she might start taking it out on your friend in there."

Patterson stepped aside to let Jesse past. She followed him into the living room and watched while he set up the meal in front of Esther. When she was ready to eat, Bauer said his good-byes and stood up, promising to visit her again soon.

Out in the hallway, Patterson turned to him. "How did it go?"

"Good," Bauer said. "Esther sounds a lot more settled than she did the last time we were here. Said she hasn't seen her visitor the last couple of nights."

"Jesse said the same thing."

"You think the situation resolved itself?" Bauer asked as they walked to the front door and stepped outside.

"Maybe. We'll see." Patterson glanced down at the lock box hanging on the door handle. She reached out and checked the release latch. The box didn't open. The key inside rattled when she shook it. She observed the lock box for a moment more, then followed Bauer down the steps.

FIFTY

IT WAS while they were driving back to the field office after visiting Esther Cutler that Patterson had an epiphany. They had taken a detour to pick up a late lunch, and afterward, Patterson was looking out of the window and wondering how long it would take Bauer to get back to his old self.

And there they were. A row of white cargo vans sitting in a line next to a DIY superstore located off the highway.

"Pull off at the next exit." Patterson craned her neck to look back at the vans as they cruised by at sixty-five miles an hour.

"Really?" Bauer clicked his indicator and changed lanes. "What did you see?"

"Rental vans."

"Costa already checked the rental agencies. It was one of the first things he did after that eyewitness identified a white van speeding away from the scene. It didn't go anywhere."

"Right. Because he was checking regular car and truck rental places. I bet he didn't think to try DIY stores."

"Why would he?"

"Because they rent trucks and vans, too."

"Of course." Patterson got the impression that Bauer

would have slapped his own forehead if his hands weren't on the steering wheel. "Exit is coming up. What am I looking for?"

"You need to backtrack when you come off. It's a big box DIY store visible from the highway. Place called Hammett's DIY and Garden Superstore."

"Never heard of them," Bauer said as he steered the car onto the exit ramp. At the bottom, they came to a traffic light. He waited for it to turn green, then turned right. "Want to get me some directions to make this easier?"

Patterson obliged. Her phone plotted the route, and the virtual assistant was soon giving directions. Five minutes later, they pulled into the DIY store parking lot.

"Where did you see the vans?" Bauer asked.

"Over on the far side of the store," Patterson replied.

Bauer drove through the parking lot and circled the store until he found the vans parked in a row. There were other vehicles there as well. Excavators, backhoes, and stump grinders. There were also box vans and pickup trucks. None of the vehicles bore the name of the store or any advertising delivery. Patterson found this unusual because most DIY superstores she had visited wanted to advertise their name in as many places as possible and a rolling billboard out on the streets was an opportunity not to be missed.

"Seen enough?" Bauer said, circling the rental vehicles a second time.

"Sure. Let's go inside and ask some questions."

"Way ahead of you." Bauer steered back to the front of the store, found a space close to the entrance, and they made their way inside.

After a brief conversation at the customer service desk, they learned that the tool rental desk further down the store behind the cash registers was responsible for van rentals.

When they got there, a skinny kid of about twenty-three

years old wearing a Hammett's reflective vest that looked three sizes too big greeted them.

When Patterson introduced herself and Bauer and flashed her badge, the kid took a step backward and scurried behind the counter as if he wanted to put something solid between himself and the feds.

"What can I help you with?" He asked in a squeaky voice.

"Those vans out back behind the store. Do you rent them?" Bauer asked.

"Sure." The kid pointed to a plastic sign on the wall that listed hourly, daily, and weekly rates for a host of vehicles ranging from mini excavators and trenchers to trailers and box trucks. Halfway down, beneath the rates for flatbed trucks, was a line dedicated to cargo vans.

"How long has the store been here?" Patterson asked.

"About twelve months." The kid scratched his nose, then examined the end of his finger before dropping his arm to the side again. "We're a regional store. Started out in Florida and expanded across the Gulf Coast states. This is one of only two stores in Texas so far. The other one is in Fort Worth."

"Why aren't the vans marked?" Bauer asked.

"They should be. But the company that does the vehicle wraps is running behind. They've barely finished with the Louisiana stores, and those opened almost three years ago. Who knows when they'll get around to us."

"I see." Patterson wondered if they had just stumbled upon a break in the case. It was a long shot, but she couldn't help feeling a tingle of excitement. She nodded toward a computer terminal sitting on the counter. "If I gave you a list of dates, could you bring up all the cargo van rentals that coincide?"

"I don't know about that." The kid chewed his bottom lip. "I'm not supposed to give out information to folk."

"We're the FBI, son. We're not folk." Bauer raised himself to full height and fixed the kid with a steely gaze.

"I get that, but I still can't do it. Don't know how. I'd have to call a manager."

"Then get your manager over here," Patterson said.

"Oh. Right." The kid snatched a walkie-talkie sitting on the counter. He spoke into it, then put the device down after a brief conversation. "Mr. Michaels will be here shortly."

Patterson thanked the kid, who scurried off to deal with a customer at the other end of the counter. A couple of minutes later, a rotund gentleman wearing a store vest that looked as small on his ample frame as the kid's vest had looked big came around the corner.

He extended a hand as he approached Patterson and Bauer. "Jerry Michaels. I'm the rental department manager. How can I help you?"

Patterson explained what they wanted.

Michaels shook his head. "No can do."

"Let me guess. You don't know how to operate the computer either," Bauer said.

"Oh, I know how to use it, alright. But I can't let you see those records. Privacy and all. I give you access to our booking system, I'll end up fired. Unless you have one of those order things."

Patterson didn't understand what he was referring to at first, but then it clicked. "You mean a search warrant?"

"Yeah, that. One of those."

"Look, Mr. Michaels, this is just an informal inquiry at this point. We don't have a warrant, but we would very much appreciate it if you would do your civic duty and let us check a couple of dates against the rental records for your cargo vans so that we can eliminate them as being used in a crime."

"You think one of our vans was used to commit a crime?"

"We don't know. That's what we're trying to find out," Bauer said.

"What kind of crime?"

"The abduction of a fourteen-year-old girl."

"Well, now, that changes things. My own girl just turned fourteen. Can't imagine how I'd feel if someone did such a thing to her. I'd be beside myself."

"Then you'll let us see the records?"

"Look, I can't give you unlimited access. I already told you, I'd lose my job. But if I were to bring up the master page showing all the van rentals for a particular period and the screen just happened to be turned in your direction, would that help?"

"I believe it would." Patterson smiled.

"Give me a minute." Michaels glanced around to make sure he wouldn't be seen, then he went behind the counter and approached the computer. As he passed by the skinny kid, he stopped and spoke to him. "Aaron. I'm going to show these people a couple of things on the computer. If you breathe a word of this to anyone, I'll make sure you're cleaning out the customer toilets on the hour every hour until the day you retire. Got it?"

The kid nodded.

"Good." Michaels shuffled along the counter to the computer. "What do you want to see?"

Patterson gave him the date of Amy Bowen's abduction.

He tapped into the computer and turned the monitor toward them. "Only a couple of daily rentals for the cargo vans on that date, but some weekly rentals, too."

Patterson leaned close and looked at the data displayed on the screen. There was a column with date ranges for the rentals, next to a first initial and last name, followed by either the letter F or D. The writing was small. The screen must have contained fifty entries displayed in two columns, including dates before and after the target date.

"Can I see more detail than this?" Patterson asked.

"Sorry." The manager shook his head. "Without that

warrant, this is the best I can do. And you have to make it quick, too. If my manager comes in while I'm doing this, my ass is toast."

"Understood." Patterson took out her phone and snapped a quick photo of the screen, then asked him to display the records for the date of the previous abduction. She did the same for the other two, working in reverse until she got back to Shawna Banks, the first victim. She took a photo of each page without taking the time to study them. The last thing she wanted was for anyone to get fired. She thanked the manager.

"My pleasure," said Michaels. "If you ever get that warrant and want to see more, come back and ask for me."

"We'll do that." Patterson had one more question. "Just out of curiosity, what do the letters mean after each rental? The F and the D."

"Tells us which store the van was rented from. F is for Fort Worth, and D is for Dallas."

Patterson thanked the manager again and stepped out of the tool rental area and back into the store. Maybe, if they got really lucky, there would be a name on the rental lists Patterson had photographed that matched all the abduction dates. And then they would have a solid lead other than Duane Snyder, who was looking less like the Butterfly Killer and more like a regular sleazebag with each passing day.

FIFTY-ONE

THAT NIGHT, Patterson sat in the hotel room and scrolled through the photos she had taken of the computer monitor in the tool rental area of the DIY store. She was looking for a pattern that would lead her in any direction other than Duane Snyder. But there was only one entry that stood out among all the rental contracts listed.

S. Francis.

This person had a cargo van rented on each of the abduction dates. But when she looked at the entries above and below those dates, she noticed more rentals on dates that had nothing to do with the case. Not only that, but whoever S. Francis was, had rented the van for a week each time. It was a tantalizing nugget. But considering the number of rental dates that did not coincide with abductions, she struggled to make sense of the pattern. If the van had been rented only during periods that coincided with girls going missing, Patterson could argue that there was a substantial link to their case, but as it was, the rental dates looked more like coincidence.

It was still worth following up, though, and she intended to do that at the earliest opportunity. The problem was that with only a first initial and last name to go on, she didn't know where to begin. The obvious solution would be to go before a judge and get a search warrant for the records in question. But to do that, she needed to prove justification. And any judge worth their salt would point out the same issues she was already contemplating. People rented trucks and vans all the time for their business. Just because some of those rental dates fell within the purview of her investigation by virtue of frequency did not automatically make those people suspects.

Patterson scrolled through the rental screen photos again, hoping there was something she had missed, but no matter how hard she looked, she ended up back at the same name. S. Francis.

Frustrated, Patterson put her phone down and turned the TV on. She took a shower, lingering under the hot water for a long while. She had found that inspiration often struck when she was showering, but tonight she came up blank. Returning to the bedroom, she changed into her nightclothes and watched TV with pillows propped up behind her back until she grew weary. Turning the TV off, she cleaned her teeth and was about to climb into bed when her phone rang.

It was Grant.

At that moment, her heart leaped into her throat, and she considered sending the call to voicemail. The incident with Bauer in the motel room was still fresh in her mind, and although it was crazy, she wondered if Grant had somehow found out about it. But then she shook the feeling off and answered.

"Hey."

"Hey. I was thinking about you." Grant's baritone voice was familiar and welcome. "What are you up to?"

"It's eleven-thirty at night. What do you think I'm up to?" Patterson replied, ignoring the small voice in her head that told her he was snooping. "I was about to climb into bed."

"Ah. I should've called earlier."

"No. It's fine. I love hearing your voice."

"Me too." Grant paused. "How's it going in Dallas?"

"Slow. I thought we had a viable lead on the Butterfly Killer this evening, but I'm not sure it means anything. Which puts us back to square one. Except for Duane Snyder, and the more I think about him, the more I'm convinced he isn't our man."

"I'm sorry to hear that."

"Yeah. I was hoping to wrap this up quickly and get back on Julie's trail. It's driving me nuts that I have a hot lead in Amarillo, and I can't follow up on it because I have to work this case."

"That hot lead will still be there when you catch the Butterfly Killer," Grant said. "It's been sixteen years. This isn't getting any colder."

"I know. But it's frustrating. I get a new lead, and then SAC Harris orders me onto this serial killer case. And don't get me wrong, I know it's important. I know lives are at stake. But there are so many other agents that could work on this who are just as qualified as me."

"Comes with the territory. Marilyn Khan reinstated you, which means you are once more subject to the vagaries of FBI bureaucracy."

"Maybe I was better off on my own."

"You really believe that?"

"No. I don't," Patterson admitted. The freedom of being unshackled from the FBI had meant she could be her own boss, going where she pleased when she pleased. But it also came with limitations, not the least of which was her inability to use the Bureau's connections and resources. At least without running the risk of being drummed out of the job as a rogue agent abusing her authority. Given the choice, she preferred being on the inside looking out more than the outside looking in.

"Have you spoken to your dad recently?" Bauer asked, changing the subject in the way he always did when he thought the conversation might veer into sticky territory.

"We keep in touch," Patterson said. "He misses me."

"He's not the only one." Grant cleared his throat. "I hope this quest of yours doesn't last forever."

"I know." Patterson felt a lump form in her throat. At that moment, all she wanted to do was hold Grant and tell him how much she loved him. Except he was fifteen hundred miles away. The chasm between them felt wider than ever. "You must be due some time off. Why don't you come and see me in Dallas for a few days?"

There was a pause on the other end of the line. "I'd love to, but it's hectic here. You know what it's like."

"Yes, I do. And you'll never get away if you won't make the time. The Bureau would work you seven days a week, fifty-two weeks a year if you let them. Take a couple of days off and come see me. They owe you that much."

"We'll see," Grant said.

"Okay." Patterson could tell by the tone of his voice that it wasn't going to happen. When they were together in New York, it was easier. They could snatch an evening here or a night there and convince themselves they were putting an appropriate amount of effort into their relationship. But Patterson's quest to find her sister had highlighted a problem she hadn't considered before. They were both so dedicated to their jobs that it consumed their personal lives. Worse, she wasn't sure how to fix it.

"You still there?" Grant asked after a brief silence.

"Yes." Patterson yawned. "I'm tired. I think I'll go to bed. Talk again soon?"

"Sure." If Grant sensed Patterson's unease, he didn't show it. "Love you."

"Love you, too," Patterson said, and then she hung up.

FIFTY-TWO

HE WOULD RETURN TONIGHT JUST like he always did. Amy Bowen knew this as surely as she knew her captor would end her life at some point soon. In the meantime, she huddled in her cell and waited while blackness swirled around her. She should have been afraid, but she wasn't. The darkness had become her friend. When her captor turned off the light in the tunnel outside her cell and left her in the pitch black—something he hadn't done at first but now did after every visit—it meant she couldn't see those photographs on the wall. Pictures of a girl wearing butterfly dresses just like the one her captor made her put on. Pictures of a girl with brunette hair that fell above her shoulders just like Amy's. At least, since he had cut it. That her captor was trying to make her look like the girl in the photos was obvious. Why he was doing so was not.

It didn't matter.

Amy knew how these situations always ended. With a body discovered on some scrap of wasteland. The thought that her end would come that way terrified her at first, but she had arrived at a strange acceptance of her fate since the failed bid for freedom. It wasn't that she wanted to die, but more that she understood it was inevitable.

Even so, when she heard the metal door open at the end of the tunnel, and the light clicked on, she felt the familiar rush of dread. Would he sit there and read his book while she bathed, then make her put on that horrid dress so he could stare at her? Would he cut more hair off? Or would he do something even worse this time?

As it happened, the visit was for none of those things. He carried a glass of milk and a plate with a cheese sandwich on cheap white bread. The sandwich was cut into four quarters. After making her stand near the back wall—probably because he didn't trust her not to attempt another escape—her captor unlocked the cell door and placed the offering on the ground, then backed up and locked it again. He stood with his arms folded and watched her as she eyed the gift with distrust.

"Don't you want your supper?" He asked.

Amy shook her head despite the hunger gnawing at her. She didn't want to give this man the satisfaction of watching her eat and drink because it felt like the milk and sandwich were something more than just sustenance meant to keep her alive long enough to fulfill whatever sick plan he harbored.

"Eat the sandwich. It's your favorite."

"No it's not." Amy felt a prickle of fear. Was this man delusional?

"Well, it's all you're getting tonight."

Amy still didn't move.

"Suit yourself." The man walked to the bars, kneeled down, and reached through. He plucked a quarter of the sandwich from the plate and stood again, then ate it with obvious delight.

Amy looked at the remainder, and it was all she could do to stop herself from pouncing on it.

"The longer you wait, the less food you'll have." Her captor approached the bars again and dropped to one knee.

"No. I'll eat it." Before he could reach through and take more, Amy scrabbled forward. She grabbed the plate, picked up the glass of milk, and backpedaled to the far wall. It only took a minute to consume the sandwich and wash it down.

All the while, her captor watched with a curious look of affection on his face. When she was done, he smiled. "That's my girl. Bring me the plate and glass."

Amy crossed the cell and held the items out at arm's length. For all she knew, he was going to make a grab at her the minute she was close enough. But he just took the empty plate and glass instead and pulled them back through the bars, turning the empty plate sideways so it would pass through.

After that, he stood unmoving for a few minutes. Then he retreated down the tunnel without saying another word and turned off the light again. When he closed the metal door, cutting off the last glimmering shaft of illumination from beyond, Amy was plunged back into blackness.

FIFTY-THREE

WHEN PATTERSON ARRIVED at the field office the next morning, Bauer was already there with the usual cup of coffee in his hand. Another cup sat on the opposite desk, waiting for her.

"Got your usual," he said, watching as she went around the desks and sat down.

"Thanks." Patterson wondered if Bauer would be back to his old self today. It certainly appeared that way so far. "Any fresh developments since last night?"

"If there are, no one's told me." Bauer leaned forward and peered over his laptop screen. "How about you? Did anything come of those van rental records from the DIY store?"

"Not sure yet. There was one name that cropped up around the dates of each abduction, but who knows if it means anything? S. Francis. They rented a van for the week of each abduction date, but they also rented a van on weeks that didn't have any relevance."

"Which means it could be a coincidence."

"Or it could be part of a bigger pattern we're not seeing

because we don't have enough data. We need more than just a first initial and surname."

"You heard the tool rental manager. The only way we'll get that is with a warrant."

"And we'll be hard-pressed to find a judge amenable to rubberstamping a warrant application based on nothing but a few coinciding dates and a hunch."

"We could try our luck with going to the store's corporate office and asking nicely," Bauer said.

"How many times has asking nicely ever worked for you?" Patterson asked.

"Not as often as I wish it did," Bauer admitted.

"Exactly. Until we have reason to believe S. Francis is involved in abducting and killing those girls, we'll have to chalk it up to coincidence. I bet if we looked through rental records for other items like tools and ditch diggers, we could find a few coinciding dates as well. It wouldn't mean those people were guilty of a crime, just that they rent a lot of equipment."

"Which brings us back to our one and only suspect."

"Duane Snyder." Patterson sipped her coffee.

"Right. I did a little sleuthing myself last night after I got home."

"You didn't spend the evening with Phoebe?"

"She was busy." Bauer gave Patterson a look that she interpreted as a warning not to go there after what almost happened in the hotel room. But he didn't voice it. Instead, he dove right back into his previous line of thought. "I got to thinking about Darlene Rourke and her affair with Snyder. She must've spent a great deal of time in that cabin. Don't you think?"

"I suppose."

"Which is why I called the diner and spoke to Maggie, our friendly cashier. Unlike the guy in the tool rental department, she was more than willing to help. She looked up the work schedule over the past several months. Darlene Rourke was working on each of the abduction dates."

"I'm not sure what that proves," Patterson said.

"Nothing on its own. But here's the thing. All four abductions occurred right before the weekend on either a Thursday or a Friday."

"Which is when Duane Snyder would be heading out of town for his cabin," Patterson said, understanding where Bauer was going with this. "If Darlene was spending time at the cabin after her shift ended, she might have seen or heard something without realizing it."

"Exactly. Always assuming Duane Snyder is our man, and as you said, it's far from conclusive."

"But worth a look on since we have no other leads," Patterson said. Then something else occurred to her. She opened her laptop and brought up the digital Murder Book, then went to the entry about the first victim. "On the day Shawna Banks went missing, Snyder was installing an AC unit for a homeowner in the town of Kaufman."

"So?"

Patterson switched to her browser and brought up a map of the area around Dallas. Kaufman was forty minutes southeast along the route to Snyder's cabin. Another coincidence? "What time does high school finish in these parts?"

"Beats me. But I can find out." Bauer turned to his own laptop and pecked at the keyboard. "Three-thirty."

Patterson thought for a moment. "The homeowner let Snyder in and then went back to work. She didn't come back until later that evening. He was alone in the house all afternoon and would have had time to drive back to Dallas and snatch Shawna, then take her to his cabin and get back to the job site before the homeowner returned."

"I don't know, Patterson," Bauer said. "That's a mighty tight window."

"But it could be done. And here's the thing. Snyder said the job took longer than he expected, which was why he was still there when Jodi Banks reported her daughter missing. Did it really take longer, or did he step out for part of the afternoon?"

"The only person who can tell us that is Duane Snyder, and I can't imagine he's going to be cooperative after everything that's happened."

"Let alone that lawyer of his," Patterson said.

"Jameson Screed."

"Which brings us back to Darlene. Who knows? Maybe she saw or heard something and doesn't realize it."

"You think she'll talk to us?" Bauer asked. "I can't imagine she's thrilled right now since we ruined her relationship with Snyder and then discredited her rape claim, leaving her open for charges of filing a false report and wasting police time."

"The only way we'll know is to go and see her." Patterson was already standing up. "How do you fancy another drive down to Athens?"

Bauer grimaced. "I guess it was inevitable from the minute I started poking into Darlene's work schedule."

Patterson slapped him on the back as she headed for the door. "And that's what you get for being conscientious."

FIFTY-FOUR

IT TOOK ALMOST three hours to make the hour and thirty-minute drive from Dallas to Darlene Rourke's apartment thanks to a jackknifed tractor-trailer on US-175. By the time they arrived, Patterson was feeling restless and frustrated. She jumped out of the car and stretched to work the kinks from her sore back and legs. Bauer did the same. They had spent too much time in the car over the last several days driving back and forth, and it was taking a toll.

When they reached Darlene's second-floor apartment, Patterson knocked and waited for a response. When no one answered, she knocked again.

"Maybe she isn't home," Bauer said.

Patterson went to the second-floor railing and looked across the parking lot. There, parked under the shadow of the building, was an old Honda with faded blue paint. Patterson recognized it. "Her car's here."

"She could have gone somewhere on foot, or a coworker picked her up." Bauer leaned over the railing and looked at the car. "Or she doesn't want to answer the door."

"Maybe." Patterson went back to the apartment and banged

on the door with her fist. "Darlene? It's Special Agent Blake. Open up."

This time, she got a response. But it was not from Darlene's apartment. The door across the landing opened, and a middle-aged man with a sagging gut and thin greasy hair appeared. He was wearing shorts and a white T-shirt with a brown stain on the front. "You looking for Dee?"

"Yes." Patterson turned to face him. "You are?"

"Sawyer Reed." The man sniffed, wiped his nose with the back of his hand, then rubbed it on his shirt.

"Have you seen Darlene this morning, Mr. Reed?" Patterson asked, holding up her badge.

"You cops or something?"

"FBI," said Bauer. "Answer the question. Have you seen her today?"

"Nah. Not since last night." He shook his head. "Heard her come in around ten. Must've been working at the diner. But that ain't all I heard."

"What do you mean?" Bauer asked.

"She had a late-night visitor because I heard 'em over there. Raised voices like they was arguing, then she was shouting at someone to get the eff out."

"You heard an argument?"

"Sure. I guess. Wasn't the first time, either. There was some guy here the other day banging on the door and hollering. I came out and asked what his problem was, and he told me to eff off. Went back into my apartment and I was glad I did. Cops showed up not long after and dragged him off."

"We know about that incident," Patterson said.

"Yeah, well, guess he must've come back."

"It was the same man?" Patterson didn't like where this was heading.

"Don't know for sure, but I think so. Couldn't make out much over my TV other than muted voices. Couldn't even really tell who was speaking. Know what I mean? Until Darlene started screeching at whoever was over there, that is. I heard that clear enough."

"And you didn't go over and check on her?" Patterson asked.

"After the last time? Hell no. Figured it wasn't my problem. Keep to myself. Know what I mean?"

"How long was this going on?" Bauer asked him.

"Ten, maybe fifteen minutes. Wasn't too bad at first, but it got out of hand fast, although that was all Darlene. Then it got real quiet all of a sudden. I guess whoever was over there must've skedaddled. Good thing too. It was almost midnight."

"What made you think it was the same man as before if you didn't see or hear him over at Darlene's?" Patterson asked.

"Cuzz I looked out my window after it all calmed down. Wanted to make sure nothin' was going to flare up again. And I saw him walkin' across the parking lot. Only he was coming toward the apartment, not away. Figured he must be coming back for round two, but I never heard nothing more, so I went to bed."

"I see." Patterson nodded. "And you're sure Darlene hasn't left the apartment since?"

"Sure as I can be. But it's not like I sit here watching her door or nothing."

"Thank you, Mr. Reed," Bauer said. "You can go inside now. If we have any more questions, we'll come and get you."

"Whatever." Reed shrugged and closed his door.

Bauer turned back to Darlene's apartment. "I've got a bad feeling about this."

"Me too." Patterson gripped the door handle. It turned. The door swung inward. "Not locked."

"Between that and what our friend over there said, I believe that gives us probable cause to enter, wouldn't you say?"

"I would." Patterson slipped the Glock from her shoulder

holster and held it in the low ready position. The sub-compact backup weapon Bauer had given her felt heavy against her ankle. She was glad it was there. She stood to the side of the door, next to the frame, and peered into the apartment. "Darlene Rourke? This is the FBI. If you can hear me, I need you to answer."

Bauer was standing on the other side of the door with his own gun out. "Miss Rourke. Armed federal agents. We're coming in now."

Patterson waited to see if there was a response. When none came, she stepped around the doorframe and into the apartment.

The front door led straight into a living room, with an open-plan kitchen beyond separated by a breakfast bar. To the left of the kitchen was a nook big enough for a small table and chairs. To the right of the kitchen was a short hallway with two doors. They were both closed.

The first thing Patterson noticed was the lamp sitting on an end table beside the sofa. It was on. Next to this was a half-full beer bottle on a coaster. A ceiling fan turned in lazy circles.

"Not looking good," Bauer said, following Patterson into the apartment. "Not looking good at all."

"Darlene?" Patterson called out again. "Miss Rourke? Are you in here?"

No answer.

"Look." Bauer pointed to the coffee table in front of the sofa. The ashtray they had seen on their last visit was still there, but also something else. A bright red smear on the corner of the table. "Blood?"

"There's more here," Patterson said, nodding toward a crimson streak on the tile floor near the kitchen. More streaks led into the hallway. There was what looked like blood spatter on the wall.

Patterson reached into her pocket and pulled out a set of

latex gloves, which she put on. If something had happened to Darlene Rourke, and it looked like it had, she didn't want to contaminate the scene. She went to the hallway, stepped around the blood, and opened the closest of the doors. It was a toilet. The other must be the bedroom.

She waited for Bauer, then pushed it open before coming to an abrupt halt.

Darlene Rourke was lying on the bed with her legs draped off the side. She was on her back with one arm by her side and the other across her stomach. But it was the blood-soaked uniform blouse, still sporting her name tag from the diner, that told Patterson all she needed to know.

Bauer followed her in and stopped in his tracks. "Shit."

Patterson remained silent while she regained her composure, then she cleared her throat. "Well, that explains why Darlene didn't answer."

Bauer sighed. "Yeah. I guess."

FIFTY-FIVE

AN HOUR after Patterson found Darlene Rourke lying on her bed drenched in blood, the apartment complex was a hive of police activity. Athens PD had cordoned off a wide area in front of the building, and her neighbors were removed from their apartments and asked to wait behind the police line. They had also been interviewed one-on-one by uniformed officers, who then fanned out around the complex to speak to other residents further afield.

A forensics team was on its way from Dallas because Athens wasn't big enough to have its own department. There was also a mobile command center on the way. Not to mention Detective Costa, who wanted to be on hand in case Darlene Rourke's murder ended up linked to the Butterfly Killer.

Patterson and Bauer stood next to their car and watched the action while doing their best to keep out of the way. They had given statements to a homicide detective by the name of Connor, who took command of the crime scene from them, and they were now waiting for his go-ahead to leave. That permission arrived via Detective Voss, who came striding across the parking lot with a resolute expression.

"Just once, I'd like a visit from you guys to mean I'm not in it up to my neck," she said, closing the gap.

"Believe me, we feel the same way," said Patterson. "Anything Darlene Rourke might have been able to tell us about the Butterfly Killer just went to the grave with her."

"You think she was silenced?" Voss asked.

"Impossible to know." Bauer shrugged. "But I've got a pretty good idea who the prime suspect for this is. The neighbor saw Duane Snyder out in the parking lot after the argument that led to her death."

"You've got to be kidding me." Voss rolled her eyes. "This guy just can't stay out of trouble. An accusation of rape. Then attempted assault. Now it looks like he's gone and murdered someone."

"Which is why we need to get over to his cabin ASAP." Patterson was getting itchy feet. The longer they waited, the more chance Snyder would be in the wind.

"We already have a couple of units on the way there. But if you want to join them, be my guest. Connor says you're free to go. If he has any more questions, he'll route them through your field office."

"Fantastic." Bauer clapped his hands. "Sounds like our cue to get out of here."

"Maybe I'll join you," Voss said. "I'm the department's answer to a special victims unit, and our erstwhile victim is dead, which means I'm kind of a spare wheel at this point."

"Be our guest," Patterson said.

"Great. Mind if I catch a ride?" Voss asked, glancing toward the Bureau car. "I came over here with Connor, and he ain't leaving anytime soon."

"Hop in." Bauer pulled the car keys from his pocket.

Five minutes later, they were cruising away from Darlene Rourke's apartment complex and heading in the direction of Duane Snyder's cabin. As they went, Detective Voss called the units already on their way and told them to hold at the end of the trail leading up to the cabin.

When they got there, a pair of cruisers were parked along the side of the road. Bauer pulled over behind them and jumped from the car. He went to the trunk and removed a pair of tactical SWAT vests with FBI patches on the front. He handed one to Patterson, and she put the heavy body armor on, making sure it was tight before getting back into the car.

After securing his own vest, Bauer climbed behind the wheel and turned to Voss in the backseat. "You good?"

Voss understood what he was asking. "Already wearing a vest under my shirt. All good."

Bauer pulled around the cruisers and waited for them to swing onto the road behind him, then turned onto Snyder's property and started slowly up the trail.

———

The cabin looked just like it had on their previous visits, except Patterson noticed a dark green Jeep Wrangler parked under the lean-to carport. After Bauer brought the car to a halt, Patterson jumped out, gun drawn, and made her way toward the cabin.

She mounted the front steps with Voss and Bauer right behind while the uniformed officers circled around the back of the cabin to cut off any potential escape route.

The three of them took up positions beside the door before Patterson knocked and announced their presence. "Duane Snyder. Armed federal agents. Open up."

For the second time that day, she received no answer.

Patterson knocked again. When she still didn't get a response, Bauer reached across and tried the handle. Locked.

Patterson turned to the window, but heavy curtains blocked her view.

"You want to go in?" Bauer asked.

Patterson knew what he was thinking. They did not have a warrant to arrest Snyder or search his property. It would take two days or more to get one of those, even if they rushed it through the system. By that time, Snyder could easily have made it to Mexico and disappeared. But they might not need a judge's approval. An eyewitness had placed Snyder at the scene of the crime, which gave them probable cause to believe he was involved in Darlene Rourke's murder. That meant they could pursue him based on exigent circumstances—no warrant required.

"Let's do this," Patterson said, stepping out of the way as Bauer squared up to the door.

He backed away to give himself enough room, then placed a well-aimed kick a couple of inches to the right of the door handle. The door slammed back on its hinges, sending splinters of wood flying.

Bauer's gun was already up and aimed at the opening, just in case anyone came charging toward them.

Patterson spun around the doorframe with her own gun at low ready and entered the cabin, quickly scanning her surroundings for signs of an occupant. She saw none. "Clear."

Bauer stepped past her and made straight for the stairs leading up to the open loft area above. "Clear up here, too."

Patterson checked the bathroom and then approached the door leading to the old root cellar. It was still damaged from the last time they were there and opened easily. She pulled a flashlight from her vest and shined it down into the darkness. Seeing nothing, she descended under the cabin. The cellar was empty, just like the rest of the building. Snyder was gone.

FIFTY-SIX

WHEN DETECTIVE COSTA SHOWED UP, he came bearing gifts. A pair of search dogs along with their handlers. By that time, more uniformed officers had gathered to assist in the search for Duane Snyder, and a mobile command center had been set up under a tent in the clearing next to Snyder's cabin. After a briefing led by Detectives Voss and Costa, the searchers fanned out across the property and the surrounding parcels of land. They weren't just looking for Snyder. Amy Bowen might be out there somewhere too, and although no one spoke the sentiment out loud, they all hoped the Butterfly Killer's reign would be brought to an end with Snyder's apprehension.

Patterson was convinced he was still close by. His Jeep was parked under the carport next to the cabin, and Dallas PD had already confirmed that his cargo van was behind his estranged wife's home. Her own car was there as well. If Snyder had fled in a vehicle, it wasn't one belonging to the family.

Snyder's property had been divided up into quadrants, with each assigned to a different team. Patterson and Bauer were on team three, searching the northeast section of his property and beyond. It was a daunting task made worse by the rough woodland terrain.

They searched for five hours, combing the woods for any sign of Snyder or a hiding place, but as the sun dipped low on the horizon, Patterson was forced to concede that they were not going to be successful. At least not today.

"We should head back," she said to Bauer as they trudged through a dry creek bed choked with fallen branches and forest debris. "If we keep going much longer, we risk losing the light, and I don't want to be lost out here at night."

"I was thinking the same thing," replied Bauer, walking several feet to her right.

Further afield to their left and right, they could hear the other searchers on their team, six Athens PD officers. Bauer had been assigned as team leader and wasted no time getting on his walkie-talkie and instructing everyone to head back to the cabin.

Patterson was disappointed. She had hoped to find Snyder in short order, but the vastness of the property had beaten them today. As they trudged back, her spirit sagged. Despite the late hour, the air was hot and humid. She felt sticky and gross under her tactical vest and couldn't wait to remove it, which she did as soon as they arrived back at the clearing.

While she was stashing the vest in the trunk of Bauer's car, Detective Costa ambled over.

"Something you should see," he said, then turned back toward the cabin and motioned for her to follow.

When she entered he led her to a small desk sitting next to the loft stairs. The drawers were open, and the contents had been spilled. Costa pointed to a pile of kid's drawings. "We found these at the back of a drawer. Looks like Shawna made them when she was younger."

"What am I looking for?" Patterson asked.

"Take a look through them. You'll see."

After putting on a pair of gloves, Patterson picked up the drawings and leafed through them. There were twenty or more, all drawn in crayons. Patterson guessed Shawna must have been around six or seven years old when she made them, judging by the crude execution. One showed a house with a pair of figures standing outside that were labeled 'mom' and 'second dad'. Another drawing depicted what looked like a Christmas tree with presents underneath. The scrawled message beneath read, 'happy holidays to my second dad.'

Patterson shrugged and looked at Costa. "Am I supposed to see something in these drawings because if so, I'm missing it."

"You haven't gotten far enough yet." Costa motioned for Patterson to keep looking.

Patterson sensed Bauer enter the cabin and come up behind her.

"What are you doing?" He asked, peering over her shoulder.

"Beats me," Patterson said, leafing through several more drawings. Then she stopped. Halfway down the pile was an image of a man, a woman, and a pair of children standing between them. Patterson assumed these were Jodi, Duane, Shawna, and her younger sister. But it was what else the drawing contained that gave her pause.

Butterflies.

Eight of them crowding the white space above the family. Some were yellow, others red. One was drawn in bright green crayon. Patterson's gut tightened. She leafed to the next page to find another butterfly drawing. This time the entire sheet was consumed by a pair of vibrant insects drawn in weaving colored lines. Underneath was a message, presumably to Snyder and written in young Shawna's shaky hand.

'Thank you for marrying mommy. Now I have a second daddy.'

Patterson dropped the pictures back on the desk and stared

at them, unsure what to make the discovery. "You think this is a motivation for the butterfly dresses?"

"Hard to say. If nothing else, it shows that Shawna was into butterflies when she was a kid."

"And that's probably all it means," said Bauer. "I bet lots of girls that age draw butterflies." He picked up the sheets and looked through them. "Three of these drawings have ponies in them. Another two have dogs. It's coincidence, people. We're seeing what we want to see." He threw the drawings back on the desk.

"Maybe," said Costa. "Or maybe not."

Bauer turned toward the door. "When the pair of you have finished chasing shadows, I'll be waiting outside."

Patterson watched him leave. "Sorry about that. He gets cranky when he's tired."

"Nah. He's probably right. Coincidence." Costa gathered the drawings back into a neat pile. "You and your partner should get out of here. Find yourselves a hot meal back in town before everything closes. We'll post a couple of uniforms here tonight in case Snyder comes back to the cabin."

"What are *you* going to do?" Patterson asked.

"Lay my head down in the first motel I come to and get some sleep. I want to be back here at first light. You should do the same. Let's catch this bastard, Butterfly Killer or not."

FIFTY-SEVEN

THEY CHECKED into the same motel they had stayed at a few nights before. Bauer booked them in for two nights, figuring that after long hours of searching the following day, they wouldn't be up to the drive back to Dallas, even if they located Snyder.

As they were heading across the parking lot to their rooms, they encountered Detective Costa, who had found his way to the same motel.

"Great minds think alike," he said at their approach.

"It's also the only motel between Snyder's land and Athens," Bauer pointed out.

"True. And I was happy to find it." Costa pushed his hands into his pockets. "Gotta say, I'm surprised to see the pair of you here, though. I would've thought you'd be in swankier digs, what with that bulging federal expense account and all."

Bauer snorted. "Don't make me laugh. I'll be lucky to get this place reimbursed."

"That bad, huh?" Costa strolled next to them with an athletic bag in one hand. Either he kept his own go bag or had possessed the forethought to pack for an overnight trip before leaving Dallas. When they reached a room on the ground floor mid-block, he stopped. "This is me."

Bauer and Patterson continued on. Their own rooms were at the end of the block on the second floor. Bauer waited until Patterson had unlocked her door and then mumbled a quick good night before hurrying to his own room and disappearing inside.

The suddenness of his departure surprised her. She wondered if he was thinking about what had almost happened here only a few nights before.

Patterson entered her room and dropped her go bag on the bed. The first thing she had done after their last overnight trip was to put one together and stash it in the trunk of Bauer's Bureau car.

She took a quick shower, then gave her dad a call.

He was overjoyed to hear from her, and they talked for an hour before she found herself unable to stay awake. After that, she set an alarm on her phone for five a.m., roughly an hour before sunrise, when the search for Duane Snyder would resume. Then she climbed into bed and was asleep almost before her head hit the pillow.

FIFTY-EIGHT

THE NEXT MORNING a little after six, they gathered at Duane Snyder's cabin for a second day of searching. There were fewer officers this time. Budget cuts had forced the police department to limit overtime, and after expending so many resources the previous day, they could not afford to pull them from other duties.

Still, more than half the property had been searched already, with no sign of the fugitive. Patterson had wondered if Duane would try and sneak away in the Jeep during the night. Put more distance between himself and the authorities. But the two shifts of Athens PD officers who stayed at the cabin to guard against that very outcome reported no unusual activity. That didn't preclude the possibility that Snyder had changed his location, moving from an un-searched area into one they had already scoured, which was why the search dogs were back again. They had briefly picked up his trail the previous day, but it had amounted to nothing. If Snyder was on the move, Detective Costa hoped the dogs would detect the fresh scent and zero in on him.

Patterson listened to the morning briefing while she

258

munched on a breakfast sandwich and sipped coffee provided by the Lonestar Skillet. They had wasted no time in mobilizing to cater the search for Snyder once they heard of their coworker's fate. Patterson was glad for the sustenance and was on her second coffee when they broke to enter the woods.

Patterson and Bauer were assigned to the same quadrant as the previous day, along with a pair of police officers she hadn't met before. Yesterday they had been eight. Today they were four.

Even so, they covered ground faster than the previous day because both Patterson and Bauer were now familiar with the terrain, at least until they reached the point where they had turned back when it started to get dark.

From here on in, the woods were unexplored. They moved forward slower, fanning out as before to cover the maximum amount of ground. Patterson could see the other members of her team through the trees, each of them moving forward in their own lane. They carried on this way for a couple of hours, crisscrossing the landscape to no avail.

Patterson didn't want to admit it, but she was losing hope. They must have been near the edge of Duane Snyder's property by now, and there was no sign of him. She wondered if he was even on the property by the time they started the search. He could have hitched a ride out of town and been hundreds of miles away before they even discovered her body. He might even have stolen a vehicle. If that was the case, then this whole search was nothing but a waste of time. Then, just when she thought they weren't going to find anything, the trees parted to reveal a narrow trail that cut a lazy U shape through the woods.

She gathered their group together to discuss options. It was already one in the afternoon, and the temperature was soaring. If they didn't find something soon, they would have to return to the staging area and let a fresh team take over. But Patterson didn't want to do that. Not yet.

She pulled a water bottle from her vest and took a long drink, then turned to Bauer. "What do you think?"

"If you ask me, we've stumbled across an old logging trail."

"You think we're still on Snyder's land?" The woods extended for miles in every direction, and there was nothing to mark the boundary between parcels.

"Hard to say." Bauer shielded his eyes from the sun. "Even if we're not, it doesn't matter. He could be anywhere."

"Where do you think this trail goes?" Patterson asked.

"Beats me." Bauer took out his phone and checked their location on Google Earth. After a moment, he pointed back in the direction from which they had come. "You can't even see the trail on satellite imagery. Too much tree canopy. But Snyder's cabin is about half a mile a mile due east of here. I'd say it's a fair bet this is still his land."

Three-quarters of a mile. It didn't sound very far to Patterson, but their zigzagging search pattern meant they had walked much further than that. "You think Snyder knows about this trail?"

"I'd bet money on it."

"I wonder where it goes?"

"The only way we'll know is to follow it," Bauer said. "Only question is, which direction?"

"How about both?" Patterson turned to the two officers and told them to follow the trail in one direction while she and Bauer took the other.

They set off, making easier progress now they were on clear ground. The trail weaved through the woods for what felt like at least a mile, turning back on itself in a meandering fashion. At one point, they were forced to scramble over a fallen pine that blocked their path. Not long after that, Patterson noticed the trail getting narrower. Then it petered out entirely, leaving them facing a wall of trees.

She stopped and looked around. "Guess we reached the end of the road."

"At least we know where it went," Bauer replied. "Nowhere. We should—"

A sharp crack split the air.

Bauer grunted and twisted sideways. Then he went down hard, even as a second shot rang out.

FIFTY-NINE

PATTERSON MADE a frantic dive for cover, ending up behind a tall pine tree that offered less protection than she would have liked.

"Marcus." She looked around, frantic, but couldn't locate Bauer at first. Then she saw him slumped against a tree with a pained look on his face. She sagged with relief. The bullet must have impacted his body armor. Painful for sure, but it would only leave a bruise. Except he was clutching his shoulder, and blood seeped through his fingers. When their eyes met, she mouthed a silent question. "How bad?"

"Don't know," he mouthed back. "Not good."

Patterson took a deep breath. She would be no good to Bauer if she couldn't think straight. The first thing she must do was locate the shooter and then reach Bauer to assess his injury.

She was sitting with her back to the tree. The trunk was just wide enough to shield her from view, but any movement would reveal her position. She reached down slowly and pulled her gun from its holster, then took a moment to center herself.

The shots had come from ahead of them in the trees beyond where the trail ended. But she had seen no one ahead of them.

Not even any movement. Which meant the shooter was concealed.

She pushed herself up against the tree trunk to a standing position, then risked a quick peek in the direction the shots had come from. She pulled her head back just as another crack rang out. A bullet whizzed through the air mere inches from her hiding place and smacked into a nearby tree.

Patterson cursed under her breath. She still hadn't located the shooter. But at least she had confirmed the direction of fire.

Bauer had drawn his weapon and was holding it awkwardly in his left hand. His right arm hung at his side, and she could see a crimson stain spreading down his arm. She had to reach him and see how bad it was. But the shooter had them pinned down.

Then she heard heavy footfalls getting louder. At first, she thought maybe the shooter had broken cover, but then she realized the footsteps were coming from the direction of the trail. She looked around to see the other two members of their search team racing up the trail with guns drawn.

Patterson waved them off, but neither one saw her. At least, not until it was too late. As the closer of the two cops reacted to her warning, another shot echoed through the trees. The lead cop went down hard and didn't move.

Shit.

The second cop twisted sideways in a frantic bid for cover, even as he popped off a couple of rounds in the general direction of their assailant.

Patterson shifted position while the shooter was preoccupied. Given the amount of open ground between them, she didn't stand a chance of reaching Bauer. But if the shooter didn't know where she was, it might be possible to scope out his position. She dove to the right, away from the trail and into a thick expanse of undergrowth. Twigs raked her face, and thorns scratched her arms as Patterson pushed through the understory and circled around.

Now she had a better view of the woods beyond the trail. It was no wonder they hadn't seen their assailant. There was a structure tucked in between a pair of tall pine trees. It was constructed of wood with a low roof, and at first, Patterson thought it was a tiny cabin, but then she realized that instead of windows, it had narrow horizontal slits. Camo netting draped the roof and walls. This was no primitive cabin. It was a ground blind—a concealed structure designed to hide hunters from their prey. And right now, the prey was her.

But she had one advantage. Whoever was in the blind, and she felt sure it was Duane Snyder, didn't know where Patterson was. That gave her a tactical advantage. All she had to do was stay out of sight and circle the structure until she could find a way in and take him down.

Patterson flattened herself low to the ground and squirmed forward on her hands and knees. The blind was about forty feet away, positioned to afford the shooter within a perfect line of sight to the end of the trail. She cursed her stupidity. They had walked right into Duane Snyder's field of fire. Now one man might be dead, and Bauer was probably bleeding out.

But at least Snyder had stopped shooting for now. Probably because his targets had all taken cover, and he didn't want to waste ammunition. But if he caught even a flicker of movement, Patterson had no doubt the bullets would fly again. Which was why she had to be careful. The hunting stand had a wide field of vision, and the shooter could easily take a shot in her direction if he realized where she was and what she was doing.

The going was slow. Patterson crawled forward on her stomach and ignored the rocks and branches that scraped her skin as she went. After what felt like too long, she poked her head up and risked a look to get her bearings. She was almost halfway around the hunting blind. She could see the back of it now. Even better, Duane Snyder must still be focused on the trail because there were no shots in her direction.

Now all she had to do was cover the short distance between her hiding place and the blind, then gain access before Snyder realized what was happening. And she had to do it quickly because two members of her party were down, and she didn't know their status.

She pushed the thought of Bauer dying from her mind. At that moment, she needed to focus. Patterson studied the hunting blind. There was a narrow door at the back of the structure, but Snyder might have locked himself in. Breaching the door was an enormous risk. As soon as Snyder realized what was happening, he would almost certainly turn and shoot blindly through the back of the structure, and that would be deadly. But it was a chance she must take.

Patterson checked her surroundings one more time, then scrambled to her feet and sprinted to the blind. She gripped the door handle and was relieved to find it opened easily. She flung the door wide and took a step back to bring her gun up. Only to find herself looking down the barrel of Duane Snyder's rifle. Then he pulled the trigger.

SIXTY

PATTERSON THREW herself sideways away from the door just as the gun went off. She landed hard on the ground. The air rushed from her lungs, and for a second, she couldn't move. Then she pulled herself together and rolled to point her gun at the empty door.

She expected Snyder to come charging at any moment with his rifle. Instead, she heard a familiar voice.

"Special Agent Blake. You okay?"

It was Detective Costa.

Surprised, she scrambled to her feet and approached the door to see Duane Snyder standing there with the rifle at his feet. Costa stood behind him on the outside of the blind, his own gun raised at Snyder through the narrow horizontal window.

"Care to help me secure the suspect?" Costa asked when he saw her.

"Happy to." Patterson stepped into the small hut and slid the rifle sideways with her foot, out of Snyder's reach. She took a pair of handcuffs from her belt and reached around him, pulled his hands behind his back, and cuffed him. Then she marched him out of the blind as detective Costa and the second officer in her search group came around the side of the structure to assist.

"We'll take it from here," Costa said, grabbing Snyder by the shoulder. He handed him off to the officer as more officers arrived. Costa gave Patterson a once over. "You good?"

"I'm fine. I have to find Marcus." Patterson raced around the side of the blind and through the trees to the head of the trail. When she got there, Bauer was sitting up against the tree. His tactical vest was on the floor next to him, and he was holding his hand against a wound to his right shoulder. His shirt was soaked with blood. Kneeling next to him was Detective Voss.

"He'll be okay," she said, standing up as Patterson approached.

"Let me see," Patterson said, dropping to the ground next to Bauer.

"Hey. What Voss said. I'll be fine. It's a scratch."

"It's not a scratch. There's a big hole in your shoulder." Patterson wasn't sure whether to cry or laugh. She turned her head to look down the trail. "What about the officer?"

"He'll be fine." Voss put a hand on Patterson's shoulder. "The round impacted his ballistic vest. Knocked him off his feet. He'll have a hell of a bruise, but other than that . . ."

"Wish my vest had stopped a bullet," Bauer said, grimacing. "An inch to the left, and I would've been fine."

"Or you would've ended up shot in the throat," Patterson said. "Then where would you be?"

"Gee. Look on the bright side, why don't you?"

"Just pointing out that it could have been worse."

"Yup." Bauer tried to stand, but Voss ordered him back down.

"Not so fast. Paramedics are on the way. You need to sit still and wait for them."

"C'mon. Like I said, it's—"

Voss waved a finger at him. "I swear if you say it's just a scratch . . ."

Bauer looked at Patterson. "She's worse than you."

"Thanks." Patterson laughed. "I think."

"Was it Snyder?" Bauer craned his neck to look toward the hunting blind.

"Yep. Thank heavens help arrived when it did, or I probably wouldn't be here now." Patterson squinted up at Voss. "How did you get here?"

"Are you kidding me? Every searcher out here heard those gunshots. Figured you might have flushed him out." Voss turned her head toward the hunting blind. "Wow. That thing is really well camouflaged. If you didn't know it was there, you'd walk right past it."

"Yeah," Patterson said. "Tell me about it."

She slumped back against the tree next to Bauer and closed her eyes, exhausted. Ten minutes later, the paramedics arrived.

SIXTY-ONE

FOUR HOURS after their encounter with Duane Snyder in the woods, Patterson was standing in a hospital waiting room and pacing back and forth. The paramedics had patched Bauer up as best they could on site, but there was only so much they could do. When he arrived at the hospital, they had taken Bauer straight into surgery. Now she was waiting for news on his condition and growing more frustrated by the minute.

"Special Agent Blake?"

Patterson turned to see a doctor with wavy blonde hair and brilliant green eyes striding toward her. In his hand was a clipboard. Patterson wondered if this was standard issue for all doctors, presented to them on the day they graduated medical school along with their diploma to make them look more serious.

"I'm Doctor Hammond."

"Hello, Doctor Hammond," Patterson said. Her throat was dry. A swarm of butterflies danced in her stomach. "Is he okay?"

"Well, he has a hole in his shoulder, so I can't quite go that far."

"Sorry. I mean, is it serious?"

"Serious enough but not life-threatening." Hammond pulled a pen from the clasp at the top of the clipboard and tapped it against the sheets of paper clipped there in an uneven staccato rhythm. "He was a lucky man. The bullet missed the subclavian artery, which could have caused him to bleed out if it was not treated quickly. It also missed the brachial plexus. That's a nerve bundle that controls arm movement. If the bullet went through there, Special Agent Bauer might have been looking at early retirement on medical grounds."

"He'll recover then," Patterson said, slumping with relief.

"He should, thanks in part to the weapon that shot him. A fairly low velocity .22 rifle. Of course, it would have been exponentially better if the bullet had hit his body armor instead of impacting high and to the right. It would have stopped a bullet like that with no trouble at all."

Patterson couldn't help but smile. Bauer had said the exact same thing back at the scene. "When can I see him?"

"He's in recovery right now. As soon as I'm satisfied with his progress, we'll move him to a room. You can see him then."

"Thank you, doctor."

Hammond flashed a wide smile to reveal impossibly white teeth. "You're welcome. Now, if you'll excuse me, I have other duties to attend to."

Patterson thanked the doctor again. She watched him depart, then sank down into a chair. All the stress of the last several hours drained away, leaving her exhausted and fragile. Duane Snyder was in custody, and even though Bauer got hurt, no one else died. Of course, there was still the matter of Amy Bowen and the Butterfly Killer. But she was happy to let Detective Costa and his team take the reins on that one for the time being. They were still scouring Snyder's property on foot, by helicopter, and with drones to make sure they hadn't missed anything.

She closed her eyes and let the exhaustion take control. She must have fallen asleep because the next thing she knew, a female voice was calling her name. Patterson opened her eyes to find the nurse standing over her.

"Special Agent Blake?" said the nurse. "Sorry to disturb you, but I thought you'd want to know. Special Agent Bauer has been moved out of recovery, and he's in his own room now if you would like to see him."

"Absolutely." Patterson jumped to her feet. She glanced at her phone to see that another hour had passed.

"If you'd like to come with me," said the nurse.

Patterson followed the nurse out of the waiting room and down a corridor that smelled like bleach. When they came to a nurses station, her guide stopped and conversed briefly with the nurse behind the desk, then led Patterson off again until they arrived at a closed door. Mounted on the wall next to the door was a small whiteboard with Bauer's name written on it in red ink.

"Here we are," the nurse said, opening the door and moving aside to allow Patterson entry. "Fifteen minutes. No more."

Patterson thanked the nurse and stepped into the room.

Bauer was lying with the bed raised at thirty degrees. A machine next to him beeped. There was a drip in his arm and a cord running from a monitor on his finger. His eyes were closed, but when Patterson entered, he opened them.

"Come to check that I'm still in the land of the living?" he asked in a hoarse voice.

"Are you kidding me?" Patterson said, crossing to the bed. "You're having too much fun annoying me to go anywhere."

"That's so true." Bauer smiled, then winced. "Ouch. You wouldn't think that smiling would hurt your shoulder. News-flash. It does."

"Then don't smile, moron."

"Sage advice." Bauer's eyes almost closed again, but he

forced them back open. "I know you'll hate to hear this, but you might have to continue the investigation on your own, at least for a few days. I told the doc I'd be fine to leave just as soon as my head cleared, but he wasn't down with that."

"You'll be in here at least a couple of nights," Patterson said. "And I don't want to hear you complain about it. You just got shot. You could have died."

"You talked to the doctor?"

"Of course I did. I've been sitting in that waiting room since they brought you in."

"Aw. I think you like me, after all." This time, Bauer refrained from smiling.

"You know I like you." Patterson placed her hand on his. "Even if you are infuriating."

"You're not the first person to say that." Bauer cleared his throat. "I hate to ask this because I'm not sure I want to know the answer, but did the doc say if I'll ever play piano again?"

"If you're going to trot out that old joke about not being able to play it before, we've all heard it." Patterson squeezed his hand. "But if you're asking, will you be able to hold a gun again —keep your job—then the outlook is good. He said the bullet didn't hit anything vital on its way through. You shouldn't have any nerve damage."

"That's a relief." Bauer slumped back into the bed. "I figured someone would have been along to fill me in by now, but all I've had are a couple of nurses who claimed they didn't know anything. I was beginning to think it was bad, and no one wanted to tell me."

"No such thing. I'm sure they're probably just busy."

"That must be it." Bauer's eyes were closing again.

Patterson squeezed his hand one more time. "You look beaten down. I'll let you rest."

Bauer mumbled something she didn't understand.

"Take it easy and do as the nurses tell you." Patterson

headed for the door, then she turned back. "You scared me today. I was afraid that . . ." She let the words trail off, not wanting to vocalize the fear that had clutched at her.

It didn't matter. Bauer was out for the count. The only response she got was a hearty snore.

Patterson stepped into the corridor and retraced her steps back to the waiting room. When she got there, Phoebe was rushing in from the other direction, looking flustered.

"Oh, thank heavens you're here," she said, spotting Patterson. "I got here as soon as I could. Is he okay?"

"He's fine. Sleeping like a baby," Patterson reassured her. "The doctor said there was no major damage. He'll be back on his feet before you know it. Shouldn't even impact his job."

"That's such a relief."

For the second time in the last fifteen minutes, Patterson saw the anxiety drain away.

"I can't believe he went and got himself shot," Phoebe said, wiping a stray tear from her cheek. "I appreciate you staying until I got here."

"Are you kidding? I wasn't going anywhere until I knew he was out of the woods," Patterson replied. "But I'll head out now you're here. It's been a long day."

Phoebe nodded. "Of course. I'm going to stay here all night. I'm not leaving Marcus on his own."

"He'll appreciate that. Although it might be a while before you get to see him. He's asleep. I think they put painkillers in his drip, which made him woozy."

Phoebe wrapped her arms around Patterson, giving her a tight hug. "Thank you for being here. I mean it."

Patterson returned the hug and then pulled away as an image of Bauer kissing her in the hotel room popped unbidden into her head. She felt like a heel. "I have to go. Call me if you need anything."

"Sure." Phoebe gave her a wan smile.

Patterson stepped around her, eager to escape, and hurried away toward the exit.

SIXTY-TWO

ON HER WAY back to the motel, Patterson took a detour to Athens police headquarters. She wanted to make sure Duane Snyder had found his way into a ten-by-ten cell.

When she got there, Patterson was surprised to find a haggard-looking Detective Voss still hard at work.

"How's Special Agent Bauer?" Voss asked, looking up from her desk as Patterson entered the detective's division and walked toward her.

"Good, considering," Patterson said. "He's out of surgery and resting."

"Glad to hear it." Voss watched Patterson settle into a seat on the opposite side of her desk. "I just got an update from Detective Costa. There's no sign of the girl on Snyder's property. They scoured every inch, even brought in cadaver dogs. If she was there, we would have found her."

"And Snyder?" Patterson rubbed her temples. She had a headache, probably brought on by dehydration.

"Claims to know nothing about the missing girl, and honestly, my gut tells me he's telling the truth."

"Except that we found butterfly drawings at the cabin."

"Doesn't prove a thing. Lots of little girls draw butterflies. Now, if we'd found a dress with a butterfly print on it inside that cabin, or a pillowcase with embroidered roses that matched the one found at the last crime scene, that would be a different matter. Besides, I'm not even sure you still think Snyder's the Butterfly Killer. I can see in your eyes."

"It would make everything so much easier if he was."

"When was catching killers ever easy?"

"Just once, it would be nice."

"I hear you."

"We'll know for sure soon," Patterson said. "Detective Costa messaged while I was at the hospital waiting for news about Special Agent Bauer. Dallas forensics brought his van in earlier this evening. They're going over it with a fine-tooth comb. If there's even a single hair from Amy Bowen in the van, they'll find it."

"There you go."

"What about Darlene Rourke?" Patterson asked. "Is he claiming innocence on that, too?"

"Actually, he's not claiming anything at all because that slimy lawyer of his showed up again, and he clammed up. Not that it would do him any good. We found the murder weapon at Darlene Rourke's apartment. A metal lamp base. His prints are all over it. Not to mention everywhere else in the place."

"Fingerprints don't prove anything in this instance," Patterson pointed out. "He was having a relationship with her, and we know he's been to the apartment at least once before. Chances are he'd been there many times."

"True. But we have an eyewitness that places him at the scene, and his prints are on the murder weapon. He had motive and opportunity. And he opened fire on yourself and Bauer, not to mention my officers. Hardly the actions of an innocent man."

"Where is he now?"

"Sitting in one of our cells. Jameson Screed isn't going to

spring him so easily this time. We've already charged him with Darlene Rourke's murder, plus assault with a deadly weapon and attempted murder for what he did today. I'm sure there will be a bail hearing, but given the circumstances, I can't imagine any judge in their right mind would let him walk before trial."

"That's one thing, at least."

Voss leaned back in her chair and put her hands behind her head. "Honestly, for the life of me, I don't know what he was thinking, holing up in that hunting blind. Looked like he was in it for the long haul. He'd stashed bags of chips, peanut butter, bread, bottles of water, and at least twenty cans of soup, beans, and vegetables. Anything he could grab from the cabin. He had a sleeping bag and a couple of battery-powered camping lanterns, too. Plus, about two hundred rounds of ammo for that rifle of his."

"Who knows? Maybe he figured we wouldn't find him, and he could lie low until we took our search somewhere else."

"Or he was just a dumbass criminal who figured he could hide in the woods, and everyone would forget about him."

Patterson laughed at that. "Wouldn't be the first time."

"Right?" Voss chuckled. "You heading back to Dallas tonight, Special Agent Blake?"

"I'm beat." Even the thought of driving that far made Patterson wilt. She was running on empty. "I still have a reservation at the motel for one more night. I'll probably head back over to the hospital in the morning anyway to check up on Marcus."

"In that case, you'd better make yourself scarce and get some rest." Voss nodded toward a wall clock on the other side of the room. It was after ten. "There's nothing else you can do tonight."

"What about you?"

"I still have paperwork to finish before I can bid my desk farewell for the evening. Reports don't write themselves."

"Don't stay too late," Patterson said, standing up. "No one's even going to read those reports until tomorrow at the earliest."

"You make a good point." Voss kicked her chair back and stood up, then grabbed her jacket. "Let's both get out of here."

SIXTY-THREE

IT WAS after eleven when Patterson arrived back at the motel. She turned on the TV and found a local news channel. The media had wasted no time in reporting on Darlene Rourke's murder and the subsequent manhunt on Duane Snyder's land. She wondered how they knew so much, so quickly. But it wasn't unusual. Any half competent news organization had contacts within the local police department, and it was likely someone there had fed information to them. This was born out by the number of references to sources that would not speak on the record. A giveaway that someone who should not be talking had slipped information into the hands of a willing reporter.

Patterson left the TV playing in the background while she showered and then climbed into bed. The room was not as comfortable as the hotel back in Dallas, but right now, she didn't care. Patterson was beyond exhausted, both emotionally and physically. Her headache was worse, too. She popped a couple of painkillers and washed them down with an entire bottle of water before turning off the TV and sending a good-night text to Grant. He replied a few minutes later with an uncharacteristically long message in which he said how much he missed her. He also promised to call her the next day, time permitting.

Patterson put the phone down and turned off the lamp. She lay in the darkness, unable to sleep. Her mind would not shut off. The day's events rolled through her head like a dark tide. Even though Bauer ended up in the hospital with a gunshot wound to his shoulder, they had gotten lucky after walking into Snyder's ambush. One or both of them could easily have ended up in the morgue instead.

She didn't want to think about that.

Patterson turned the light back on and went to her overnight bag. She took out a book she had been reading on and off for the last several weeks. A thriller her father had given her after he finished with it. She wasn't much into that kind of fiction, given her job, which was why she was only on chapter six. She forced herself to read for the next forty-five minutes until her eyelids grew heavy.

She closed the book and placed it on the nightstand, then turned off the lamp again. But sleep still would not come. She was thinking about the Butterfly Killer and the ticking clock winding down to the discovery of the next body. Amy Bowen was out there somewhere, scared and alone, and Patterson was no closer to finding the teenager than she had been on the day Amy was abducted. It was frustrating.

But there was something else, too. She still felt she was missing something. Some elusive thread dangling at the back of her subconscious that she could not catch hold of and pull. It had been bothering Patterson for days, but she could not reel the stray impression in, no matter how hard she focused on it. But at least the headache was gone, and for that, she was grateful.

Patterson gave up. She took several deep breaths in through her nose and out through her mouth. With each exhalation, she was releasing the tension in her muscles. And as she did this,

Patterson banished all thoughts of the Butterfly Killer from her mind and imagined an endless sandy beach with waves lapping the shore and an azure ocean beyond. Palm trees lined the beach, reaching up into a cobalt blue sky with only the barest hint of fluffy white clouds. She could almost feel the breeze through her hair and the sand under her toes. It was a technique that had worked for her in the past. It was her happy place. A Mindscape of peace and tranquility. Before long, she fell asleep.

SIXTY-FOUR

PATTERSON JOLTED awake and sat up. It was still dark. The digital clock on the nightstand told her it was ten past five in the morning.

The pillowcase.

That was the thread she hadn't been able to grasp. It was the vintage pillowcase found at the scene of the last murder. The same pillowcase that was used to smother the third victim, Susie Tomlinson.

Patterson grabbed her phone and brought up the photos sent by Detective Costa. She had seen a similar pillowcase somewhere else. Not the same, maybe, but close enough. At Esther Cutler's townhouse, when her caregiver was changing the sheets.

Patterson stared at the photos. Could it be?

There was only one way to find out. Visit the old lady and see for herself. Patterson closed the photo app and brought up Phoebe's phone number. Her finger hovered over the dial button, but she resisted. It was so early. Yet she didn't want to wait. The hour-plus drive back to Dallas would eat up enough time, especially since Patterson would hit rush hour in the city, even if she left now. And Phoebe was at the hospital, anyway. It was unlikely she was getting much sleep.

Making up her mind, Patterson swung her legs off the bed and stood up, then hit the green call button.

Phoebe answered after only one ring. "Special Agent Blake. Why are you calling so early? Is something wrong?"

"No. Nothing's wrong," Patterson reassured her. She was about to dive straight into the reason for her call when another thought occurred to her. "How's Marcus doing?"

"He's okay. In pain. They changed his dressings a couple of hours ago and administered more meds. After that they let me in to see him for a few minutes."

"How are you holding up?" Patterson asked.

"I wish they had more comfortable seats in this waiting room, but other than that, I'm doing fine. The SAC called after you left last night. He was really sweet. Sounded worried. Said I should stay here for as long as necessary, so that's what I'm going to do. He asked about you, too, and I told him you looked beat." Phoebe drew a long breath. "Did you only call to ask about Marcus or was there something else?"

"There is something else," Patterson replied. "I know this is a strange request, but I need to visit your grandmother. Like right away."

"I thought you said nothing was wrong." There was a note of panic in Phoebe's voice.

"And there isn't. But I need to check a hunch."

"Is it to do with her imaginary visitor?"

"I'm not so sure he is imaginary," Patterson said. "And I think there might be a connection to the Butterfly Killer. That's what I want to check on."

"What?" Phoebe's voice quivered. "How could that be?"

"I don't know yet. I'd rather not go into detail until I'm sure. This could be nothing but my overactive imagination playing tricks."

"Are you still in Athens?"

"Yes. At the motel. I'm going to check out and drive back this morning. Figured I'd leave right away."

"You'll hit rush hour."

"I know that. But I don't want to wait."

"If you can make it there in time, her caregiver comes in between eight and nine to get her up and make breakfast."

"I'll get there," Patterson said.

"Okay. I'll call the agency and let them know you're coming." There was a moment of silence on the other end of the line. "Should I be worried about this, Special Agent Blake?"

"No. Your grandmother isn't in any danger, at least as far as I know," Patterson reassured her.

"That's a relief. Will you keep me informed?"

"Of course." Patterson was already getting dressed. She held the phone between her shoulder and chin as she pulled on her pants. "Do me a favor and keep quiet about this to Marcus. Okay?

"Sure. If you want me to."

"I do. You know how stubborn he is. If he thinks something is going down, he'll probably try to check himself out and race back to Dallas."

"That sounds like him. What if he asks where you are?"

"Just tell him I'm busy dealing with the fallout from yesterday. Whatever happens, I don't want him to stress out. He needs to stay calm and let that shoulder heal."

"I'll make sure Marcus stays right where he is," Phoebe said. "If he's on as much medication as earlier, he won't be in any condition to go anywhere, anyway."

"Thank you. This might be nothing. In that case, I'll drive right back and come to the hospital."

"I hope it's nothing," Phoebe said. "I don't know why you think my grandmother's nighttime visitor has something to do with the Butterfly Killer, but that thought terrifies me."

"I know it does but try not to worry." Patterson checked the time. "I have to go. I'll keep you in the loop."

"Okay." Phoebe sounded relieved.

Patterson went to hang up, but then Phoebe spoke again.

"Wait. I just thought of something. Let me give you the lockbox code. That way, you can get inside if you need to, even if Jesse isn't there."

"Text it to me," Patterson said.

"I'll do that right now."

"Great." Patterson hung up and finished getting dressed, then she grabbed her go bag and hurried from the room. After a quick visit to Bauer's room to collect his belongings, she checked them both out. Fifteen minutes later, she was on the road and heading back to Dallas.

SIXTY-FIVE

JESSE THE CAREGIVER was already at Esther's townhouse when Patterson arrived two hours later. As she expected, traffic had been hell. Every major artery of the city was clogged with bumper-to-bumper vehicles crawling along as the residents of the Big D scurried to their offices and retail establishments across the DFW metropolitan area to start another day.

Esther was already sitting up in her chair when Patterson entered the living room. When she saw the FBI agent, her eyes lit up. "Special Agent Blake. How lovely of you to drop by."

"Phoebe called and told us you were coming," Jesse said as he fussed over the old woman, making sure she was comfortable before setting up a TV tray and placing a breakfast of scrambled eggs and bacon before her.

"I was in the area and thought I'd stop in and say hello," Patterson lied.

"Where's that handsome partner of yours?" Esther asked.

"He can't be here today," Patterson told her.

"Shame. If I were sixty years younger, Phoebe would have a

fight on her hands over that man, granddaughter or not. I'll tell you that much."

"Now, Esther. That's no way to talk." Jesse grinned at Patterson. "She can be a handful."

"You should've seen me when I was younger," Esther quipped without a moment's hesitation.

"You're incorrigible," Jesse said to her, moving the tray closer so she could reach the food. He straightened up and turned to Patterson. "Phoebe said you want to check on something."

"That's right. It won't take long, and I won't get in the way."

"Take all the time you need." Jesse sat in a chair next to the old woman and watched her eat. "I'll be here keeping Esther company."

Patterson nodded and moved off toward the bed at the far side of the room. She slipped her cell phone out and compared the photos of the pillowcase to the ones on Esther's bed. They were close, for sure, but they were not a match. Esther's pillowcases were embroidered with pink flowers and scrolling greenery along the open edge. The pillowcase that had been used to murder Susie Tomlinson was embroidered on the edge with red roses, and there was a lace trim.

Patterson was disappointed, but it had always been a long shot. What chance was there that Esther's late-night visitor was a serial killer and not just a product of her aging imagination? The answer was obvious. Zero percent. After all, there must be a thousand pillowcases like that in the city adorning the beds of every octogenarian. More than likely, the killer had picked up the pillowcase in a thrift store or a vintage shop. Somewhere they could purchase it without being easily traced. Then she remembered something.

When she and Bauer had searched the house on their first visit, she had noticed an open drawer in the master bedroom.

Inside the drawer were bed linens and pillowcases just like the ones she was now looking at on Esther's bed.

Jesse was still tending to the old woman who was almost finished with breakfast. Patterson motioned to him and pointed upstairs. "I'll be back in a minute."

She rushed out into the corridor and took the stairs two at a time. In the bedroom she approached the dresser. The drawer was closed now. Patterson slid it open to find neatly folded sheets and pillowcases. There, sitting on the top, was one that she recognized.

"Holy crap," she said under her breath, removing the pillowcase and laying it on the bed that hadn't been slept in for years. When she compared it to the photos on her phone, she couldn't believe her eyes.

The pillowcases were a perfect match.

A chill wormed its way up her spine.

She turned back to the drawer and rummaged through it looking for a companion pillowcase but couldn't find one. She opened the drawer above to find more bedding, but the missing pillowcase was not there, either. The top drawer contained clothes. She turned her attention to the only other piece of furniture in the room capable of holding linens. The wardrobe. But when she opened it, all she found were coats and dresses on hangers. There were boxes stacked on the floor of the wardrobe underneath the hanging clothes, but when she dug through them, they turned out to be knickknacks like old photographs and ornaments wrapped in newspaper for storage. A few were shoe boxes with the shoes still in them.

Patterson closed the wardrobe and went back to the bed. Was the pillowcase in the photo part of the same set as the one spread out in front of her on the bed? If so, how was that even possible?

She needed to find out. Patterson snatched up the pillowcase and ran back downstairs. When she reached the hallway,

Jesse was walking to the kitchen with the empty plate in his hands. She followed him in and showed him the pillowcase.

"Do you recognize this?" She asked.

"Sure. It's one of Esther's old pillowcases. Why?"

"Where's the matching one?" Patterson asked.

Jesse looked perplexed. "I assume it's in the drawer, along with all the others."

"It's not. Do you keep bedding anywhere else in the house?"

Jesse shook his head. "Only if it's in the laundry, and I know the matching pillowcase to that one is not there because I always use matching pairs. If one is folded and put away, the other should be with it."

"It's not," Patterson said. She didn't mention the photograph on her phone of the matching pillowcase found at the scene of Susie Tomlinson's murder. For all Patterson knew, Jesse had taken it. "I searched every inch of that bedroom."

"Then I don't have an answer," Jesse said. "Sorry."

SIXTY-SIX

THE FIRST THING Patterson did after leaving Esther Cutler's townhouse was to call Detective Costa and fill him in on what she had discovered. He was intrigued but baffled. It would be a major breakthrough if the pillowcase found at the crime scene really was the twin to the one in the old lady's drawer, but he wanted more information. Esther Cutler was obviously not the Butterfly Killer. Apart from the obvious fact of her gender and age, both of which did not fit the profile, she could barely walk. Which meant someone else must have removed the pillowcase. The question was, who?

Patterson intended to find out. Her next step, she told Costa, was to dive into the background of anyone who had contact with Esther or access to her home. That meant the caregivers and, by extension the agency they worked for, which kept the lockbox code on file. She would also check Esther Cutler's neighbors. She even intended to do a background check on Phoebe, mostly to eliminate her, because Patterson didn't believe for one second that Phoebe was the killer. That last one would be easy. As an employee of the FBI, Phoebe had already been subjected to numerous background checks.

After hanging up with Costa, Patterson drove back to the field office and went straight to the windowless box that she shared with Bauer. She sat down and looked across the desk at the empty chair opposite. The office was quiet and empty without him there. Patterson hated to admit it, but she missed Marcus Bauer.

Shrugging off the maudlin feelings, Patterson turned to her laptop. She started with Phoebe, asking HR for an updated background check after clearing her request with Walter Harris. The SAC had hesitated, wanting to know why an FBI agent was investigating a member of their own organization, but once Patterson explained her motives and what she had found, Harris green-lit the probe and instructed human resources to make it look like a routine update to her employment file. The last thing he wanted, Harris told Patterson in no uncertain terms, was Phoebe thinking any of her coworkers suspected her of such a heinous series of crimes. Morale was important in the FBI, not to mention trust.

With the easiest and arguably most unpleasant task taken care of, Patterson turned her attention to more likely suspects. She started with the caregivers. When she phoned the agency, they told her that Jesse was responsible for Esther Cutler's welfare five days a week, and a woman named Lisbeth took over on his days off or if there was an emergency that Jesse could not respond to. They were more than happy to share the work schedules of both caregivers in order to avoid even a hint of impropriety by any of their employees. They also assured Patterson that only a handful of people had access to the code for the lockbox hanging on Esther Cutler's door. Patterson was able to discount the admin staff because all of them had rock-solid alibis for one or more of the abduction dates. The same was true of both caregivers. Their work schedules cleared them in short order since both worked Thursdays and Fridays and were tending to clients—the agency was very particular about not calling its customers patients—during the time frames of the abductions.

That left few suspects and no one Patterson could identify as being privy to the lockbox code, which Phoebe changed monthly. She started with the neighbors closest to the town-house. The ones on each side. On the left-hand side were Helen, Benjamin, and their two kids. Patterson and Bauer had met both parents on previous visits to Esther's townhouse. It didn't take her long to find out that their surname was Forrester.

On the other side was a couple in their mid-forties. Matt Eaton and Darren Janeczko, and she started with them. But it went nowhere. Matt and Darren both worked as actors for a local repertory theater company and were out of town until late August. Since the troupe didn't stage productions over the summer, they had gone north and found work at a summer theater in Maine. It took Patterson all of ten minutes to confirm that they were eighteen hundred miles away when Amy Bowen was taken.

The suspects were whittling down fast. But when Patterson turned to Benjamin and Helen, she found an unexpected connection. At first, it appeared the neighbors on Esther's left would end up eliminated as easily as the caregivers and those on the right. She ran a check through the usual databases, including the National Crime Information Center or NCIC, which collected and preserved, among other things, the crim-inal histories of offenders from all over the United States. It was available to state, local, and federal law enforcement agencies across the country, who not only used it as a valuable source of information but also helped maintain it by adding records. But there were no hits for either Benjamin or Helen.

She also ran their names through NICS, the National Instant Criminal Background Check System, which was used by firearms dealers to make sure purchasers did not have a crim-inal record. Again, she came up empty.

Finally, on a whim, she did a general web search. And this was where she struck metaphorical gold. Most of the links relating to Helen were for social media profiles and background check websites that lured people in with the promise of juicy details about their friends and loved ones.

But Ben was a different matter. She found a newspaper article from earlier in the year about the church he attended and the charitable foundation they had founded to build homes for low-income individuals. Ben was featured prominently because he was one of the more enthusiastic team members, often working four days a week, including weekends. He was also one of the volunteer supervisors on the project. There was even a photograph of him, standing with a hammer in his hand near a white van beyond which was the skeletal frame of the house they were building. But it was the church he attended that drew Patterson's attention.

St. Francis of Assisi.

She took out her phone and found the photo she had taken of the rental screen at the DIY store. One name had stood out to her when she was going through the list of rentals. A name that coincided with the dates of each abduction. S. Francis.

She looked back at the article with a flicker of dread. That could not be a coincidence, especially since Benjamin was standing in front of a white cargo van in the photograph. A vehicle that could very well have been a rental.

But it was still all circumstantial. Patterson needed hard answers. It was time to have another chat with Helen and Ben Forrester.

SIXTY-SEVEN

HELEN FORRESTER WAS at home when Patterson arrived on her front doorstep, but Ben wasn't. She was surprised to see the FBI agent and asked if everything was okay with Esther next door. Patterson assured her that it was and showed the concerned woman her FBI credentials, then asked if she could come inside.

"Oh, right. Absolutely. Come on in," Helen said, moving aside so that Patterson could enter. "I thought you were coming around to visit Esther because you were friends with her granddaughter, Phoebe."

"We were," Patterson replied without elaborating. She stepped inside and stood facing Helen in the hallway. "This is about something else."

"Does that mean you're here in an official capacity?"

"I'm making inquiries related to a case I'm working on, and I'd like to ask you some questions, if you don't mind."

"Goodness. We're not in trouble, are we?" Helen asked, giving a nervous laugh. "I can't for the life of me think why the FBI would be interested in us. It's not like we're running around robbing banks. We barely even go to the movies or eat out. If our lives were any more boring we'd fall asleep living them."

"It's just a few routine questions, mostly about Benjamin's work with the church. Specifically, the charitable foundation he's involved with."

"I see. Is the foundation in trouble?" Helen lifted her hand to her mouth.

"I'm not at liberty to say," Patterson said, letting the assumption stand. "Are your children at home, Mrs. Forrester? Danny and Samantha."

"No, they're not," Helen replied.

Patterson nodded. She didn't want to ask questions about Ben with his kids around. "Good."

"What would you like to know?"

"Well, for a start, I was wondering what Ben does there."

"He's one of the volunteer supervisors. He makes sure people know what they're doing and where they're doing it. Keeps the job site in line."

"But your husband isn't actually in the construction business, correct? The last time we were here you said he was an accountant."

"That's right."

"And you also said he only works three days a week in the family business."

"Yes. He works for his dad. He comes from a long line of accountants who expected him to get his degree then join the family business. Truth is, he hates accounting. Finds it boring. He tried to quit several years ago and do something else, but his father begged him to come back. He did, but on his terms, which were three days a week, and no more than that."

"And he fills the rest of his time with volunteer work."

"Yes. He's always been good with his hands even though he's not a licensed contractor or anything. He finds working at the charitable foundation to be the best way he can honor his calling from God."

"Could you just confirm to me . . . the church you attend that runs the charitable foundation is St. Francis of Assisi?"

"That's right."

"Does the foundation ever use rental vans?" Patterson asked. "Specifically white cargo vans?"

"I believe they do," Helen answered. "They use them to move construction materials and such."

"Why don't they just buy a van? Wouldn't it work out cheaper in the long run?"

"It would if they were paying for them. But the pastor solicits donations from local companies. The DIY store provides materials and van usage as part of their own charitable efforts. The store donates a block of rental vehicle hours every month. It works out well for everyone."

"Is Ben in charge of the van rentals?" Patterson asked.

"I really couldn't tell you." Helen shook her head. "But it's possible. He handles a lot of things. He's pretty much the pastor's right-hand man."

"What days does Ben work on the housing project?"

"It depends on if they need him, but he's free Thursdays through Sundays."

"So he could end up volunteering with the foundation on any or all of those days?"

"Yes." Helen frowned.

"Have you ever noticed your husband acting strangely after volunteering at the foundation?"

"I'm not sure I know what you mean by that," Helen replied.

"Does he come across as preoccupied or worried?"

"Never." Helen's frown deepened. "Look, if this is about the foundation, maybe you should talk to them. If it's about my husband, I'd like you to tell me."

"Like I said, I'm just making routine inquiries. Filling in gaps."

"That doesn't answer my question. Is this about Ben?"

"We're not investigating any particular person," Patterson answered. She had pressed Helen enough and decided to back off. What she really wanted to do now was take a look around. Maybe she would see something that would solidify her suspicions. "Would you mind if I used your bathroom?"

"Yes. Of course. It's on the second floor. Up the stairs and turn right."

"Thank you." Patterson started up the stairs. As she climbed, she was aware of Helen's gaze on her back. She made her way down the hallway to the bathroom and stepped inside. After a suitable amount of time, she pulled the flush and stepped back out.

She heard Helen moving around downstairs. It sounded like she had gone into the kitchen. The townhouse had three floors. Patterson paused a moment longer, then headed for the next set of stairs. She crept up as softly as she could. There were only three rooms on the third floor. The first was another bathroom. The second was an office for Ben. She stepped inside. There was a desk in the middle of the room. Bookshelves lined the back wall. She went to the desk and searched it but found nothing that would point to Ben Forrester as anything but a mild-mannered accountant. She went to the bookshelves and searched those, too, with the same result. All she saw were journals of case-law and assorted nonfiction books that ranged from autobiographies of politicians and a couple of Supreme Court judges to do-it-yourself manuals.

She stepped back out into the hallway and paused, listening for any sign that Helen was coming upstairs. When she heard none, Patterson crossed to the other door and opened it. This was the bedroom of a teenage girl, presumably Helen and Ben's daughter, photos of whom graced the walls of the hallway downstairs alongside her younger brother.

Patterson didn't have much time before Helen would miss her. She walked past the bed to a desk under the window. There were school textbooks stacked on top, along with a couple of notepads. A ceramic pot contained pens and pencils. There was one other piece of ceramic on the desk. A butterfly with its wings spread fired in an iridescent glaze. Patterson picked up the small object and turned it over in her hands before putting it back, then turned her attention to a four-drawer chest on the wall opposite the bed with a flat-screen TV sitting on it. The drawers were full of underwear, folded sweaters, blouses, and pairs of jeans.

There was nothing out of the ordinary.

The only other place Patterson hadn't searched was the closet. She approached the louvered doors and reached out to open them, just as an angry voice spoke behind her.

"What the hell do you think you're doing in here?"

SIXTY-EIGHT

PATTERSON WHIRLED AROUND.

Helen stood in the doorway with her hands on her hips. Her mouth was a thin line. "You shouldn't be in here."

"I'm sorry," Patterson said, stepping away from the closet. "I used the bathroom down the hallway, and this door was open. It reminded me of my own bedroom when I was a kid." The excuse was flimsy, and Patterson knew it.

"Why didn't you use the bathroom on the second floor?" Helen eyed her with suspicion.

"You said the bathroom was upstairs, I just assumed . . ."

"This is our daughter's room. We don't like people in here."

"I didn't mean to intrude."

Helen's face softened. "Don't worry about it. Why don't we go back downstairs?"

"Sure." Patterson breathed an internal sigh of relief. She pointed toward the desk and the decorative ceramic insect. "Your daughter likes butterflies."

"That was a gift from her grandmother. Samantha was so shy when she was young, but then she found her voice. Came out of her cocoon like a butterfly. That's what we used to call her growing up. Our little butterfly."

"Really?" Patterson took one last look at the girl's bedroom before Helen led her down the hallway and back downstairs. When they reached the bottom, Patterson stood in awkward silence.

"Do you have any more questions, Special Agent Blake? If not, I really am very busy."

"No more questions." Patterson made a move toward the front door, then turned back. "How's the renovation coming?"

"What?" A perplexed expression passed across Helen's face.

"Your husband said he was turning part of the basement into a man cave. Somewhere he could watch football."

"Oh, that." The puzzlement fell away. "He's getting there. Another few months, maybe."

"I'd love to see it," Patterson said, her gaze flitting to the basement door near the kitchen. "My dad back in New York has been wanting to turn his basement into a man cave for years. Might give him some ideas."

"I'd like to show you, but I can't. Ben keeps the basement door locked and the key on him. He doesn't want Danny going down there when he's not here. Says there are too many power tools. The kid is fascinated with that stuff. You know what boys are like."

"Right. Where is your husband now?"

"At the church attending a planning meeting for the next phase of construction on the housing project."

"Maybe next time, then."

"Yes. Next time." Helen steered Patterson toward the front door and out onto the stoop. "Have a nice day, Special Agent Blake."

"You, too." Patterson descended the steps and walked to Bauer's car. She slipped behind the steering wheel just in time to see Helen close the door. Then Patterson sat there for a while, lost in thought. Her cop's sixth sense told her something wasn't right. She wondered what she would have found in Samantha's closet if Helen had not interrupted her. A butterfly dress, perhaps? It was impossible to know. But Patterson knew one thing. Benjamin Forrester and his activities deserved more scrutiny. By the time she pulled away from the curb, Patterson had decided what she was going to do next.

SIXTY-NINE

BY FIVE O'CLOCK THAT EVENING, Patterson was back at the townhouse and sitting a little way down the road in the lime green Corolla that Grant had arranged for her back in Chicago. Neither Benjamin nor Helen Forrester had ever seen it before. All the previous times that she and Bauer had visited this street, they had come in her partner's newer and more comfortable Dodge Charger.

Patterson was prepared for a long night. She had purchased snacks and a cup of hot coffee at a convenience store, along with two cans of cold brew for later. This was not her first stakeout, and she knew that come midnight, she would be glad for the jolt of caffeine the cold brew provided.

Earlier that afternoon, before returning here, she had updated a skeptical Detective Costa and told him her plan.

"Are you sure it's worth spending the night sitting in your car all alone?" Costa had asked. "All your evidence is circumstantial. For all you know, Benjamin Forrester is exactly what he appears to be. A loving father dedicated to volunteering at his church."

"I'm right about this," Patterson replied. "My gut tells me something is off."

"Even if you are right, what makes you think that sitting outside of that townhouse will do any good?"

"I don't know that it will. But if Benjamin Forrester is the Butterfly Killer, he isn't going to be too pleased that an FBI agent was asking questions. Especially when he finds out that Helen caught me snooping around upstairs."

"Which was a stupid thing to do. It amounts to an illegal search. That could jeopardize any case we build against him."

"Don't worry. I handled it."

"What were you thinking?"

"I was taking an opportunity." Patterson didn't feel she needed to defend herself. "And if my visit prompts Ben into making a rash move, like trying to move Amy Bowen, it will have been worth it."

"You're taking a huge gamble."

"I don't think so. The evidence is there. He rents vans on behalf of the charitable foundation his church runs. Vans he could use to abduct those girls, and no one would be any the wiser. Not only that, but law enforcement might overlook rental vehicles from somewhere like a DIY store because they aren't immediately obvious."

"Yeah. We did overlook it. Thanks for pointing that out." Costa sounded miffed.

"Not blaming you. Just saying," Patterson said before pressing on. "Then there's the daughter. She had a thing for butterflies. Even had a little ceramic butterfly on her desk because it was her nickname growing up. That's another connection."

"Still tenuous."

"And what about the locked cellar door? For all we know, he has Amy Bowen captive down there."

"Yeah . . . right. And his wife never noticed a teenage abductee being held under their house?"

"I don't have all the answers yet, but I'm right. I feel it."

"And Esther Cutler?" Costa asked. "How does she fit into all of this?"

"I haven't figured that out yet, but there is a connection. I'm sure."

"Because of the pillowcase."

"Even you have to admit, it's a hell of a coincidence that Esther Cutler would own a vintage pillowcase that exactly matches Susie Tomlinson's murder weapon. Especially since the matching one is missing."

"I'll give you, it's intriguing. But I still can't see how it all fits together."

"That's what I'm hoping to find out."

She heard Costa sigh on the other end of the line. "If you really want to waste your night, go ahead."

"Even if nothing comes of this and Benjamin Forrester is innocent, it won't be a waste," Patterson replied. "Eliminating a suspect is a good thing."

"I agree. But I still think staking out that townhouse is a waste of time. Nothing's going to happen." Costa took a quick breath. "But if it does, I expect you to call for backup. Your partner is out of action, and the last thing I need is another FBI agent with a bullet in them."

"Don't worry," Patterson assured him. "If I'm right, and Ben Forrester panics and reveals himself, I'll call it in."

"Make sure that you do," Costa told her before hanging up.

That conversation had taken place almost two hours before, and now, as she sat in the car and contemplated the long hours ahead, Patterson wondered if the detective hadn't been right. Maybe it was a waste of time to sit staring at Benjamin Forrester's townhouse in the vain hope her visit earlier in the day would spook him. But she was determined to go through with it. And not just because she trusted her gut but also because Amy Bowen was still out there somewhere, alone and afraid, and Patterson couldn't bear the thought of going back to her hotel room for the night and doing nothing.

SEVENTY

HE HADN'T VISITED her all day since bringing a bowl of thin oatmeal to her for breakfast, and Amy Bowen was grateful for that. He had also left the light on in the tunnel outside her cell, which meant she could see the photographs taped to the back wall. That was not so pleasant. The longer she had been down there—because Amy believed she was indeed underground—the more disturbed she had become by those photographs.

Amy didn't know if she was the first captive to be held here, although she guessed not because her captor appeared so comfortable with his crime. The girl on the wall had not been a captive, though. That much was obvious by the locations of those photos. Some of them were indoors. A living room at Christmas. A girl's bedroom. Others were taken at the beach or park. Not the kind of places you took an abducted girl to photograph her. Not that it mattered. Amy was more concerned with her own situation than that of those who came before her. Even if it raised the question of what her captor had done to them. She thought she knew the answer to that, too, but preferred not to think about it.

That was how Amy passed her day. Trying not to look at the photographs on the wall or think about the fate that awaited her.

She wondered when her captor would show up again. He normally visited her at least twice a day—more if he wanted her to bathe and put on one of the butterfly dresses. But something was different now. She knew this because it was past the time he always brought her supper. Even though Amy did not have a phone or watch, she possessed a good sense of how late it was, thanks to the hunger pangs that gnawed at her stomach.

Then, just when she thought he would leave her alone all night, she heard the bolt being drawn back on the metal door at the end of the tunnel. Moments later, he stepped into the pool of light cast by the bulb hanging from the tunnel ceiling. But he had no food, and there was a strange expression on his face.

He thrust a butterfly dress through the bars and tossed it toward her without waiting for her to come and get it. Something he never did. He didn't like the dresses to touch the floor.

"Put that on," he instructed in a gruff voice. "Do it quickly."

Amy didn't want to. She hated undressing in front of him. It made her feel dirty. Not to mention embarrassed. But she needn't have worried because he turned and strode back toward the door.

When he got there the man paused.

"I'll be back in fifteen minutes. I expect you to be ready."

"Why?" she asked in a small voice. "What's happening?"

"Time for you to go," he said. Then he stepped through the door and slammed it shut.

Amy looked at the dress lying on the floor. And then she cried because whatever hope remained that she would live through this nightmare had all but vanished.

SEVENTY-ONE

IT WAS one a.m. when Patterson saw the light in the upstairs windows. But not those of the townhouse belonging to Benjamin and Helen Forrester. This light was in Esther Cutler's bedroom.

Patterson had been sitting half reclined behind the wheel of the Corolla and doing her best to stay awake. Both cans of cold brew coffee had gone hours ago, and now she had to rely on her own resolve to keep her eyes open.

When she saw the light, Patterson sat up and leaned forward over the steering wheel to get a better view. At first, she thought it might be nothing more than a reflection of car headlights. But then she realized there was no traffic on the street and the light did not reflect anywhere else. Judging by the way it bobbed around, this was not a reflection from some external source. This was a flashlight. It shone first in one window, then the other, as if someone were moving around the room.

Patterson slipped from the car and checked she had a flashlight of her own, then she pushed the car door closed without making a sound. As she hurried across the street toward the townhouse, she sent Detective Costa a text message to appraise him of the situation. As she reached Esther Cutler's front door, there was a reply.

'Stay where you are and wait. I'll send backup.'

Underneath the message were three animated dots. Costa was still typing. A second message came through.

'Don't engage.'

Patterson didn't bother to reply. There was no way she was leaving Esther Cutler on her own in that house with an intruder. She opened the text message below Costa's. This one was from Phoebe Cutler, sent the previous day when they were at the hospital. It contained the lockbox code.

Patterson retrieved the key and slid it into the lock. The door opened with a barely perceptible squeak of hinges.

The hallway beyond was dark and empty.

Patterson drew her gun, then stepped across the threshold, leaving the door ajar for Costa's backup whenever they arrived.

The light had come from the second-floor master bedroom. Patterson knew this because she had already figured out what lay behind each of the townhouse's front windows.

The living room door was open. Patterson went to it and poked her head inside, intending to alert the old lady of her presence. But Esther Cutler was fast asleep and snoring in her bed at the back of the living room.

Patterson went back to the stairs. She stopped and listened. Only Esther Cutler's faint snores and the tick of a clock somewhere deeper in the house reached her ears.

She paused a moment longer, gathering her nerves, and put her foot on the bottom stair.

A clattering sound in the kitchen made Patterson jump, and she almost squealed out loud, barely stifling her reaction in the nick of time. She froze, letting her thudding heartbeat return to normal. Then she realized what had startled her. It was the sound of ice cubes falling into the tray under the automatic icemaker in Esther Cutler's freezer. In other circumstances, she would have laughed at the timing, but not here and now.

Patterson steeled herself and started up the stairs. She knew they creaked and kept her feet to the far edges of the treads to minimize the pressure on the boards. It worked. Mostly.

She climbed with caution, aware of the swirling darkness around her and the hidden dangers within. She stopped twice to listen but still heard nothing but the familiar sounds of an old house.

She gripped her gun tight when she reached the second-floor landing and resisted the urge to slip the flashlight from her pocket and turn it on so she could see better. Unless the intruder had rushed back downstairs and somehow escaped in the time it took Patterson to cross the road and enter the house, they must still be up here.

To her left, another flight of stairs went to the third floor. For all she knew, the intruder had heard her enter and fled upward. Or they were behind one of the closed doors leading off the landing.

Patterson crept forward and approached the master bedroom. That door stood half open. She pushed it wide with her toe, aware that the intruder might be hiding behind it, ready to slam it back on her as she entered.

The room beyond came into view. It appeared to be empty. That didn't mean it was. Patterson stepped inside. No one was waiting behind the door. She scanned the room. And then she noticed something odd. The bottom drawer of the dresser between the windows was open. The same drawer within which she had found the pillowcase earlier that day. Patterson had closed it.

Any last doubt that the light was nothing more than a reflection cast by some unseen external source vanished. Someone had been up here. They probably still were.

Patterson made a quick sweep of the room to make sure no

one was hiding under the bed or inside the wardrobe and retreated to the bedroom door.

Her mouth was dry. She wished Costa's promised backup would arrive. Maybe she should have waited like he asked. But that was never an option. Not with Esther Cutler alone in the house with an intruder. The old woman had been right, after all. Someone was sneaking around, and Patterson resolved to find them.

She tensed her finger, resting against the frame of the Glock, and stepped back into the hallway, intending to search the room opposite.

She didn't get that far.

A flicker of movement danced at the corner of her eye from the direction of the third-floor stairs. Patterson swiveled on the balls of her feet but before she could bring up the gun, a black shape barreled out of the darkness toward her, much too close.

SEVENTY-TWO

THE INTRUDER CRASHED into Patterson before she could react. She was driven back by the painful impact and almost lost her balance but regained her feet at the last moment and lifted the Glock, ready to defend herself against another onslaught.

"FBI. Stop where you are," she shouted, dropping into the firing stance. But her attacker had no interest in pressing his attack. He was already on the stairs and racing down to the ground floor, no longer bothering with stealth.

"I said stop." Patterson sprinted forward and all but launched herself down the stairs. At the bottom, she paused, and for a brief moment, thought that her attacker had fled out the front door, which was now standing open. But then she glimpsed movement at the other end of the hallway, near the kitchen. He had tried to throw her off by throwing the front door wide to make her think he had escaped that way, but in reality, he was hiding in the pass-through pantry that led to the cellar.

"Who's there?" came a groggy voice. It was Esther Cutler. The noise must have awoken her.

"It's okay, Esther," Patterson shouted out as she advanced on the pantry with her gun raised. "It's me. Patterson Blake. There's nothing to worry about."

A small whimper of fear was her only response, but there was no time to comfort the old woman. Patterson couldn't let the intruder escape. Which begged the question: why had he chosen to head for the pantry instead of taking the easy option of fleeing out the front door? He wanted Patterson to take the bait and go in that direction, but still . . . it didn't make sense.

It made even less sense when Patterson reached the pantry and stepped into the doorway. It was empty. There was only one place the intruder could have gone.

Patterson hurried past the shelves stocked with condiments and spices and canned foods and approached the cellar door. She gripped the handle with one hand and pulled it open, while keeping her gun trained on the darkness beyond.

This time no one rushed her from the shadows.

Patterson took out her flashlight and turned it on, then shone it downward. The cellar steps descended into gloom. The intruder must be down there somewhere, but he wasn't on the stairs.

Patterson started down, sweeping the flashlight left and right to make sure no one ambushed her a second time. When she reached the bottom, she stopped and assessed her surroundings.

The cellar looked just like it had on her last visit there. There was a rocking chair, an iron bed frame, and a bunch of card-board boxes stacked in one corner. The homemade workbench that must have belonged to Esther's husband loomed out of the shadows when her flashlight swept across it. Finally, she came to the only piece of large furniture in the cellar. A cabinet pushed against the far wall. What she didn't see was any sign of the intruder.

Patterson flipped the switch at the bottom of the stairs. Pale yellow light pushed the darkness away.

She moved further into the cellar and stood in the center near a brick column that supported the ceiling above, then turned full circle. Patterson was mystified. Unless the man had become suddenly invisible, she was alone.

That wasn't possible.

She knew he hadn't escaped through the front door. She had seen him run into the pantry and, by extension, into the cellar beyond and below. There was no other place for him to go. But people didn't vanish. So where was he?

Patterson studied her surroundings. There wasn't even a window he could have climbed out of. Baffled, she searched the entire cellar, starting with the heating oil tank that stood under the stairs. But there was not enough space between the tank and the wall for anyone to hide. Likewise, it was impossible to crawl underneath. It was too low to the ground. She checked the pile of boxes stacked in the corner with the same result and peered under the workbench, even though she could already see no one was crouching there.

She approached the cabinet. It was about five feet tall and three feet wide, with four large drawers containing a variety of hand tools from box planes to screwdrivers and a rusty manual hand drill. The cabinet, which someone had turned into a makeshift toolbox, looked old and must have been down there for a long time. It was also obvious that no one could conceal themselves within it. Patterson was about to turn away, disappointed, when she noticed something else about the cabinet. It was sitting on small metal casters attached to the bottom frame. The cabinet was on wheels.

Patterson drew a sharp breath.

She slipped her gun back into its holster, pocketed the flashlight, and took hold of the cabinet. Then she pulled.

The cabinet moved an inch, then another. Then it swung out in a wide arc to reveal a brick wall.

Patterson's heart fell. There was nothing there.

But then she glanced down and in that moment she knew where the intruder had gone. Because attached to the back of the cabinet was a short length of rope, which trailed across the floor and into a rough hole knocked out of the brickwork. A hole big enough for a person to crawl through. Beyond it was more darkness.

SEVENTY-THREE

PATTERSON DROPPED to her hands and knees and pushed herself through the hole. The sharp edges of bricks dug into her back as she squirmed to the other side. She was expecting a cramped space behind the wall but was surprised to find she could stand up straight. She reached out and felt around, touching cold brickwork to her left and right. She reached into her pocket and withdrew the flashlight. Turning it on, she found herself in a narrow tunnel with a vaulted ceiling. Behind her was a blank wall, but the tunnel ran in the other direction for at least fifty feet before ending at a metal door, its surface rusty and pitted with corrosion.

To Patterson's left, opposite the hole through which she had crawled, was another door, this one much newer. It stood open an inch or two. Was this where the intruder had gone?

Patterson slipped her gun from its holster, then nudged the door open with her toe. Beyond was more blackness. She clutched the flashlight and stepped into the space beyond the door.

It was a cellar just like the one she had come from, except this one was in a better state of repair. The brickwork had been painted white, and the floor was smooth new concrete. A partition wall with a door divided the space, making the room she currently occupied smaller than Esther Cutler's basement by half.

Patterson went to the door and opened it, aiming her flashlight beam into the space beyond. This part of the basement was older, with a large oil tank at one end. Sticks of furniture and boxes lined the walls. There were also a couple of children's bicycles and a large metal tool chest. To her right was a staircase that led to the home above. If she climbed the stairs, Patterson was sure she would find herself in a familiar hallway. One she had carried trays of flowers through only a few days before.

Which meant the intruder she had chased down into Esther Cutler's basement and beyond could only be one person. Patterson's hunch was correct. Benjamin Forrester must be the Butterfly Killer, although what his motives were, she was not yet sure.

Patterson turned back around. If Amy Bowen was being held captive here, it would not be upstairs. It would be somewhere less obvious. Like behind that metal door in the tunnel. She started back toward the door leading to the tunnel, and as she did so, her flashlight beam swept across the wall ahead of her.

Then she stopped.

She had thought the basement room was empty, but that was not the case. Hanging on the wall ahead of her was a large, framed photograph of a teenage girl with hair that fell to her shoulders and gorgeous blue eyes. She was standing in front of a building that looked like a church. St. Francis of Assisi, perhaps? But it wasn't the location that caught Patterson's eye. It was the white dress the girl was wearing. And the butterflies printed on it.

Patterson stared at the photograph for a long moment,

wondering why it was hanging down in the cellar. But when she dropped her flashlight beam, the answer was obvious. Underneath the framed image was a narrow wooden table upon which stood a small wooden box surrounded by several fat round candles that had burned down and pooled wax on the table's surface. Two smaller photographs in silver frames had been placed on the tabletop on each side of the box. And in both of them, the girl was wearing a different butterfly dress. In front of the table was a bench like those found in a church. It was arranged so that whoever sat upon it could view the macabre tableau. A pair of kneelers, also like those used in a church, sat in front of the bench.

Patterson's breath caught in her throat.

This was a shrine.

She stood frozen for several seconds, trying to make sense of what she was looking at. Even though the candles were not lit, Patterson could imagine the effect when they were. The flickering flames would illuminate the portrait hanging above in a dancing orange light while whoever had built this shrine kneeled before it and raised their eyes to the object of their devotion. Samantha Forrester.

Curious, Patterson approached the table and looked down at the wooden box. She reached out and opened it. Inside, tied with a piece of red ribbon, was a lock of hair.

Patterson recoiled in horror. She closed the box and took a step backward, the hairs on the back of her neck standing up.

This was more than she ever expected to find.

She studied the shrine for a few moments longer and then took out her phone. There was only one reason anyone would build a shrine like this, but she needed confirmation. And she knew who could provide that answer, assuming there was any cell service down under the townhouse. Patterson was relieved to see one bar. Not great, but it would do. She placed her call, praying she would get an answer, then lifted the phone to her ear.

Phoebe Cutler picked up after four rings.

"Special Agent Blake?" Phoebe sounded groggy, as if she had been asleep, which made sense. It was the early hours of the morning.

"Phoebe. I know it's late, but I need you to answer a question." Patterson kept her voice low. She didn't want anyone in the house above to hear her. "It's important."

"Um, okay. Shoot."

"Your grandmother's neighbors, Ben and Helen Forrester."

"What about them?"

"Tell me about their daughter."

"Samantha? She was a lovely girl . . . always happy and smiling. Used to bring cookies around to Gran every week. She would visit with her sometimes, too, and read to her while Jesse made dinner."

"Where's Samantha now?" Patterson asked.

"She's dead. Hit by a car while riding her bike almost three years ago. It was so awful. Those poor parents. They were heartbroken."

Patterson fell silent. She stared at the shrine.

"Special Agent Blake?"

"Sorry. I'm still here."

"Why are you asking about Samantha Forrester?"

"No reason. Just a hunch I wanted to confirm." Patterson thanked Phoebe and told her to go back to sleep and returned the phone to her pocket. Then she stepped back into the tunnel and started toward the metal door at the other end, beyond which she suspected Amy Bowen was being held captive.

SEVENTY-FOUR

PATTERSON ADVANCED along the tunnel with her flashlight in one hand and gun in the other. She didn't know where Benjamin Forrester had gone or if he was still down here, but she wasn't taking any chances. She reached the metal door. There were two hefty barrel slide bolts affixed to it that looked newer than the rest of the door. One at the top, another at the bottom. But they were not drawn, and the door stood open a crack. Patterson resisted the urge to charge right in. she paused, listening for any sound of movement from the other side. When she heard none, she pulled the door toward her and raised the flashlight.

Beyond the door was another tunnel, swathed in darkness. This one was wider and taller, with a curved ceiling that arched overhead. It reminded her of a subway tunnel in New York, except there were no train tracks, and it dead-ended fifty feet away in a wall built of different colored bricks that looked newer than the rest of the tunnel. Next to this wall was a single chair, illuminated in eerie chiaroscuro by the flashlight's beam.

Patterson stepped beyond the doorway and swung the

flashlight around. Iron bars divided the tunnel straight down the middle. The space on the other side of the bars was further partitioned in the other direction into a row of holding pens . . . or cells. Three of them, each with its own heavy door. The bars looked as old as the door she had just passed beyond. They were thick with corrosion. The reason soon became obvious. Water dripped from the ceiling in several spots, and Patterson could see wet patches on the mottled concrete floor.

She moved further into the tunnel. The flashlight beam danced across the bars, sending crazy shadows skittering across the floors and walls, before picking out a shape huddled in the middle cell.

A teenage girl squinted back at her against the bright light, face twisted with fear. Patterson recognized the face instantly from photographs provided by Amy Bowen's parents, although her hair was cut short, and tears streaked her cheeks.

"Oh my God." Patterson rushed forward and gripped the cell door, tugging on it. "Amy."

At first, the girl didn't reply, then she stood and approached the bars. "It won't do any good. He locks the door."

"I'm going to get you out of here," Patterson said, noticing with horror that Amy was wearing a butterfly dress just like those of the last three victims . . . and the girl in the cellar portrait.

"He's here," the girl said, breathless. "You have to run. Now. Before it's too late."

"I'm not leaving without you," Patterson replied, but even as the words left her mouth, she sensed a rush of air to her rear.

Amy screamed.

Patterson swung around and lifted her gun at the same time. The flashlight beam lanced through the darkness, briefly illuminating Benjamin Forrester as he loomed behind her with a heavy wrench held above her head. A wrench that was sweeping down fast. Patterson's finger tensed on the trigger a fraction too late. Before she could get off a single shot, the wrench found its target, and Patterson's world exploded in white hot pain, followed by merciful oblivion.

SEVENTY-FIVE

WHEN PATTERSON WOKE up she was lying on a hard cold floor. Her head felt like it had been split in two. She reached up and touched the spot where it hurt. Her fingers came away bloody.

"Samantha never warned me about you. Otherwise, I would have been better prepared," said a voice in the darkness.

Patterson raised her head and pushed herself up from the floor. It took a while for her eyes to adjust before she realized it wasn't totally dark. Her surroundings swam into view. She was in one of the tunnel cells. Amy Bowen occupied the cell next to her. The girl looked on with baleful eyes.

Weak yellow light spilled from a bare bulb hanging from the ceiling beyond the bars. The voice came from a man sitting in the bulb's glow. He straddled the chair Patterson had seen when she entered the tunnel, one leg on each side and the back pressed against his chest. His arms leaned on it, and his chin leaned on his arms. It was Benjamin Forrester.

"What are you talking about?" Patterson said, scrambling to her feet. She approached the bars. "Your daughter is dead. How could she tell you anything?"

"She speaks when I pray." Benjamin's mouth curled up into a parody of a grin. He touched his temple with an extended finger. "I can hear her in my head. She wants to come back. To be a family again. She told me what to do."

"What did she tell you to do?" Patterson asked, not sure she wanted to know the answer. Afraid she already knew it.

"Find a vessel. Give her a new body so she can live again. So our girl can come back to us. God isn't ready for Samantha to be in heaven yet. If we find the perfect vessel, God will send her back."

"That's why you took Shawna Banks."

"Yes. But she wasn't pure, so I had to find another."

"Why wasn't she pure?" Patterson asked.

"Because Samantha rejected her. I asked her why. I prayed so hard. Night and day. But she would never say."

"So you kept taking girls and killing them when they didn't become your daughter?" Patterson asked, horrified.

"What other choice did I have?" The smile faded from Benjamin's face. "They have to be right for our little girl. I make them look like Samantha. Dress them in her favorite clothes. But I can't change what's on the inside." A tear rolled down Benjamin's face. "I can't make them worthy."

"That must suck so bad for you," Patterson said. An image of Benjamin Forrester kneeling in front of the creepy shrine in his basement and praying to his dead daughter flitted through Patterson's mind. "Whatever made you think you could bring Samantha back in the first place?"

"She came in a dream. Instructed me to build the shrine. Said that if I prayed to her, she would answer. That we could be together again. But it didn't happen. Not at first. I prayed for months on end with no reply. I begged her to speak to me again, told her how much I missed her, and then, just when I was giving up hope, she did. Her voice rang in my head. She promised to return like Lazarus rising from the dead. Except there was nothing for her to come back in. Unlike Lazarus, her body was gone. Cremated a week after she died. But my Samantha knew what to do."

"You're not a well man, Mr. Forrester." Patterson moved close to the bars and peered between them. "Why don't you let me out of here, and we'll get you some help."

"You don't understand. You don't have faith."

"It's not about faith, Benjamin. It's about not hurting any more girls. This has to end."

"You're right. It does." Benjamin's gaze shifted toward Amy, cowering at the back of her cell under the wall of photographs. He stood and pushed the chair away. "She's no purer than the others. Samantha doesn't want her. That's why she has to go away. And now you'll have to go with her."

"You don't mean that, Ben," Patterson said. "Think about what you're doing."

"I have thought about it. It's all I think about twenty-four hours a day," Ben said. He went to the metal door. "I suggest you do some praying of your own. Both of you. I'll be back soon."

Then he stepped into the tunnel beyond the door and slammed it closed.

SEVENTY-SIX

PATTERSON WATCHED the door close with a mixture of relief and dread. For all his outwardly amiable persona, Benjamin Forrester was a cold-blooded killer. Worse, he was obviously insane. The grief of losing his daughter had led to a psychotic break, and no amount of reasoning would bring him back. That much was obvious. Benjamin was delusional, and he had retreated into a comfortable place to justify that delusion. He believed his daughter was speaking to him and that God had said it was not yet her time. Like Lazarus, she would rise from the grave. If only Ben could find a suitable host to replace her own cremated remains.

An obviously religious man prior to Samantha's death, Benjamin had taken those beliefs and turned them into a sick parody through the grief that ravaged him. Instead of praying to God, he was kneeling in front of that grotesque shrine and praying to his dead daughter instead. His faith, which should have been a source of comfort, became a demon riding his back.

And now Patterson was on the receiving end of that delusion, along with his latest impure vessel. Amy Bowen.

They had to escape before Benjamin came back, or they were both dead, and it would be Patterson's fault. Spooked by her visit earlier in the day, Ben must have panicked and decided to get rid of his captive. Which was why he waited until the early hours of the morning and snuck into Esther Cutler's home next door to get another pillowcase with which to smother Amy. If Patterson hadn't seen his flashlight in the upstairs window, the girl might already be dead.

But she wasn't, and Patterson intended for it to stay that way. But to survive, they had to escape the crumbling tunnels.

Ben must have discovered the tunnels under the converted warehouse building during his basement renovation and decided to use them. Tunnels the Santa Fe Railroad Company had built over a century before to move merchandise under the streets of the city. They were later used by everyone from prohibition bootleggers to the Army in World War II. That was also how he accessed Esther's townhouse next door. The narrow space between Benjamin's cellar and his neighbor must once have been a larger entry point to the tunnel complex. All Ben had to do was install a door in his own cellar and knock through the brickwork to gain access to Esther's townhouse. After that, he could come and go as he pleased with his victims because Esther was bedridden, and even if she saw him, no one would believe her. Not even his wife had any idea. That was why he kept the basement locked. If Helen discovered the tunnels, he would be caught.

Patterson tugged on the cell door. As expected, it was locked, and even though the bars were corroded, it was mostly surface rust. They held strong against her efforts to break out. But all was not lost. Ben had taken her gun and phone. No surprise there. But he had made a mistake born out of ignorance. Her right ankle was heavy when she walked because her backup weapon was still strapped there in its holster. He hadn't thought to check for a second gun. Or maybe he had checked but didn't think to look down there. She breathed a silent thanks to Bauer for arranging the Glock Sub-Compact. That gesture would probably save her life and that of Ben Forrester's latest victim.

She went to the bars dividing her cell from Amy's. The tunnel light was still on, and she could see the teenager huddled near the back wall again, under the creepy photomontage. No doubt she was terrified. "Amy, sweetie, I'm going to get you out of here."

At first, the girl didn't respond, but then she lifted her head. "We can't escape. I've already tried."

"This time it will be different," Patterson promised. She reached down and drew the small Glock from her ankle holster. "I want you to stay where you are right now and cover your ears because it's going to get loud, okay?"

The girl looked at her but didn't respond.

"Tell me you understand," Patterson said. There was only one way they were going to get out of the cells, and it was not Patterson's first choice. She would need to shoot the locks. That would make a lot of noise and might alert Ben to their escape attempt.

"I understand," Amy said in a small voice. She lowered her head and pressed her hands to her ears.

Satisfied, Patterson retreated to the middle of the cell. She didn't want to be too close to the door when she shot out the lock but still needed to be close enough to guarantee her aim in the lowlight environment.

She dropped into a firing stance and aimed the gun, then squeezed the trigger.

Sparks flew from the metal plate covering the door lock. Small pieces of metal flew in all directions.

The boom was even louder than she expected in the

confined space. It reverberated off the walls and ceiling and left her ears ringing.

When Patterson tugged on the door again, it opened with a grind of rusty hinges.

She stepped out into the tunnel beyond. Her first thought was to repeat the procedure with Amy's lock and release the terrified teen, but she was worried Ben had heard the gunshot. She waited a moment to make sure he was not rushing back down. After all, her service weapon was missing. Patterson didn't want to take a bullet in the back trying to free Amy. That would help neither of them.

She backed away toward the bricked-up tunnel wall and lifted the Glock in a two-handed grip. There was only one way in or out of the tunnel. She aimed the muzzle toward the metal door and waited.

Her instincts were correct.

Someone was on the other side. She could hear them drawing back the slide bolts. Then the metal door swung open to reveal Ben Forrester. In his hand was her service weapon, and it was pointing straight at her.

"Drop the gun and put your hands in the air," Patterson snapped. "Do it now."

But Ben didn't drop the gun. Instead, he rushed forward with a snarl. The Glock waved wildly in his hand. He pulled the trigger.

The bullet missed Patterson and zinged off the iron bars to her right.

Patterson didn't wait for him to fire again. She squeezed the trigger of the Glock sub-compact twice in quick succession, sending a pair of bullets hurtling toward her enraged assailant. A two-round center mass double tap, just like the instructors had trained her at the Academy. If Ben had kept going, a third would have swiftly followed. You don't leave an assailant

329

standing to shoot back and kill you. But it wasn't necessary. Benjamin Forrester crumpled and dropped to the ground.

Behind him stood Helen.

She looked at Patterson with a mixture of disbelief and anger on her face. "Why did you do that?" She asked, as if the answer wasn't obvious. "He was only trying to bring our little girl back. That's all."

SEVENTY-SEVEN

ONE WEEK LATER.

At four in the afternoon on a rainy Friday, Patterson occupied the same chair in the office of Dallas SAC Walter Harris as she had done on the day she arrived in the city several weeks before.

"The Serial Killer Queen strikes again," Harris said, with a bemused smile on his face. "I swear, I don't know how you do it. You snagged two unrelated killers in the same investigation."

"I guess it's a gift," Patterson replied with a grin of her own.

"And got your partner shot in the process."

"That wasn't my intention."

"Obviously. Doesn't make you any less dangerous to be around, as I'm sure Special Agent Bauer will agree."

"Marcus knows how dangerous the job can be. Duane Snyder would have opened fire on whoever came close to that hunting blind."

"I'm sure you're right. And he'll spend a long time behind

331

bars because of it." Harris paused before continuing. "You'll probably have to come back and testify when he goes on trial. You realize that."

"Given how slowly the justice system works, I hope to have finished my search for Julie by the time that becomes necessary," Patterson said.

"Not to mention Benjamin and Helen Forrester." Harris picked up a case file from his desk and flipped through it. "Who would have thought that such a quiet, churchgoing couple would be such monsters?"

"Grief causes people to do strange things."

"That it does." Harris dropped the file back on the desk. "The photos of that shrine give me the creeps."

"It was worse in person, trust me."

"They actually thought their daughter would rise from the dead if they found her a suitable body to inhabit?" Harris shook his head. "Lord help me."

"I think that's the point. They were hoping the Lord would help them."

"I don't know if there's an afterlife or not, but if there is, those two are taking the express elevator all the way down." Harris rubbed his chin. "Ben Forrester will probably get there way ahead of his wife."

"Either way, he's not going to hurt anyone else," Patterson said. Ben Forrester had been on life support for a week. He was clinically dead when the paramedics arrived in his basement lair, and by the time they brought him back the damage had been done. Even though both her bullets had missed his heart, Ben had stopped breathing which meant his brain was deprived of oxygen. Cerebral hypoxia. Now he was brain dead and being kept alive only by machines, at least until those machines were turned off.

"One thing I don't understand is why they felt the need to

come and go through Esther Cutler's house instead of their own."

"I didn't understand that either," Patterson said. "Until I looked around the back of the townhouses. The neighbor on the other side of Helen and Ben had installed an outdoor security camera to cover their back entrance. The wide-angle field-of-view also caught the back of the Forrester's townhouse."

"But not the townhouse belonging to Phoebe's grandmother."

"Correct. It was the only way they could avoid being seen bringing their victims in and out. Ben would abduct the girls using the van rented by the church, which meant there was no link back to him. Then he would drive the van around the back of the townhouse and leave the girls there until the early hours of the morning. All he had to do after that was sneak up into Esther Cutler's home, go out her back door, and bring his victims in that way."

"Except that Esther saw him on more than one occasion."

"And no one believed her because she was old and bedridden. Everyone assumed she was just dreaming it and her eyesight wasn't good enough to recognize her neighbor in the darkness."

"Why take pillowcases from her home to commit the murders?"

"Easy access. Not to mention that it would be impossible to trace them unless you knew where they were coming from." Patterson thought for a moment. "Also, I think he was squeamish. This was not some cold and calculating psychopath. It was a man lost in his own psychosis. Smothering those girls was neat and clean. There was no blood."

"If Esther's granddaughter wasn't an admin for the FBI, he might never have been caught," Harris reflected. "Even then, he could have gotten away with it if you hadn't made the connection with those pillowcases."

"I'm just happy I did." Patterson had thought long and hard about how easily Ben and Helen Forrester could have slipped through the cracks and gotten away with their crimes. "Amy Bowen is alive and back with her parents because of it."

"For which I'm sure they are more than grateful." Harris leaned back and folded his arms. "I had a long chat with Marilyn Kahn on the phone this morning."

"Really?" Kahn was Patterson's SAC back at the New York Field Office. A sudden panic gripped her. "You're not planning to assign me another case, are you? We had a deal. If I helped catch the Butterfly Killer, I could continue my search for Julie."

"Take it easy, Special Agent Blake," Harris said. "I have no intention of reneging on our deal, even if I would rather keep you here. You are an asset to the FBI, despite your frustrating penchant for bending the rules."

"So why were you talking to SAC Kahn about me?"

"How many kidnap victims have you saved from certain death over the last six months?" Harris asked, deflecting from her question.

"Um . . ." Patterson shrugged.

"Don't be modest, Special Agent Blake. It doesn't become you."

"Sorry."

"The answer is three. If you add in Claire Wright, who wasn't technically abducted, it's four," Harris said. "Which I'm sure you already know."

"That's my job."

"It's also remarkable. Four people are still alive directly because of your actions."

"I'm not sure where this is going," Patterson said.

"Then I'll enlighten you." Harris leaned forward. "I've recommended you for the Medal of Valor."

"What?" Patterson could hardly believe her ears. The FBI Medal of Valor was awarded to agents who performed exceptional acts of heroism and put their own lives at risk to save others. Patterson had never thought of herself in that manner. "I don't deserve it."

"That's funny. I got the impression Marilyn Kahn thought the same thing, although she never outright said it. But don't let that worry you. Kahn's a bitch, but until she makes deputy director, there's nothing she can do about it."

"I don't know what to say."

"How about a heartfelt thank you?"

"Thank you." Patterson tried not to smile but couldn't help herself.

"That's more like it," Harris said. "If you ever fancy a change of pace from New York, call me, and I'll put in a transfer request. I could use an agent like you at this field office, and I'm sure Special Agent Bauer would concur."

"I'll keep that in mind," Patterson said, standing up. "Will there be anything else?"

"Not at the moment."

Patterson thanked SAC Harris again and turned toward the door. When she got there, he addressed her before she could step into the outer office.

"Special Agent Blake?"

"Yes?" She turned around to face him.

"Good luck finding Julie. I mean that." He met her gaze with steely eyes. "And stay safe out there."

SEVENTY-EIGHT

"THERE'S the woman of the hour," Bauer said when Patterson arrived back at the small and featureless office she shared with her partner. "I hear congratulations are in order."

"News travels fast." Patterson sat at her desk.

"It does when your girlfriend is the ASAC's admin."

"Ah. Insider information."

"Something like that. Besides, it's not like I have anything better to do than listen to office gossip."

"Desk duty getting you down, huh?"

"It sucks." Bauer had been put on three months of desk duty while his shoulder healed. "But it's better than ending up forced into a ridiculously early retirement."

"And don't you forget it."

"I won't." Bauer fell silent for a moment. "You're really leaving us, huh?"

"The time has come to move on," Patterson said.

"Right. You still heading for Amarillo to find Mark Davis?"

"That's the plan." Patterson had intended to leave for Amarillo weeks before to find the bass player for the band Sunrise, who Julie had traveled there with sixteen years ago, along with other members of the band. But SAC Harris had put her search on hold. Now though, she was eager to take up Julie's trail once more.

"Can't say I won't miss you."

"Yeah, right." Patterson chucked. "I bet you can't wait to see me drive off into the sunset. I've been a royal pain in your ass."

"I won't deny that. But I'll still miss you." Bauer cleared his throat. "We had our moments."

"We certainly did." The romantic near miss at the motel flitted through Patterson's mind even though she would rather have forgotten it. "I'll miss you, too."

"Well, shucks." Bauer feigned embarrassment. "Oh. I almost forgot. Detective Voss called with an update on Duane Snyder while you were up with SAC Harris. Forensics pulled another set of partial prints at the scene of Darlene Rourke's murder. You'll never guess who they belonged to."

"Jodi Banks," Patterson said.

"Huh. How did you know?"

"Wild guess."

"Well, you guessed right. They were very curious about that, so they brought her in for more questioning. They also had another chat with Snyder."

"And?"

"Jodi refused to say anything. Pleaded the Fifth. Snyder claimed Jodi was at Darlene's apartment that night. He said she went there to confront the other woman, and Darlene called him in a panic. He went over there to find the two of them going at it. Convinced Jodi to leave, which she did. After that, he somehow got into an argument of his own with Darlene, which got even more out of hand and ended with her death when he bludgeoned her with a lamp base."

"That doesn't sound right. And it will be easy to verify. If Snyder is telling the truth, there should be a call from Darlene on his phone."

"There is. But wait until you hear this. They pulled a partial print from the lamp base. It was a tentative match for Jodi. But there wasn't enough for it to be conclusive."

"Shit." Patterson rubbed her temples. "She did it. Jodi Banks killed Darlene because she was angry about the affair and wrecking their marriage."

"That's a leap."

"Is it though? Think about this. She drives there and confronts Darlene. Things get out of hand. She smacks Darlene around the head with a lamp base and kills her."

"And then Jodi panics and calls the only person who can help, even though they aren't talking."

"But she has the forethought to use Darlene's phone, so she wouldn't be tied to the scene," Patterson said. "That's why after overhearing the argument, the neighbor saw him walking toward the apartment, not away from it. He did the only thing he could to help the woman he still loved. Told her to leave, then staged the scene to look like he committed the murder. He wiped down the murder weapon, presumably missing a partial print, and planted his own fingerprints."

"Why not just try to dispose of the body?" Bauer asked. "He has a lot of property on which to bury Darlene."

"Because he knew that even if he disposed of the body he would be the number one suspect if Darlene Rourke disappeared. He also knew he could never clean the crime scene well enough to remove every spot of blood and trace evidence. Modern forensics has a habit of catching people even without a body. Not only that, but a cadaver dog would find a fresh corpse in those woods in short order."

"So he fell on his own sword, metaphorically speaking. Took the blame so that his wife wouldn't have to." Bauer rubbed his chin. "I don't know, Patterson. That's a doozy of a scenario."

"Are you saying I'm wrong?"

Bauer frowned. "I wouldn't go that far. Athens PD is going to have a hell of a job proving it, though, unless either Jodi Banks or Duane Snyder change their tune."

"I wouldn't hold your breath."

"She's going to get away with murder, isn't she?"

"It looks that way."

"Yeah. You know what, unless someone asks for assistance, which they won't, it's not our problem anymore." Bauer looked at Patterson across the desks. "I'm going to miss you. Things won't be the same around here."

"I'll miss you, too," Patterson admitted. "But hey, I'm not gone yet. How about we get pizza and a few beers? You can send me off in style . . . I mean, unless you have another hot date with Phoebe."

"I don't." Bauer stood and grabbed his jacket from the back of the chair. "And even if I did, I'd cancel. Let's go."

SEVENTY-NINE

THE NEXT MORNING, Patterson was ready to hit the road. Her car was packed, and she had said her goodbyes. She was eager to pick up her sister's trail and see where it led her. But as she climbed into the lime green Toyota Corolla, her phone rang.

It was the last person she expected to get a call from. Claire Wright. Patterson hadn't heard from her since they spoke in the hospital after Ryan Gilder tried to kill her. It had only been a few weeks ago, but it felt like so much longer to Patterson. A lot had happened in the time since.

"Miss Wright, how can I help you?" Patterson asked, answering.

"It's more how I can help you," Claire said. "Are you still in Dallas?"

"For another hour. I'm driving to Amarillo today."

"Mark Davis?"

"Yes. I'm eager to see what he knows about Julie and where she went next."

"That's kind of why I'm calling," Claire said. "Since I got out of the hospital last week, I've been thinking a lot about Julie and what happened back then. It jogged my memory. I have something to give you."

"What is it?"

"I'd rather wait and show you in person. I have an apartment now. Arranged it while I was still in the hospital, with some help from a friend. Didn't want to spend even one more night at Ryan's place. Not that he's there, of course, but I don't need those memories. I got all of my stuff yesterday morning, and I've been unpacking ever since. It was in one of the boxes. I can give you the address."

"Can you text it to me?" Patterson asked. She was burning with curiosity. "I'll swing by on the way out of town."

"Sure. I'll do it right now." Claire said goodbye before ending the call. Less than thirty seconds later, Patterson received a text message with her address.

———

Claire Wright's new apartment was in a complex north of downtown and close to the route Patterson had intended to take out of the city. When she knocked on the door, Claire answered immediately.

"Special Agent Blake." Claire let her in. "I'm so glad I caught you before you left town. If not, I would have mailed it to you, of course. But this is better."

"You haven't said what you found yet," Patterson replied, taking in her surroundings. The apartment was small, with a living room, kitchen combo, and a bedroom in the back. There wasn't much furniture yet, and boxes were stacked in every room, but Patterson thought it would be perfect for Claire to make a fresh start. "I assume it's related to Julie."

"Yes. I was thinking about that concert all those years ago and how your sister hung out with me, even though she was older. She was really nice. I liked her. Then I remembered something. On the day she left, Julie gave me a gift to remember her by. I've kept it all these years, but to be honest, I'd forgotten. When I got my possessions from Ryan's house, I went through the boxes and found it again. I'd like to give it to you now."

"What is it?" Patterson asked, her heart beating fast.

"Here, I'll show you." Claire led Patterson into the bedroom. There was a brown moving box on the bed surrounded by what looked like folded posters, items of clothing, and various sentimental tchotchkes. The sort of things a teenage girl would adorn her room with. Claire looked at the items with misty eyes. "This is all the stuff I packed up from my childhood bedroom when my parents sold the house. I haven't looked at it for years. Just kept toting it around from place to place in this box." She singled out a piece of clothing—a faded blue T-shirt with the phrase 'live your best life' printed on the front in a lighter blue font—and held it out to Patterson. "This was Julie's. She said it was one of her favorites. She was wearing it the first day I met her and wore it again at the music festival. I really liked it and had told her so more than once. On the day Julie was leaving, she pulled it out of her bag and gave it to me. I'm sorry it's so faded. I wore it all the time for a couple of years after that and always thought of her."

"I remember this T-shirt." Patterson took the garment and held it up. She pressed it against her chest and, for a moment, thought she could sense her sister's presence in the room with her. She swallowed a tremble. "This really was one of Julie's favorites. I never thought I'd see it again."

"It's yours now." Claire smiled. "A little something to spur you on while you look for her."

"I can't take this. She gave it to you." Patterson tried to hand the T-shirt back.

Claire shook her head. "No. I want you to take it. That T-shirt was never mine. Not really. I was just caretaking it for your sister . . . And for you."

"If you're sure." Patterson felt tears welling at the corner of her eyes.

"I'm more than sure." Claire's eyes were moist now, too. "Find your sister and give it back to her. Bring Julie home."

"I will." Patterson clutched the T-shirt. "I don't know what to say. Thank you for this."

"It's my pleasure." Claire walked to the door. "And it's the least I could do after all you did for me. You saved my life."

Patterson didn't know how to respond, so instead, she reached over and embraced the other woman in a tight hug before releasing her. "When I find Julie, I'll let you know."

"I'd appreciate that." Claire watched Patterson walk to her car and climb in before waving to her. "Good luck."

Patterson waved back and started the car, then steered out of the parking lot with the T-shirt lying on the passenger seat next to her. It was another link to Julie. It hardened her resolve to find her sister, if not in Amarillo, then somewhere. This was why, with tears in her eyes and that thought on her mind, Patterson pointed the car north and into the unknown.

A NOTE FROM A.M. STRONG

THE TUNNELS UNDER DALLAS.

The Santa Fe Railroad tunnels under downtown Dallas are a real thing. They connected four warehouse buildings that made up the Santa Fe Freight Terminal and were used to ferry merchandise out of the city. Later, after the railroad company abandoned them, they were repurposed to move troops during World War II, and there are even rumors of prohibition bootleggers using them to store and move illicit liquor.

I was fascinated with these tunnels, many of which are still there, lying forgotten under a hotel, luxury lofts, and even a federal building. But they didn't quite fit the bill for what I had in mind for this book. Which is why I invented a fifth building further afield and linked by a branch line. This became the converted warehouse Esther Cutler lives in. And the tunnels underneath provided a suitably creepy place for a killer to roam. So please don't email saying I got the history of Dallas wrong. I already know that. But hey, that's what artistic license is all about.

Until the next book...

A.M. Strong

READY FOR MORE PATTERSON BLAKE?

Read the next book in The Patterson Blake FBI Mystery Thriller series.

Never Let Her Go

Patterson Blake is in more danger than ever before...

Following the clues of her sister's disappearance to Amarillo, FBI Special Agent Patterson Blake is hopeful she will finally learn the truth about Julie. But there's a problem. The man who might hold those answers has been accused of a heinous crime. One he claims to be innocent of.

When Patterson starts to dig into the case, she stumbles upon a dangerous conspiracy that threatens to not only derail her search for Julie but could also get her killed.

With the clock ticking and her life in danger, Patterson must unravel a plot bigger than any she has ever encountered, even as forces she cannot control close in around her with one aim . . . to stop her by any means necessary.

ABOUT THE AUTHORS

A. M. Strong is the pen name of supernatural action and adventure fiction author Anthony M. Strong. Sonya Sargent grew up in Vermont and is an avid reader when she isn't working on books of her own. They divide their time between Florida's sunny Space Coast and a tranquil island in Maine.

Find out more about the author at
AMStrongAuthor.com

Made in the USA
Las Vegas, NV
15 May 2023

72111628R00208